Mythvoluti

Part 1

Living the Oollaballuh!

Written by Vas Constanti

ISBN: 978-1-291-43796-6

www.publishnation.co.uk

About the author

Vassos Constanti was born in London in 1967 where he still resides. His childhood was greatly influenced by his aunt and uncle who worked for the RSC as costume and set designers respectively, and family holidays to Cyprus and his beloved Crete, where he fell in love with mythology. He went on to study at the internationally renowned Guilford School of Acting, graduating in 1990 with distinction. He has performed on the stage in the West End as well as nationally and in Europe, and has also featured as an actor on television.

The ideas for Mythvolution came about in 1992 when Garston was born in a series of letters.

"With circumstance and fate you face the fear behind your eyes!"

It took a while to get here!

At the beginning of a novel there is usually a page where the author writes a thank you to everyone! It usually consists of a list of names that, to the reader, mean nothing at all because very little explanation is ever given. And so, I wanted to remedy this and explain further.

In helping me get the ideas out of my head and onto a page, I would like to thank, Grant.

In aiding me take those ideas and place them in the right order, I would like to thank my chosen guinea pig readers, Lyn, Mac, Pip, Elise and Kris.

For being supportive during the entire process, I would like to thank, Jane, Grant, once again, Elizabeth Buchan, Paul Spyker, Andrianne Neofitou, Caroline Green, Lee Whelan, Stephane Anelli and Publish Nation.

For their talent, I would like to thank Andre Cutress, Celeste Leal, Elise Leal and Scott Gaunt.

I would also like to dedicate this novel to the memory of some friends that the world lost too soon, Kieran, Paul, Ray and the lovely Cara.

For Vincent.

Mythvolution:

Noun:

The doctrine that the true story of the creation of the known Universe is not quite as recounted in the Bible, especially the first chapter of Genesis, but due to the probability that mythology may not be a myth after all and is responsible for evolution.

Mythvolutionism:

Noun:

As Mythvolution but with an ism!

Mythvolutionist:

Noun- adjective:

A believer in the doctrine of Mythvolutionism and a 'nut nut!'

UNLOCK A MIND, UNMIND A LOCK, IT'S THE SAME AS THE BEGINNING OF THE END!

From the very first moment that man took a barefoot step upon the Earth, he has struggled to understand his thoughts and dreams, fathom their meaning and comprehend how they relate to a personal existence. He has lived through epic moments of darkness and often scavenged for a mere glimpse of light. With the weight of gravity upon his shoulders, he has habitually been led to believe in the 'rivers of plenty,' where he imagines that one day he will glide blissfully beside angels of self-preservation and disregard a speculated life. Historians, archaeologists, theologians and geologists have, for so long, hunted for answers to man's future by reading scripts from the past, a past that was once made so simple by self-imposed or natural borders. In doing so, they have helped man learn everything he has concerning the floating rotating sphere that he survives upon. Their findings, however, are frequently interpreted differently and so now, with a mind twisted and poisoned by contradictory beliefs, man's lonesome search for sustainability regularly leads to self-destruction. What he considers to be correct is often, without a doubt, incorrect and increasingly harmful to life on this beautiful, benevolent world. It has now become abundantly obvious that the continued threat from his own marauding kind has left him with very few alternatives.

Today, those who are considered to be the saviours of mankind are frequently locked away! They are condemned to live a life not meant for anyone, anyone at all. From desks and laboratories they watch in misery, as the world becomes a desecrated grave for a myriad of the globe's inhabitant species. These saviours recognise that most of mankind is mercifully unaware of the devastation it's creating and thus, it is they alone who struggle with the guilt of circumstance, as man and Mother Nature battle for life.

***

Our tale does not resonate from a small municipal state with the power of self-righteousness, or even an alternative universe where the masters of realm and time have jousted for thousands of years in a city you, or I, are familiar with. We don't catch a mode of transport from a split portal in space to get there in an instant for assembly, take a leap of faith through reflective glass, or even stumble down a badger hole! We simply look to the heart of the Cheshire countryside where a workplace for the saviours of man masquerades as an elegant Georgian Manor House. Pradgonne Manor is a fine example of British heritage and period architecture that stands majestic in its surroundings. Secluded by rambling hills and musty scented dew-dropped woodlands, it is bestowed a natural security while its reverence draws the bite from the January frost.

Through its ostentatious, black, heavy, double front doors, a grand sweeping stairway and sea of varnished parquet flooring welcomes you into the belly of the beast. Its grandeur allows ample space for all of the tall gilded mirrors and pre-Raphaelite masterpieces adorning its decorative plaster framed walls. Ornamental ceramics flood the eye from every tabled surface and sturdy oak doors conceal elevators and rooms of mystery that only the saviours of man may enter. The hallway itself has the grace to be the only traditionally decorated and architecturally accurate room in the house, and it isn't even a room!

PROJECT COMMUNE

A tall, thin, pointy nosed man in a crisply creased, sharply cut, grey suit stepped back from the retinal recognition sensor on the wall beside an unsuspicious door marked 'NO ENTRY,' and turned to the crowd of reporters standing behind him. The door effortlessly slid open to reveal a land of brushed steel, glass and chrome.

"Just follow me please and don't touch anything," said the grey suit.

As the group of reporters walked through the huge room, they were astounded to find they were being followed by a cluster of happy clicking dolphins swimming gleefully behind a glass wall running the entire length of one side of the room. At numerous workstations robots with countless arms, carefully handled microscopes, beakers and test tubes whilst conducting various experiments and storing the results.

"Wow. Who runs all of this lot, all these robots?" asked a gawky member of the press.

"They are mainly self-aware. They look after themselves most of the time. There is the odd person running around in a white coat here and there in the Manor though," the suit replied.

He led everyone to a door at the far end where he peered into yet another sensor. The door slid open and everyone again followed him in, but this time into a room that was constructed like a surgical viewing gallery.

"And there they are down there, on the Grid. The Grid is actually exactly that, a large flat, 40 foot square white granite floor. It comprises 1600 individual tiles with their defining borders being made of an exposed wafer thin steel alloy. This in turn, as you can see, is surrounded by a gem beading running symmetrically from edge to edge of each separate tile."

"The beading?" said a voice.

"Brightly polished precious gem stones, submerged like broken glass in a thin trickling stream; and that deep red glow; well that, that's our classified liquid, water mostly and a little bit of something else!

The truth is, it can be quite dangerous in there and that's why Vincent here, hello Vincent," he didn't reply, "controls everything from behind this large safety glass wall."

Vincent Russell was twenty years old and a little different from other guys his age. His dark swarthy looks, shiny, glossy wavy hair, eyes of pitch and lean physique made him an extremely handsome catch, that is, if he knew how to be caught! He was also more than a little geeky, with an IQ that was seriously off the charts. His demeanour could be described as laid back, if not horizontal and he was kind in nature, but not really at home with the human race. He needed someone, a girlfriend perhaps, who could show him the world and take him in hand; remind him to comb his hair and shower on a regular basis. All of this was perhaps typically the result of too much work and not enough play! Private schooling and personal tuition, a life in front of a computer monitor and social skills learnt from watching re-runs of Star Trek had made Vincent far from ordinary!

Vincent gave a nonchalant wave, his half eaten lollipop popped over his shoulder. The suit continued patronising the world's media.

"And that, that cube hanging from the ceiling in there with screens on its four sides, well, that's 'The Cube'. Our subjects are all connected to it; I mean they're wired in; metaphorically speaking that is, via infrared, Bluetooth and laser technology. Our subjects have also been fitted with microchips that can store terrifyingly large amounts of information."

"Wow! And the ceiling?" asked another member of the press.

"Double Glazed Solar panelled glass, with our classified liquid pumped between its panes!" replied the pointy nosed man.

"What's the liquid called?" asked another.

"Solar Powered Articulating Functional Fluid."

"SPAFF!" said a tabloid reporter, after a beat.

"Yes, SPAFF for short I suppose," replied the pointy nosed man with exasperation.

There was a snigger and a scratching of pen to paper....

"So being solar powered means that, whatever you're presenting us with tomorrow will only function during daylight hours?" asked yet another reporter.

"Err no, please tell me you're not seriously asking me that

question?” the grey suit sneered. “The power can be stored, don't be an idiot! We use solar power because it’s friendlier to the environment. That by the way is the invisible and very visible enigma that surrounds us.”

The press stared at him blankly, the suited guide continued.

“Quickly moving on. Our experimental subjects are also fitted with a kinetic, self-serving, recharging battery cell!”

“Oh. You mean like a watch?”

The grey suit applauded sarcastically.

“Yes it’s simple, for their individual microchips and other bits and pieces; it will all make sense tomorrow. Ok then, shall we? If you would like to follow me through to the conference room I can brief everyone on tomorrow’s events.”

The door closed behind the suit and the reporters.

Vincent sat back in his chair, and flicked a switch, another buzzer sounded.

“Hi guys,” said Vincent.

Voices returned through a dozen, wall hung, surround speakers.

“Hello Vincent, hi Vincent, Vincent, dude, buddy, morning sweetheart, good morning Vin, Vinnie, hey mate, Yo fella, alright sexy!”

“Yin, Yang, what about you two?”

“*Greetings human,* how is your *snivelling existence on* this dull *and laborious day?”*

“Guys.... finish your own sentences.”

“*You made I and I what I’s are. I’s swim in your SPAFF* and now I’s are two in *body but one* in mind, plebeian imbecile.”

Yin and Yang spoke as one in their customary thin, light insidiously sweet tone.

“Oh really, well let’s see how you are two in mind and two in body!”

Vincent stood up and pressed a few buttons, a few of the hundreds he found on the panels around him. Through the safety glass he watched keenly as a robotic arm, gently cradling a ping-pong ball in its mechanical jaws came out of the sidewall and moved purposefully across the Grid. On reaching its designated target it meticulously dropped the ball into an aquarium filled with SPAFF, a couple of stones, a bit of green stuff, a multi coloured plaster skull and two highly excited terrapins! Another robotic arm placed what can only be described as miniature basketball hoops at either end of the transparent dwelling.

"Let the games begin," Vincent announced.

"Ooh you spoil us, *wait, wait till the whistle*, don't cheat, *get lost leatherneck or you shall* feel I's wrath. Oh please you're *such a* drama queen!"

The rest of the subjects took an interest.

"Right, shut it," said Vincent.

Sniggers came from the crowd.

"Seth, you can be the referee."

"Me, cool, excellent bud sure thing."

Vincent pushed a few more buttons. A path lit up across the Grid like illuminated white squares on a giant crossword puzzle! Seth shuffled along it to the Terrapin stadium, passing the others on the way.

Seth, a grey buck rabbit with a white bushy tail, had a bounce to his stride like a 1970s soul singer. He lived in his own little world daydreaming most of the time but he was harmless enough, in fact he was a pussycat!

The truth was that he, like most of the others came from a different part of the facility. To put everything into context, all you need to know about Seth is; he is male, allergic to cigarettes and he feels that ruby lips by Revlon is too gaudy and clashes with the colour of SPAFF! You see he 'worked' in the smokers' section but, due to his inability to inhale at a consistent level, was moved to cosmetics, regardless of his health! So Seth is a common rabbit who now likes wearing lipstick!

The others took their seats for the event.

Garston, a white and tan coloured gerbil, had built the seating around the terrapin abode with toilet rolls, washing up detergent bottles and other bits and bobs including a gerbil wheel that was originally placed onto the grid for experiments and tests.

Vincent pushed another button, a whistle sounded and then, they were off!

The terrapins flew, well, swam, like Olympic swimmers in a paddling pool, towards the ball flapping furiously with their flippers and thwacking each other along the way.

"Ouch you little terrapin. That's right!"

The crowd struggled to follow the action as the game escalated to a frothy frenzy. They all had to squint to see what was happening in the tank and then;

"Goal!"

"It's basket!"

"I scored, no I did."

"Seth,"

"Yes," Seth replied.

"Who scored?" asked Vincent.

"They did," Seth answered, after a little deliberation.

"Good then it's a draw."

"It was me I tell you, you ignoramus!"

"Now that's enough you two," said Vincent.

The disgruntled terrapins came to an impasse and brought their abuse to a mutter.

"Now, I have to explain what tomorrow is about," said Vincent

"*We are all shell,*" Yin and Yang replied, decidedly uninterested.

The robot arms on the Grid cleared away the homemade seating.

"You're all going to be tested and if everything goes well, you guys will give mankind a gift."

"Tested?"

"Yes Seth. When the world finds out that you can talk, be it through speakers or a typeface, then millions of people will be able to hear, but more importantly listen to you."

No one said a word.

"You, the animals," Vincent became more and more animated, "of the world will have a voice, you will save endangered species and help the planet. You'll tell us how to save the oceans and, well, it's gonna be great. The," he paused and then with real hope said, "the things mankind will learn will mean we can all be friends, and ensure everyone's survival."

"Does that mean you won't eat uz any more?" said Maurice the French-accented resonating toad that didn't quite know the difference between a zed and an s!

"Err... It's going to be great Maurice. I swear it! Look, all I can say is, that you guys haven't eaten each other yet, have you? And you should have. Believe me, if you had followed your instincts you would have, but you haven't and that's because of the qualities of SPAFF."

Mumbling came from the group.

"Guy's look, Bandi, you're a cat right, a normal, black, household pussy-cat?"

"Doh, baby, like yeah, from Alabama in the good old US of A."

"Err yes, anyway; you have been on the Grid for months now and not eaten anyone. You see, normally your instincts would have had you munch on, Garston, Seth, Albert and Escobar."

"Us why us?"

"Because you're a common grey pigeon Albert and Escobar is a kite, a beautiful bird of prey."

"What's common got to do with the price of fish, hey guv, and how come he gets the compliments?" Albert replied disgruntled but with an abundance of cockney charm and swagger.

Escobar, frowning, marched straight up a miniature ladder to the protective viewing glass divide and fronted Vincent.

"Are you talking to me? Hey hombre, I said, are you talking to me? It's lucky you called me beautiful."

"Escobar, don't be silly, you're not a New York gangster you're from all over the place, via Indonesia and you are also quite the carnivore, but you're not a gangster." Escobar huffed, Vincent continued. "Maurice, she would have eaten you too, even though you're a toad and Freak, believe me when I say, you too would make a tasty snack."

"Me, surely not. Bandi wouldn't stand a chance."

"You'd be surprised Freak," Vincent replied.

"But I am venomous, and if under attack I would bite."

"Doesn't matter, she would have you too, Freak. With her lightning reactions you would be mulch before you could strike!"

There was a thoughtful silence.

"I would choke you with my eight legs on the way down, so don't even think about a meal cat!" said Freak staring straight at Bandi!

"Bring it on Freak, tarantula spider is looking tasty!" Bandi replied.

"Stop it you two," said Vincent.

"Yin and Yang, you're food too," they were very unimpressed, "and she might even try you Spike."

"Now stop that Bluey, I'm too big."

"That may be, but, Aussie Iguana would also be on the menu. If she was starving, only Steve would be spared."

"Yeah, cos I am big and tuff."

"Big, no! Because you're a Jackahuahua and a dog, yes!"

"That's an odd breed, never heard of it, what exactly is a Jackahuahua?" asked Bandi.

"It means Steve is half Jack Russell and half Chihuahua, Bandi!"

"Oh, so why isn't he a Chewy Russell?" asked Bandi.

Vincent looked down at his keyboard and shook his head.

Spike had a moment of realisation.

"Hold on! Who are you calling an Aussie mate? I'm from the Americas!"

"You have a surfer accent." Vincent replied.

"What accent?" Spike asked.

"Never mind!"

Vincent got back to the subject in hand.

"Anyway all of this has made you, something I call, Sapienised!"

There was a hiatus in the conversation as Vincent looked at the group. Garston broke the silence.

"So let me get this right," said Garston.

Garston was enigmatic, he hardly spoke but when he did for some reason everybody listened. This was partly due to the fact that everyone had to in order to understand his thick Liverpudlian accent!

"Err, we are to undergo a test and if we pass, the world will benefit and if we don't pass the world will carry on the way it is."

"Well, yes. That's it in a nutshell really," replied Vincent.

"So we are the only animals in the world that can do this?"

"Err, well, yes!"

"Why?" Garston asked.

All of the subjects turned to Vincent and gazed up at him, all of them patiently waiting for an answer.

"As far as I know you are the only group of animals being tested in this way. You see SPAFF has created something very special. If you like, a wall-to-wall shield around you all. The solar power generates a current, which feeds the Cube, and then the SPAFF works its magic. Do you follow?" Vincent paused.

They all nodded in recognition, other than Steve who was sniffing

Seth's bottom! Vincent continued.

"Well, all of you have a couple of things that add to your uniqueness, you also all have within you individual devices that enable you to access computer and communication programmes via modern technology."

"And how did we get these devices?" Garston asked.

"Well, you all went through a small procedure. This saw a tiny microchip inserted into your individual skulls. They in turn are activated by your body's electrical impulses, via recharging kinetic cells, allowing your intelligence to be magnified and that gives you the power to communicate by means of a speech programme that I developed for you to use with the Cube, okay? The Cube is basically a computing transmitter that has got all of the bits and gadgets on it you need for each of your individual communicative devices."

"So why is the Cube in here and not out there?"

"It's in the room with you Garston, because in there it is protected from the outside world and hackers. It's a computer in a bubble if you like, and I am the only one with access. Me and a couple of bigwigs."

"Err.... what is a bigwig?" asked Spike chewing on the nub of a carrot!

"It's slang for very important person, and you could have found that out yourself by accessing the Cube with your device and searching its Oxford dictionary programme. You are all smarter than you think."

"So anything we want to know, anything at all, we can find out just by thinking about it, as long as the information is in the Cube?"

"Yes, Garston."

"Zo the cube iz a computer?" Maurice asked glistening.

"Yes."

"With no wirez powering it?"

"That's right, only solar power Maurice, and that's what keeps anything from corrupting the Cubes programme files."

Something fluttered.

"So hombre, err, how do you programme the Cube?" asked Escobar.

"I use an encrypted password and infrared keyboard in here," Vincent replied. Escobar continued.

"And the reason you hear us is because..."

Vincent cut in.

"The programme I invented to transform your thought patterns into words as you talk."

A Tarantula sat back and crossed eight legs.

"What about our voices?" Escobar asked.

"Your individual voices are coming out of these surround speakers, but each voice has been developed a little to match your individual personalities, and your brains do the rest. You ever heard a rabbit say dude, sounds awesome, yeah?"

"Well, actually, *yes we have, everyday since* that insufferable lop-eared, *passive, bushy tailed* rodent entered our *domain."*

"And you can all see in colour now too, not just black and white!"

"*Has this odious idiot got* anything interesting to contribute *other than the* obvious or *fictitious?"*

"Ah, Yin and Yang you are a little different. Everyone else is dosed with SPAFF through sunlight, as it beams down through the solar powered glass. However, you two actually have direct contact with SPAFF and through osmosis, or due to the fact that you swallow it every now and then, you have become, if you like, a rogue experiment!"

"What on earth is this anthropogenic, antiquated minded, two-legged, sugar-sucking twit on about? This *may be tantamount to slander*."

"Because you're in a tank and can't do anything out of it, you were, chosen," said Vincent.

"*Chosen, I like that* we are 'The *Chosen!'* How are we *different* from the others regarding all of this *convoluted nonsense?"*

"Well, there are two of you, but sometimes you behave as one, as you know." Vincent scratched his head and ran his fingers through his hair and huffed.

"What I am trying to say is that you two are telepathic or, as I like to call it, terrepathic. Get it?"

Everyone just looked at each other blankly.

"Oh never mind, anyway, that's why you're a separate experiment. It's the SPAFF in your bodies and enveloping you! It's creating something, taking you to another evolutionary level. Oh yeah, and your kind are usually green in colour, not white!"

Yin and yang were repulsed and indignant all at once!

"Green, how turgid!"

"You see, in the wrong hands this knowledge could be dangerous. You communicate with the others and with me by using your microchips and Bluetooth, but with each other by thinking. I also have an inkling that maybe you don't need these four walls, I mean everyone else is surrounded by SPAFF, it's in the walls, ceiling and floor but because you guys have SPAFF within you, well, one day we might just find out what you are really capable of. SPAFF was just supposed to be something to help us communicate with you, but to be honest, we don't really know what it does exactly."

"*Chosen!*"

"Sorry guvner, I don't get it. Why is the floor a grid then? And what the blighty are the shiny stones doing in the SPAFF and what…."

Garston interrupted Albert mid flow.

"The floor is a grid because it allows Vincent to place objects in, and out of the room and measure the results of experiments more accurately. The precious stones reflect and intensify the strength of SPAFF, not really necessary but a nice touch; mercury would have sufficed, poisonous though! The steel composite strips around the grid floor allow the transference of electricity to any part of the Grid and thus movement of the Grid can be regulated."

"Is that right fella?" Albert asked in his East End drool. "The Grid is run by electricity, the Cube by solar power generating electricity and the terrapins should be green? And how does he know?"

"Err yeah," Vincent replied. "Garston and Freak are also a little different."

"How?" Freak asked.

"The silk webbing that you produce is actually a power conductor, like copper wire, Freak. This," Vincent searched for a word, "miracle has been achieved by feeding you SPAFF dipped beetles. The result is that you can access information from any device your web is connected to or in contact with, like now and the Cube for instance."

Freak raised a leg in the air and asked a question. "Why do I have this then?"

"You have a steel foot, sorry claw, because I built it for you. You had lost your own in a previous incident."

"Incident?"

"Yes. When you were first brought in, you were placed up here with me, nothing different about you, but one night the caretaker freaked because you had got out and then, blah blah, you were a bit of a leg short as it was slammed in a cupboard door."

"The caretaker huh, I'll remember that. Who brought me in then?" Freak asked.

"Oh, no-one, just the cleaner. Her son was afraid of you. She said she'd bought you for him as a gift"

"I was an unwanted gift! How very sad." Freak was devastated.

"And what about me?"

Vincent looked at Garston, and paused in thought before he replied.

"Well Garston, you have all the usual stuff, and of course your left eye gives you cam vision and technology."

"Still doesn't explain everything." Garston asked.

"Ok then, well, you were found in a place called Garston in Liverpool, that's how you got your name. The caretaker brought you in when he saved you from a vicious raven attack in his garden. You had obviously escaped from a pet shop or something and were half dead and eaten, so he brought you here because he felt sorry for you and thought I might be able to help. You were fixed up and ended up in the experiment, sorry, I mean programme. Now though, you're alive, different but alive and your cam eye works great."

Garston pondered thoughtfully and then tried to remember his past.

"Why can't I remember anything?" he asked.

"All of your memories and I mean all of them, were wiped when the microchips were installed. Nothing to do with me, that was the idea of the Military."

"Military? We *are* the *Chosen!*"

"Yes the Military. Oh and Albert, in answer to your previous question, Garston knows all of this because he accessed the Cube via infrared and downloaded the information onto his own microchip. Something I recommend that you all do, so you best understand what all of this is in relation to."

"Right you are guv, no worries. What does he mean by download?" Albert asked turning to the group.

Garston, forever inquisitive, took full advantage of this

knowledge and accessed all the data the Cube had to offer by downloading every piece of information he could, every morsel. This included a schematic of the facility and how to improve the food rations!

***

The following morning, very early at about 2am, a bleary eyed Vincent shuffled up to the door marked No Entry and stared into the retinal sensor. The door slid open and Vincent trundled past the frozen in time sleeping robots and tranquil dolphin aquarium, to his room at the far end to begin a group of nighttime tests regarding speculative behavioural patterns! When he got there, he sat at his desk, pushed a few buttons and the Grid lit up.

"Dude, Vincent help us, it smellz like a Frenchman's underpantz in here!"

The Grid looked like a ransacked supermarket. Food was everywhere and a pile of something very smelly and half the size of its owner was steaming next to a mortified, pint-sized little dog. Everybody else stood huddled together in the far corner!

"I told you too much knowledge can be dangerous," Vincent chuckled. He pushed another button and watched as the world's most expensive pooper-scooper did its stuff and cleared the room of leftovers and doggy do, whilst a deodoriser filled the room with citrus odours! The huddle soon dispersed around the Grid to individual hangouts affording Vincent the time to sense that something was different! The group were one member short. Garston was gone. Vincent panicked.

"Where is Garston? Where has he gone? Bandi did you eat him? He just can't disappear," he yelled, nervously grabbing a lollipop from a storage jar.

"He hasn't," said a distinctive voice with its owner appearing through a section of floor like a magician through a trap door. "I am here," said Garston.

"Where have you been? What on earth.... this really is not acceptable." Vincent was seething. "I am sorry but I'm going to have to remove you from the programme, you may be contaminated."

"Shut up, chill out and listen," Garston said with purpose.

Vincent was dumbstruck.

"Look guys, after downloading a schematic of this place, my enquiring nature took over. I couldn't help myself. I wanted to see what the great outdoors looked like. I have no memory of it and the Cube can only access something called Google Earth, which is great, but not in real time! So, I checked out the security room, which is linked to 130 cameras, some of them are outside and some of them in here. This facility is huge. Did you guys know that there are four underground levels or that there's a bunch of dolphins in a huge aquarium living next door?"

"Of course we *did you loathsome limp minded excuse for a rat,"* someone said sarcastically!

"And what about you, Vincent? You never mentioned you lived here!"

"How do you know that?"

"Well, there's a camera in your room, actually the label under the screen says Vincent's apartment."

"You mean they've been watching me?"

"Must be!"

"Oh my! Well that's embarrassing!"

"What is?" Albert asked.

"Err… nothing," replied Vincent, who was flushed brighter than beetroot!

"Well, anyway I've filmed and downloaded something important, so watch the monitors on the Cube."

There was a quick burst of snow on the screens and then two chatting men appeared. One was wearing a long white coat and the other was dressed in an army uniform. They were talking about a movie Vincent had been watching in his room. It was the tale of a dog, named Lassie, and her life with an orphan boy on a farm, but as the conversation went on it drifted towards Vincent's programme or as they called it Project Commune. The two men were jolly and smiling, nattering on about the use of SPAFF and the microchips and how they couldn't wait for the government to put them to work with their best candidates from military school and an institution called MIT and if everything went well during today's tests, how their lives would be changed for the better and what promotions they should get, and how they were going to tell Vincent that, whatever the result, Project

Commune was a failure and the Grid would be destroyed and all of its subjects, every one, would have to be terminated!

The screen went blank and Garston broke the silence. "Well?"

Vincent turned green at the gills as he slumped into his chair.

"It iz time for us to zplit like frogspawn and get out of here," said Maurice doing a pretty good impression of a devastated French Barry White!

"We don't know how to behave in the outside world. What do we do as our species to survive in the outside world? Where are we supposed to live in the outside world? We're all gonna die in the outside world!" Spike was hysterical; his voice had escalated in pitch towards, well, madness!

Vincent jumped up. "Ok, this is what is going to happen," turning from nerd, to sugar sucking Sergeant Major. "Garston, did you find a way off the Grid to the outside world?"

"Yes, I'm afraid it's the same way that the Grid disposes of our surplus food and bodily droppings."

"Nice!" muttered Bandi.

"Well that's a start. Now guys listen carefully. I will do something up here, which will let you all access the information you will need to survive as your individual species in the outside world, however, before that you must download the code for my speech programme onto your individual chips so you can transfer it to any other computer hard drive, just in case you need it. Then you're going to all wrap yourselves in Seth's lettuce leaves and be disposed of as surplus food. Got it?"

"But what about us, we swim in your SPAFF, in this glass box! You can't *wrap this in lettuce* and pretend it's pooh! So come up *with a plan that's* viable, geek!"

"Yin, Yang, shut up," clipped Bandi.

"Thank you Bandi," said Vincent. "Now Albert and Escobar, I am about to tell you something that you may find hard to swallow, but it's true, ok?"

"Yes guv!"

"Si Baroni!!"

"YOU CAN FLY!" said Vincent.

There was absolute silence.

"Is the lad sick?" said Albert.

“No, he’s an idiot!” Escobar replied. “We know that, we just don’t need to in here.”

“Oh,” said Vincent sheepishly, “then, well, you two get either end of the “Glass box” which is actually made of a lightweight plastic, hook your talons to the lip at the top and flap like crazy. The rest of you get to one side of it and as soon as the lads get it off the floor, charge at it together. This will hopefully spill out Yin and Yang. You can then wrap them in lettuce and they can join you in the Poop Shoot! Got it?”

Sure enough after everyone had downloaded the code for Vincent’s Speech programme and finished discussing the plan, it was agreed that the Terrapin SPAFF tank was to be stormed!

Albert and Escobar took their places whilst the others lined up ready to charge.

“Ok guys, before we begin” said Vincent, “I need you to download this programme too, it’s called Internet Explorer and then I want you to find, access, and save as much information as you can regarding, well everything? Now, the Internet is an invention that allows humans to communicate over long distances and find out any information they require on any subject when they need it, so it will be helpful.”

Vincent pushed a button.

“Right, the Cube is now linked to my computer in here, which is logged onto the Internet. Your individual communication devices will now allow you to scan the Cube for any material you need. Do you understand?”

Nobody answered him.

“I said begin scanning and downloading!”

Everyone motioned in some way or another and did as they were told, concentrating on the ‘charge’ rather than what Vincent was gibbering on about, but Vincent took it all as read and started a countdown, “3, 2, 1, go!”

At ‘go’ Albert and Escobar strained and flapped for their lives.

“Come on Escobar,” said Albert.

“For the boys Baroni,” he replied.

Gritting their beaks they struggled and eventually…

Vincent glanced at his screen; everyone was hooked up to the Internet.

“Charge!” cried Spike.

In an amazing show of unity, like a squadron out of the trenches, they all bolted towards the aquarium. It was at that moment Vincent came to realise Project Commune was a great success. His subjects or rather his friends, had become the team that he had always dreamed they would, even though they were from different positions on the food chain. But then, like a multi vehicle pile up, ‘SMASH!’ everyone bashed into the side of the Terrapin SPAFFarium!

Escobar and Albert hit the ground like shot down fighter pilots whilst the charging team were sent skidding along the tiled floor, out of control. Yin and Yang however were fine! They just surfed casually out of their home, and were now flapping happily about on the Grid. With a few moans and groans everyone got to their feet, trying not to slip in the puddle of SPAFF they found themselves in.

Vincent called through the glass.

“Freak don’t move, don’t move a muscle.”

Freak, had ended up on her back still connected to The Cube via her power-conducting web.

“What’s that you’re saying?” she said getting to her feet. An odd sensation came over her as her metal claw tapped the floor!

“Ooh a tingle!”

BANG!

Electricity hit them all like lightning, zipping through their bodies amplified in power by SPAFF a thousand fold. The Cube sparked and fizzed as the current raced around the room. Vincent sprang up from his chair. The lights on the consoles around him flashed madly all at once, and the Grid began moving of its own accord. Opening and closing spaces, sweeping the area clear, dropping Ping-pong balls and throwing out food. Vincent looked on helpless.

“Hang on,” he shouted as he searched for the power breaker.

The spark-flying Cube creaked and groaned, broke free of its fixing and crashed to the floor. Shards of glass rained down and SPAFF engulfed the group. Barking, squawking and scratching, everyone swam for their lives, as the torrent poured down and tossed them around. Gasping for air, the liquid sucked each of them under one by one, through the open tiles on the Grid and into a long twisting wide waste disposal pipe. Frightened and screaming, they slid down the plastic rollercoaster shoot and eventually hurtled through a wall-flap into a large industrial bin which, in turn, through the force of the gushing surge, tumbled and regurgitated the food, creature and poop contents, onto a patch of muddy grass at the rear of the house.

In the SPAFF pool of refuse everyone rose to their claws and paws and looked around at each other to see if they were all alright. They were all fine, hunky-dory in fact but different, very different! Everyone had changed in appearance. Garston, Seth, Bandi, Albert, Steve and Maurice had become various shades of tan, however, Freak, Spike, and Escobar were now almost completely white in colour, just like Yin and Yang. The only parts of them that weren't, were their eyes, beaks, fangs and claws.

"Dude that was heavy stuff," said Seth.

"What did you say?" asked Garston.

"I said dude…."

"I know what you said. The thing is you're talking and I am hearing…without speakers and a computer."

"Yes you're right, I can too," preened Albert.

"And I alzo," croaked Maurice.

"Yeah, me too," said Steve.

The conversation ended abruptly as the group realised that Freak wasn't moving. She was lying still on her back in the sodden dirt with her legs in the air. Yin and Yang quickly crawled over, studied her condition and then, unbelievably, began to resuscitate her with CPR.

"A thousand and one, a thousand and two, a thousand and three…"

Everyone watched the slightly strange and yet, touching scene. An Escobar chirp and a Spike hiss eventually broke the silence when, miraculously, Freak spluttered back to life and began to breathe and move slowly. Dazed, she scrambled a little gingerly to her feet.

"Oh, baby we nearly lost you!"

She said nothing, just gave Yin and Yang a big scary tarantula hug.

Escobar then hopped through the grass, leaves and rubbish and carefully wrapped a talon around each of the terrapins, and then, a declaration:

"This is the end chum's! It is time for evolution to take its natural *course and for a new master race to seize grasp of this planet. Mankind will suffer for the degradation it has caused and we, the TERRORPINS, will RULE* THE WORLD. *Ha,ha,ha,ha. Ha!"*

Escobar glanced at Albert, bowed, and took off into the night sky carrying the maniacally amused Yin and Yang.

Freak, her furry body shining like silver in the moonlight, crawled over to Spike and wearily climbed up onto his back. She then speedily and with intricate artistry, furnished what can only be described as a harness and reins out of her webbing. She raised her metal claw, like a cowboy would his hat to say goodbye, and 'whoosh,' she and Spike scuttled off into the undergrowth, and were gone.

Garston was first to speak.

"The Terrapins didn't talk but I heard them. Well I did. I mean, did any of you just feel that?"

"Like voices in your head," replied Steve.

"Yeah and why didn't the others say anything, and why did they go with them?" Bandi asked.

"Maybe they couldn't zpeak and maybe zey had no choice! Yin and Yang are terrepathic remember, and it's the first time they have been out of the tank," said Maurice and then, he spoke reflectively….

"And SPAFF has done some weird poop to us all!"

"Amen!" said Garston.

"Err, excuse me you lot, but what the, shiver me timbers, ooh argh, splice the main brace, just happened?" Albert promptly stopped talking. The confused look on his face said it all. He looked at himself and then at Garston and then the others. They were all staring back at him, mouths agog!

"Err…that was very colourfully put Albert," said Garston.

"Walk the plank, or you're keelhauled, it's colourful. How the mutiny did that happen? Why am I speaking like this? I used to be so, pieces of eight, polite, maybe a little cockney but scurvy polite."

"Apparently the molecular structure of SPAFF has, through osmosis and natural intake, carried us all individually on a voyage to a dominion that is yet unexplored by the virtues of our apparent species."

"Seth?" said Steve.

"Who the crows nest made you, land ahoy, Einstein?" said Albert.

"SPAFF," said Garston.

Bandi, who had been washing herself, piped up.

"Right then everyone, shall we face the problem in hand? We have obviously all been affected by SPAFF and no doubt all of us will have some surprises in store, however we have two unscrupulous, psychotic, 'TERRORPINS' on the loose threatening to make mankind pay for whatever, and, they have allied themselves with a squawking Kite, which incidentally makes them airborne, and a Tarantula, who now rides an Iguana with the verve of Billy Crystal in City Slickers."

"Who the bilge-sucking is Billy Crystal?" asked Albert.

Meanwhile, Seth's thoughts had drifted off to a place of conundrum and so, he decided it best that he should immediately document his pondered observations and findings in a secret file in his microchip in order that he may reflect upon them at any required time:

Dear Diary,

At this time I am considering the reality that the Terrorpins can communicate by thought alone. How far can this all go? I also wonder whether something abnormal has happened to Spike, Escobar and Freak's microchip circuitry, and that this is the probable explanation for their peculiar exit. Perhaps they indeed elected to depart of their own accord in the company of the loopy amphibian twosome! The puzzle burns inside of me.

Regards Seth!

LOCATION, LOCATION, LOCATION!

Garston woke the following morning, startled by the sounds of a shrieking raven! He found himself inside a gnarly, hollowed, fallen tree trunk in the woods behind the Manor, curled up and snuggled up, between Steve and Bandi. He gave a big yawn, had a stretch and crawled over his two pals towards the daylight. Venturing warily into the open he discovered Seth and Maurice sitting side-by-side in a small clearing. They were watching through the trees as two teams of men in protective white suits and masks went about their business. One group was fishing through the twisted and broken aluminium and glass remains of what used to be a large conservatory type structure on the side of the house, while the other, with the aid of a fork lift and a winch, loaded dolphins onto a lorry for transport. Garston sat down beside his friends as the raven circled overhead.

"There's danger everywhere," he said looking up.

Seth nodded but his mind was clearly somewhere else.

Garston, keen eyed, watched the raven fly off towards the old Manor House.

"It's the Grid, or what's left of it," said Seth, "they're getting rid of it, making it look as if it never existed and where do you think they are taking those dolphins?"

At that point a large black car with dark tinted windows, pulled up sharply outside the main entrance of the house. Two men dressed in black suits, black shirts and black ties jumped out. One wore a trilby and had scars on his face, was slight in build and had a jangle to his walk. The other was a tall, burly, longhaired fellow with black leather gloves and a braided beard. They marched purposefully into the house, but less than a minute later returned, dragging out Vincent. Holding him by the scruff of the neck, they ushered him into the back of the car, throwing in a tatty sports bag after him. The car door slammed shut. The bearded man stood tall for a second and had a look around, took a sniff, opened the passenger door, slid into the front and then, the car pulled away at high speed. Vincent was gone.

"I hope Vincent's going to be alright. That was all very cloak and dagger!" said Garston.

“I’m zure he will be, he’s a bright dude,” said Maurice.

They all sat quietly, very subdued until Seth broke the silence.

“We need to find ourselves a new abode. I know we all have the information we need to survive in the outside world, but I’d prefer something with a few home comforts,” he said.

“Yes it’s a world full of predatorz and we are food!” Maurice replied.

“Where is Albert?” said Garston.

“Up here, Scurvy dog!”

Albert swooped down from the branch of a sycamore tree and landed next to the group.

“Sorry Garston I can’t, batten down the hatches, help it.”

“It’s alright Albert, you won’t be afflicted for long. I will try and cure your linguistic ailment when I get to a computer.”

“Three sheets to the wind, Seth!”

Steve trotted up with Bandi.

“What’s the plan then? Can’t live like this!” said Steve scratching an ear.

“We need to create our own base, like a Bat Cave!" said Bandi.

“A cave full of bats, what you on about?” Steve asked.

“No silly, Batman is a superhero, but he’s this millionaire Bruce Wayne too, anyway, he has a big house but underneath it is this big cave with a secret entrance and he keeps all this cool stuff in it for upholding the law. It’s called, the Bat Cave!”

“That’s it!” exclaimed Garston. “Bandi you’re a genius. Alright everyone, I am gonna open up Bluetooth so I can pass you the schematic of the house and facility underneath. We are going to build our own Bat Cave.”

“Sounds like a plan.” said Steve

“Should take about four years,” said Garston.

Seth’s ears pricked.

“What about four days?” he said.

“Seth, don’t be silly. How are we gonna do that?” said Bandi with a look of ridicule.

“We will dig down and create rooms next to rooms that are beneath the facility. One next to the food store, one next to the security room and one next to the room that has the buildings computer mainframe, and then we’ll build some rooms for living quarters, too. We will create a tunnel network between them and an exit and entrance on the surface in the woods, nice and secluded. Then we are going to order everything else we need on-line over the Internet," he paused, "I think!"

"What? Have you gone acorns on us? How are we going to do that?" asked Steve.

"Like rabbits," Seth replied.

"But we aren't rabbits are we landlubber, so we can't, can we?" said Albert.

"Ah, yes we can. All of you follow me, and quietly."

Seth set off and bounded through the shrubs into the woods, followed by the group. He eventually came to a stop in a secluded clearing.

"Now don't be alarmed guys, just do as I say. Steve, Bandi, everyone, I need you all to bow at my paws."

"What! You've got to be pulling my chestnuts mate," said Steve.

"You don't have any chestnuts Steve." Garston replied.

"I don't?" asked Steve.

"Sorry mate." Garston replied, sympathetically.

Everyone bowed to Seth, except Steve that is, who slumped to his knees with a whimper. Seth took a second and then thumped the ground with a back leg and gave a squeak.

From behind the circling trees, long grasses and ferns, eyes, ears and twitching noses soon became increasingly evident. It was shortly, abundantly clear, that the gang were surrounded by an awful lot of rabbits, hundreds and hundreds of them to be precise. Everyone froze on the spot, more than a little intimidated by the sheer number of visitors.

"I don't like this!" said Bandi.

"Hush and watch," Seth replied.

Seth stepped forward and raised his head. A grey rabbit timidly approached him through the clearing until it met him nose to nose. Seth stood his ground. The grey rabbit sniffed, and then something very odd happened, it turned to face the other rabbits that were now at least six or seven rows deep, squeaked, jumped, and thumped the ground, delightedly. All the surrounding rabbits then bowed their heads, in what seemed to be some sort of a show of respect.

"Can we get up now?" whispered Steve.

"Yes, but sit either side of me and err, slightly behind."

A path cleared through the rabbit crowd and an old haggard, ear torn buck approached the group holding a swollen root. He stopped in front of Seth and placed it down at Seth's paws and gave him a sniff. The rest of the group stood quietly still, more than a little confused by the scenario. The old rabbit then turned to the bunny horde, squeaked once more and then, bedlam! All of the surrounding rabbits started jumping up in the air and bouncing over one another everywhere.

"What the scallywag is happening?" Albert asked.

Seth turned to his friends.

"I am sorry but I have misled you," he said.

"What?" asked Garston.

"I'm not who you think I am. I am, Sethias the 9031st, rabbit king of England. And these are my subjects and our workforce."

"What?" Garston asked again.

"We, the rabbits, have been watching Pradgonne Manor for some time. It was brought to my attention, through our network of sentries posted around the countryside, and as King, I was forced to act. You see rabbits, and other animals, have been going into this building, and never coming out for some time now. So, I sneaked in as a delivery, I mean, who's going to notice one more bunny, right. However, everything after that is a muddle of make-up and smoke, I only remembered I was King this morning for some reason. I think we should get to the Manor House computer mainframe; it will help answer some of our questions."

"You're a King?" said Steve still trying to make sense of everything. "I need to eat," he said suddenly changing tack.

"You're starting to remember?" asked Bandi.

"Yes I am, though I don't know why." Seth replied.

"Zo shall we get on with it?" said Maurice.

"What about food?" Steve asked, repeating the question.

Seth replied. "Well, those of us that are herbivores are fine with the natural food around us, but you carnivores are going to have to scavenge through the rubbish. In other words, eat the leftovers that the humans leave in the bins outside the main house."

"What?" said Steve, pretty repulsed by the idea.

"It's only for a while until our home is built and we can shop on-line," said Seth.

"Right, let's get on with it then," said Garston.

"Err no!" said Seth. "You guys just stay out of the way; my rabbits have got this in hand, sorry, paw!"

***

And so the building and digging began. The rabbit workforce worked their socks off, to and fro, to and fro they toiled, disappearing and reappearing from the woods, whilst the rest of the group either, lay about discovering the great outdoors or, muddled through the Manor House bins!

***

Meanwhile, on the other side of the woods hidden in a trench by the edge of a country lane near an old cottage that had seen better days, there was a scuttling and then…

"Finally, how long *does it take for one wrinkly* lizard to get across *some woods?"*

"All night!" said Freak, creepily tugging at her webbed reins.

"Ah you can talk! Why did you not speak back at the *SPAFF spill*?"

"There wasn't much to say." Freak replied. "Where is Escobar?"

"In the middle of the Lane, he is waiting for *our lift."*

Escobar was an unusual sight. His brilliant white plumage shone brightly against the backdrop of the lane and green British countryside.

"Hush, she's coming."

A radiantly red, 1960s Morris Minor pottered up the lane at about 15 miles per hour and came to a stop just beside Escobar. The front passenger door swung open and a little old lady, in brightly coloured woollen clothes, more than any one person could ever imagine wearing, leaned over and smiled,

"Go get your friends then love," she said.

Escobar turned and fluttered over to Yin and Yang.

"Ok, Freak, don't *bite her. Now* let's get in the car."

Escobar wrapped his talons around Yin and Yang and flew straight onto the passenger seat. Freak quickly followed, leaping into the little car on Spike's back like a seasoned show jumper.

"Why is she helping us?" Freak asked from the car floor.

"Terrepathy is a powerful *medium especially with the simple* minded elderly of the human race. HA*HAHH*A!"

"You're controlling her aren't you?" said Freak.

*"Yes, isn't it fan*tastic?"

"That depends upon whether you are her or not! How did you find her?"

"That pylon thingy over there with the *telecommunication bits attached, it has that* thing called *the Internet!"*

"What happens now?" Freak asked.

"Woof, woof, bark, snort, woof, growl!"

"What's that?" said an alerted Freak her body tensing ready to strike.

"Down Roxy, down," said the little old lady.

A small curly haired mutt, of dubious origin, poked its head through the space in-between the two front seats from the back. Her coat was brown, tan, white, black, and grey in colour and she was at least an entire 10 inches tall!

"Sit down Roxy, they're our friends." said the old lady.

"What is it with people these days? " Yin and Yang asked with a certain amount of dissatisfaction, "Can no one have a dog that you *can actually call a canine and not a rodent anymore?* Don't kill the dog Freak; it may *upset the old bat. Now,* we are being taken to the *airport where* we will be loaded into executive travel cases that *we have ordered for our travel. We will then be placed upon a private jet where we will be fed our favourite meals and transported* 1000s of miles, to a place called Alcatraz Island, just off the coast of Costa Rica. There, a human entrepreneur and his flunkies will treat us like Kings. *We will* then use his fortune to do our evil bidding. H*AHAH*AH!"

"How on Earth?" said Freak.

"Again, it's this thingy, the Internet. The wet eared sugar sucking human spoke of it, remember? He was right. You can find anything. It's ability to fly through the air, touching *everything and everyone is truly marvellous,* it's a weapon waiting to *be harnessed and soon* we will harness it. HAHA*HA! We'll use it* to our advantage *anyway. HAHAHAHA!"*

"You don't have to keep doing that ridiculous evil laugh thing, it's becoming boring."

Freak, wasn't scared of Yin and Yang, after all she was deadly.

"Be careful my eight legged friend, *remember that your* mind is within the realms of our control."

"Is it? Doesn't feel like it is. I thought I made my own decisions."

"Well, why don't I and I *try something?"*

"Fine," Freak replied.

Yin and Yang chuckled with contempt; they thought it would be funny to make Freak hang from the rear view mirror like a furry air freshener.

"Go ahead, when you're ready then." Nothing happened. "Well?" said Freak.

"I's can't!"

Escobar and Spike began to whistle!

"Well it works with *them."*

"Ok, but why didn't it work on the others we left behind as well?" Freak asked.

"I and I did not try and really, I's don't care. Now I and I will try once more, with yourself.

Freak tapped her claw, smugly!

"*Wh*y, *why*!" Yin and Yang were getting frustrated.

"Not that clever are we huh? Maybe my exoskeleton is a barrier, after all I am the only one of us that has one and now, it's SPAFF penetrated; perhaps it's made me terrepathically impervious. So now who's in charge? Hahaha, blooming ha!" said Freak breaking into to chuckle.

Then quite calmly, the little old lady took off her woollen hat and dropped it on top of Freak.

"We are! Controlling weak-minded, repugnant h*umans still gives* us an *advantage* so shut it Freaky deaky. *HAHAHAHA!"*

So the 'Terrorpin' army marched on with bravado and gratification, well pottered on, until they arrived at a small airfield where a very helpful customs officer welcomed them. In fact she was almost as obliging as the old lady who dropped them off and, incidentally, very generously paid for the trip! Yin and Yang promised a fine journey, and sure enough everyone enjoyed themselves and was treated superbly during the flight. Escobar and Spike nibbled on some popcorn whilst Freak watched her favourite movie, "The Fly," and Yin and Yang, well, they read the in-flight magazines from cover to cover and discussed the appalling, extortionate costs of miniature soft toys dressed as flight attendants available from duty free.

Upon arrival in Costa Rica, the heat and the sun and a sleek white, chauffeur driven limousine greeted the group. They were driven to a nearby Marina and from there transported by private yacht from the mainland, across the picturesque Gulf of Nicoya, to their new home, a sprawling, sumptuous, cliff top luxury villa called Arcadia, on the tropical rainforest coated, privately owned, Alcatraz Island, just off the coast.

Arcadia, named after the holiday destination of the Greek Gods, was truly stunning. It was white in colour with white marble clad interiors and exotic furnishings. It was truly more than a personal residence and more than any one person could ever require. The size of a boutique hotel with rooms and staff to match, it was a millionaire's playground.

After being introduced to their new owner, a man known to other humans as Mr White, everyone scuttled off to explore and claim their own slice of sultry paradise, except Yin and Yang that is. They just sat down with Mr White on a huge white leather settee and stared at him intently.

Mr White, a handsome man in his late thirties, possibly of Mediterranean origin, was intelligent, witty and engaging. He had an air of self-confidence and possessed a spiritual dignity that only assured success could bring. He sat staring back inquisitively at his new houseguests!

"*Look into I's eyes, you ar*e getting…"

KINGS OF THE CASTLE AND THE DIRTY RASCAL!

It was a normal brisk, British morning. Dew lay blanketing the shimmering, wispy grass and a light mist was in the air, but the sun was smiling, warming everything up and to the untrained eye all was well, although there was the odd rabbit dotted about!

Inside the woods, about two hundred feet or so from the Manor House, a rabbit with a tan face peaked out of a partially hollowed, rooted tree trunk and wiggled its nose.

"Garston," called Seth. "Get the others and come here, it's time for a tour."

Garston set off and a minute later a Gerbil, a Cat, a Jackahuahua, a Toad and a Pigeon were standing inside the root system.

"Ok guys," said Seth, "this is one of the two entrances in and out. Albert if you would like to look up, you can see daylight flooding in, well that's your way in if you come in via the air. There is a small branch you can land on by the hole in the trunk. Now follow me."

Seth dived down into a small opening that was well hidden by a few tufts of grass, and the rest of the gang followed.

To their amazement, as soon as they slid through the snug opening, everything got quite roomy. They found themselves standing in a long tunnel that was at least 3 feet wide and 3 feet tall, illuminated by a string of multi coloured Christmas tree lights running above their heads as far as they could see.

"I thought I would design everything according to the largest among us. As you can see, the tunnels and indeed our home has supports made from the discarded remains of the Grid and sturdy branches collected from the woods. We are now walking downward; this is because everything we need is, of course, further underground. Now we are about to reach reception." Seth was buzzing.

The tunnel widened to form a junction. Five strong, muscular attentive rabbits were sitting in front of another five openings that were also lit with Christmas lights.

"Each of these tunnels goes to each of the underground levels of the house. These rabbit sentries are five of my best so do not fear. They are here to warn us against any intruders, such as badgers and foxes."

The sentries gave a salute.

"There is another one of these reception areas near our other entrance which is inside an old disused cottage, I will show you later."

"The old hornswaggle cottage?"

"Yes, Albert, it's on the other side of the woods, about a mile and a half away as the crow flies. It's for sale, so I suggest we tie up its purchase as soon as we can."

"Purchase! How and from who, and that's a long tunnel?"

"I have yet to work that one out Bandi, and yes it's a long tunnel. Right, now, where was I? Yes, now you each have a room that has been designed especially for your individual needs and these will be your personal quarters, other than you Albert, I thought you might like the attic of the cottage for yourself. I also thought it would be a fine look out post and as…"

"…Absolutely! Mizzen! No Jolly Roger problem, great!"

"Err, right, well, we also have a laboratory too, and a room I like to call the Green Room."

"The Green Room?" asked Garston.

"This is where we will meet, socialise and watch TV and, of course, plan strategies. It's even got your old gerbil wheel in it"

Garston didn't look that excited.

"Oh, I'm so spoilt!" he replied.

Seth continued, "I have modified our original plans after discovering more and more about the Manor House."

"What did you say before, did you say five sentries for each of the five levels?" Garston inquired.

"And did you say TV?" asked Bandi with glee.

Ignoring Bandi, Seth responded.

"There is a fifth underground level; it seems to have been sealed off, but it's there. We will investigate it some when!"

"Television! A wealth of entertainment, news and everything else invented by humans to save them from their spouses! Excellent Smithers!" Bandi said delightedly.

"Who's Smithers?" asked Seth.

"Mr Burns' sycophantic personal assistant of course!" replied Bandi, absolutely disgusted at Seth's lack of cartoon knowledge.

"How do you know that? Never mind. The sooner I can scan everybody, the better!" Seth muttered.

"But the fifth underground level is not on the schematic," said Garston, still concerned.

"It's obviously Top Zecret," said Maurice.

"Our new home or Camelot as I call it, will surprise you, however, I haven't the time to show you everything, so everyone, be prepared to download the information that I send you."

"Why did you name it Camelot, Seth?" asked Garston.

"Because no one actually knows where the historical location of Camelot is. It was the castle home of a great English Monarch, King Arthur. He and his Knights of the Round Table, used to meet there. I just thought we should name our home after it, it seemed appropriate!"

There was a pause.

"Zo we are "The Knights of Camelot," said Maurice.

"I suppose we are," replied Garston.

"Cool," said Steve.

"Yeah," said Bandi.

"Scurvy!" said Albert.

"We will all get together this afternoon for, err, a meeting; just use the rest of the morning to muse around and familiarise yourself. It's easy really, we have the Manor as the central structure and we have built everything off it and around it. The humans gave me the idea. They have a soccer stadium called the San Siro. It was initially constructed many years ago, but by building around the original structure they extended it some years later," said Seth.

"It's like every line on the Doubloons London Underground going to Davy Jones' Locker!"

"Err, yes Albert." Seth replied.

"Seth," said Garston, "I'm not happy about having a level we know nothing about. It might house something important or dangerous! I think whilst we have the rest of the morning free it should be investigated. Steve will you come with Seth and me in case we need any muscle?"

"You making fun of me buddy?" Steve replied.

"Well no actually, have you had a look at yourself recently. You have changed rather."

"Oh yez, so he haz!" voiced Maurice surprisingly.

"Look at you. You have muscles, really big ones," said Bandi.

In a piece of a broken mirror that was being held up by two grey rabbits that had strangely and stealthily pulled up behind him from nowhere, Steve turned and took a good look at his reflection!

"Yeah baby! Bring it on," he exclaimed, deliriously happy with his own physique and jumping into a number of bodybuilding poses!

"Let's go," he said.

Bandi and Maurice stayed behind to check out their new living quarters. Albert hopped around just satisfying his curiosity, whilst Garston, Seth and now a fearless Steve went to explore the mysteries of level five!

***

Everything at Arcadia was going to plan, Freak, Escobar, Spike and the Terrorpins were gloriously happy. Arcadia's main living space, a large white marble clad lounge with two sumptuous white leather sofas facing large, expansive glass doors opening to beautiful lush landscaped gardens, had become home.

Spike spent his days warming on the twisted branches of a crooked tree in one area of the gardens, which had a view of the TV in the lounge, and his nights on the twisted branches of a crooked tree indoors, which also had a view of the TV in the lounge!

Escobar had free rein to use anything or anyone as a perch and Freak, well let's just say that the rest of the garden's indigenous wildlife, from bugs to birds were becoming endangered species!

As for the Terrorpins they had discovered the cooling attributes of something called water and were now also the proud owners of a custom built super aquarium that was some ten feet long and two feet wide. It housed floating islands, tropical fish, water plants, a miniature sunken wreck, oh, and a couple of female terrapins!

"Hellllloooo ladies!"

This incredible glass wonderland sat opposite a constantly turned on and very powerful state of the art computer that enabled the Terrorpins full access to all of Mr White's bank accounts and, of course, anything else they fancied. They set about making everything 'iron clad'; just in case there was any unwanted scrutiny. Mr White was already disgustingly wealthy, but the boys were taking his millions and fast making him legitimate billions by playing internet money games, speculating on the world's stock markets and utilising various offshore high interest accounts in tax havens around the world.

"This is so much fun .Did I buy that f*actory?* I *did*. Hah*aha*ha!"

During the Terrorpin team's first week on Alcatraz Island, all of the staff were made redundant and handed enough compensation to retire on. All, but two that is. They were a couple of handy men, one big and burly and the other slight and scarred. The two men, who always wore black, would, every now and then, turn up, speak to Mr White briefly and then trundle off back to wherever it was they came from!

"They are very strange those two, where is it they are from? Who cares! Until they get in the way they can remain and disperse at their leisure! Now where was I and I. Oh yes, helloooo Ladies!"

The rest of the staff were replaced by a hand picked team of fourteen, err, let us say matronly women of a certain age, that came from different countries all around the world. They were each qualified in anything from Piloting Jets to Personal Training. There was also a younger lady that never let go of her clipboard! All of the ladies were single, either by choice, fate or widowhood and had no children to speak of.

"*This collection* of nubile totty will keep him *occupied when we are not. Hahaha!"*

They all lived onsite and were placed on rolling contracts that paid them a more than comfortable amount of money that, of course, they never needed to spend! The ladies wanted for nothing and nor did Mr White. Yin and Yang had used their powers of telepathy and now all of the ladies adored him, although oddly enough, they would have adored him without the use of mind control anyway!

***

Garston and his recognisance team had reached the end of the tunnel leading to level five but, surprisingly found themselves facing an obstacle, a concrete wall!

"Hold on, how are we supposed to get through that, and where on earth did you get, or rather, nick our equipment from if you came across a wall like this at every level?" asked Garston.

Seth laughed. "We acquired nearly everything we needed from the giant refuse bins behind the House. The humans fill them with useful bits all the time. There is also an old storage shed, too, at the rear of the house which may have been raided for the odd necessity, like the Christmas lights illuminating our facility; they must have had a tree in every department! We will invest in some proper lighting and add to what we have at a later date, when we can." Seth paused. "You see once the humans had dismantled all of the grid and binned it, a chain of rabbits industriously procured everything at night, which included the Cube and Vincent's computer, you know the one kept behind his safety glass wall! We have keyboards, screens and everything else we need and our wiring has been linked through the air conditioning vents and stud walling with a system of power conducting clips, which gives us electricity. We are if you like, a parasite feeding off the electrical supply to the Manor and our computers do the same. After getting the lot in, we just scavenged the rest of the bits we needed from the other floors in the Manor and then, I made the entrances to the tunnels smaller."

"The Cube!" said Garston.

"Yep, which now, of course, is powered by other means," Seth replied proudly.

"Other means? Oh never mind. What about the surveillance cameras?"

"A little wire snipping here, or a small power surge there, zaps out the cameras when we don't want the humans to see what we are up to."

"Smooth!" said Steve.

"Well, that's all fantastic, but what about this wall and seeing what's behind it?" asked Garston.

"I have a theory. I don't know if this will work but it might. Steve, would you mind awfully if I asked you to take a little bit of a run up and charge at the wall head-first?"

"Now listen Seth, I have always liked you but…"

As Steve nattered on, Seth wandered around him so that he and Garston were on one side, and the wall was on the other. Seth then slowly, and surreptitiously, turned his back and, 'whack,' let out an almighty kick, landing it firmly on the little dogs chest. Steve flew backwards, headfirst at lightning speed and crashed into the wall, and surprisingly straight through it!

"As I thought," said Seth.

"Interesting!" said Garston.

They both approached the hole left by the little dog and slowly poked their noses through into a large cavernous space. There was a ten-foot drop to the floor and some forty feet away in the middle of the room, a beam of light provided by a single interrogative bulb hung above a big brown tatty leather armchair. There was also a switched on television showing reality TV, a large coffee table with fruit, vegetables and nuts, that were neatly placed in piles, a couple of bottles of still spring water, a cup with a straw, a blender and a bathtub!

Garston called out with a loud whisper." Steve? Steve, you OK?"

"Yeah. Phew, it's a little funky in here. Can you smell that?" Steve replied. "No bruises or nothing, like it never happened." Steve shook the dust and rubble from behind his ears.

"Ah, but it did happen," said a mysterious, gravelly voice they had never heard before, "and Steve, I would get to the light by the chair as soon as I could if I were you, unless you want to be thrown into the sewage by a very aggressive tin can. Oh, and you would smell funky, too, if you had been here as long as I. Peeing into a bathtub, wrapping pooh in Orange peel or whatever else you can find and washing yourself with rations of spring water because of a cut off water supply, is really enough to make anyone smell funky!"

"What?" asked Steve turning sharply!

The sound of an electric motor began whirring in a distant corner and then, from the shadows, a pair of icy blue lights, like fierce slanted eyes, moved sinisterly forward, piercing the darkness.

Gradually a three-foot tall conical shaped robot eerily came into view. It had pincers, a scoop, no visible wheels, but many other intrusive and painful looking appendages, and it was heading straight towards Steve.

"The floor is censored and the Bot is here to clear rubbish or deal with me if I venture from the light. So you have three options: you are either sewage, canine kebab or you will join me in the light. All I can suggest is that when you do move, move as fast as you can," said the voice.

“Head into the light Steve, run towards the light.” Seth and Garston shouted nervously as the dangerous nature of the robot became more and more evident!

Steve took a beat and then ran for the old brown leather armchair, his legs spinning furiously on the concrete floor. The robot suddenly shifted into another gear and whoosh, it frantically chased him around the room. Waving blades and a hatchet at breathtaking ninja speed, it was soon right on Steve’s tail. Steve took a deep breath and leapt for the chair. Its scratched and tatty worn leather arms, frayed with puffs of fluff, tickled his tummy as a Bot blade just missed his nose.

“I said the light, not on the chair!” said a muffled voice.

Steve had not landed on a cushion, as he had first thought, but on, what can only be described as, a small tan coloured Macaque monkey with his jaw wired shut, wearing a bright red crash helmet!

Steve jumped to one corner of the chair startled by his new acquaintance.

“Hello I am Hannibal,” said the monkey like a bad gravelly voiced ventriloquist!

“Welcome to my home!”

“Err, hi, I am Steve”

“You are a talking dog,” said Hannibal.

“And you are a talking monkey, so how on earth are we communicating like this?” replied Steve.

“SPAFF! You are speaking the language of Vincent.”

“You know Vincent?” asked Steve inquisitively. Hannibal bowed his head.

“Yes he gave me speech, he was my friend once. I miss him.”

“So, do you know how it works?” asked Steve.

“Yes. My thought patterns and vocal sounds are put through the programme and are translated into the language of Vincent with the help of SPAFF.”

“And those who have been exposed to SPAFF receive information in the language of Vincent.”

“Of course, that’s it,” called Seth.

“Of course what!” shouted Steve in reply across the open room.

“The programme, it’s simple really,” Seth replied.

“We are all really talking in our own languages, but now, the SPAFF inside our bloodstream, reacts with the speech programme stored in our microchips and enables us all to understand one other without the aid of the Cube or, any other device. Consequently, to anyone without the speech programme, we just bark, meow, squeak and squawk.

"How can you hear us talking from over there?" said an astounded Steve.

"SPAFF that's how," said Hannibal.

"Well, shall we get out of here? Would you like to meet the others?" Steve asked.

"How many others? Oh, it doesn't matter, it is abundantly clear that it is time to eject myself from this long suffering solitude!" said Hannibal nodding excitedly. He continued after a moment of thought, "I will run around the room clockwise and you shall run around the room anti clockwise. This will confuse our robot friend and after a couple of laps, I will meet you under the hole in the wall. I will then give you a leg up to the opening."

"Err sounds simple, why have you not escaped before?" asked Steve.

"There wasn't a hole in the wall before!" Hannibal replied dryly.

"Oh yes, fine, say when then."

"When!" said Hannibal.

In a flash Hannibal shot off the chair. "Come on then." he called.

Steve took a deep breath and jumped to it. Leaping from the chair he ran at full pelt around the great room. The ominous sound of an electric motor whirring immediately filled the void. The icy blue eyes approached from the corner but this time they were flashing around in differing directions. The robot seemed crazed, if not a little bemused. Not knowing whom to follow it started to spin on the spot until Hannibal and Steve came to a stop against the wall directly beneath the hole with Seth and Garston looking on. The robot stopped spinning abruptly and faced them. Pausing in thought it seemed to weigh up its options and then, suddenly, it shot straight towards them, brandishing a carving knife drawn from a bodily-concealed compartment.

"Give me your paw," said Hannibal.

"What?" Steve replied.

"Be a good doggy and give me your paw," he said purposefully.

Steve, for some unexplainable reason felt a compulsion to give Hannibal his paw, and so he did, although a little perplexed! Hannibal took the paw and then the rest of the leg it was attached to, and tossed Steve into the air. As Steve flew upward and faced the hole in the wall, a pair of rabbit ears grabbed him by the throat and pulled him back into the tunnel. A beat later Hannibal landed directly in front of Steve, Garston and Seth, creepily, stopping dead still on the spot.

"Hello young fellow, I am Seth and this is Garston," Seth was smiling a bold smile that hid all signs of concern. Hannibal nodded shyly and said softly and gravelly with tears in his big brown eyes, "Thank you for finding me."

"Would you like to come with us to meet the group?" enquired Seth.

"Yes, please. Steve here mentioned there were more of you," Hannibal said delightedly. "It would be so lovely to have a chat with creatures other than myself."

Hannibal's head drooped and his bottom lip began to quiver.

"How long have you been down there?" asked Steve, a little worried.

"My television tells me that I have been locked away for nearly, well, nearly two and a half years now." Hannibal burst into tears and then suddenly stopped and said, "I need to be back later. Big Brother's on, and I'd like to watch it from the comfort of my chair."

"Err, sure," Seth replied a bit weirded out.

"Who is Big Brother?" asked Steve whispering to Garston on the way to the Green Room.

Garston shrugged. "I have no idea," he replied.

THE ORIGIN OF THE SPECIES

Hannibal, light on his feet, skipped down the passage happily behind Garston and Seth who were deep in conversation, whilst Steve brought up the rear.

"This doesn't feel right, there must be a reason why he was in there all by himself," said Garston.

"Yes the motive for his incarceration does seem to be evading me at the present time, as does the reason, our friend is wearing a red helmet. And why does he have his jaw wired shut? I do know one thing though, our friend has been exposed to SPAFF and I would say, quite a large amount of it!" replied Seth.

Bandi, Maurice and Albert were all watching television in the Green Room, when Seth and the others turned up:

"Hi guys, this is Hannibal. We discovered him trapped on level 5," said Seth.

Hannibal shyly raised a hand. Introductions were made, there were smiles and laughter and Hannibal began to relax and feel welcome in everyone's company. A little grey rabbit brought in a few nuts and berries and placed them on a table made of bark in the centre of the room, and then left, bowing on exit.

"I love this royalty business," said Bandi, "but any chance of some real food soon, just a tin of something?"

"I'm working on that one." Seth replied.

"So Hannibal, what the daisies were you doing on level 5?" Garston asked curiously.

"That's what I would like to know." he replied.

"What do you mean?" asked Seth. He noticed Hannibal's reluctance to answer. He smiled and then after a pause asked. "Why don't you impart what you know?"

Hannibal looked into his eyes and returned a smile.

"Well, alright then, if I just talk, you jump in with your questions, OK?" Hannibal took a pew and began to recount the tale of how his captivity came about.

"So, some time ago now, I lived with my friend Vincent in his apartment. He would go to work during the day, but pop back at lunch, and then come home in the evening. We used to talk to each other in sign language. He was my best friend. Then one day he took me to work with him, I could tell he didn't want to, but he told me that some other humans said he had to, and that's when I learnt about the Grid and the Cube. Vincent said it was all going to be alright and told me not to be scared, and he put me on the Grid."

"Were you scared?" Steve asked.

"No, Vincent was my friend so why should I have been? He said I was going to have a little sleep and when I woke up, we would be able to communicate with one another better. I remember a gas being released onto the Grid, which, was really scary, and then waking up with Vincent looking over at me from behind his glass wall with some other people. He said hello and I replied hello. It was wonderful; I was talking to Vincent through speakers in his little room. The other humans jumped around hugging and congratulating each other. Vincent told me he had fitted me with a little device and a speech programme and that's why I understood him. I shouldn't have though, I mean I am a monkey right? But, I understood every word he said. He told me about SPAFF and about receiving small doses of it through sunlight and gas and that it was responsible, apparently, for my enhanced intelligence and, well, you probably know the rest. I mean it's happened to you, right?"

"Well not exactly," said Seth.

"I know what you're trying to get at, and I'm sorry I don't have the answers. Everything was going well. Vincent and I would play puzzles and discuss all kinds of things, but then the military arrived. He," Hannibal stopped for a moment, his eyes welling up. "He tried to stop them."

"Stop them doing what?" asked Steve, who, like the others was entranced by the tale.

"I don't know, but he was shouting, No! No! A big man was holding him back and another man sat down at the window and released the gas once again onto the Grid. All I remember is waking up in the room you call level 5 with my jaw wired shut wearing this very itchy hat."

Hannibal lapsed deeper into thought.

"I miss Vincent," he said, trying to hold back the tears.

Steve seeing the Macaque bare his feelings trotted up and gave him a caring lick on the nose. Hannibal smiled and patted his newly found friend on the head in return.

"Right that's it. I can't take any more of this something has to be done. Everyone to the lab, follow me," said Seth.

The gang and Hannibal took their orders and followed Seth to the lab without question. After all, there was nothing else to do.

"Right, the lab won't surprise those of you that have taken a look around. The rest of you… hold on, how long have you lot been watching television?"

No one replied.

"None of you have seen the lab have you?"

Again there was no reply, just a shuffling of paws and a bowing of heads.

"OK. Well, feast your eyes on this."

Seth pressed a stone poking out of the wall on the right hand side of the tunnel and to everyone's amazement a hidden door clicked open and a very brightly lit room was exposed. Wall to wall white granite tiles reflected the light thrown out by row upon row of Christmas lights attached to the ceiling. In the centre of the room a raised tiled area created a tabletop, which sat directly beneath a slightly battered but fully functioning Cube.

"The Cube. It's here," said Hannibal.

"Wow," Steve mouthed.

"And Vincent's old computer is over there in the corner behind that safety glass wall."

"What? Safety Glass! Why?" asked Steve.

Seth ignoring the comments continued.

"Okay, Steve, get up onto the tabletop and lie still, the rest of you get in there behind the glass." Seth ushered everyone behind the glass wall in one corner of the room.

"How did we get this lot?" asked Garston forever curious, referring to the glass.

"It's made from the 3 largest salvaged pieces of Vincent's safety glass that we could get down here, joined together with something called liquid silicone," said Seth. "It was horrendously heavy. Now give me some room." Everyone stepped aside and Seth manoeuvred himself to the keyboard. The crowd gathered behind him.

"How are you gonna type your instructions?"

“Well I could use the speech programme, link it through, blah blah blah or, I could just do this.”

Seth’s ears pricked up. “Now don’t be alarmed,” he said.

Like the dexterous fingers of a pianist, Seth’s ears ran over the keyboard and worked the mouse faster than Bill Gate’s secretary looking for a holiday. Everybody else just quietly watched as Seth instructed the Cube from behind the glass to commence an identification scan.

“Now stay still, Steve.”

“Sure.” Steve struck a pose!

“It won’t hurt. The lights will dim and then you will be scanned.”

The Christmas lights on the ceiling dimmed and a horizontal beam of light shot out of a small compartment in the centre of the base of the Cube. The light ran down and then up the length of Steve's body like a photocopy machine scanning a document.

The room lit up.

“Right that’s it,” said Seth. “Steve, join us over here.”

Vincent’s old computer brought up a multi-layered image of Steve, his skeleton, muscles, nervous system, and organs all represented by bright individual colours. Seth’s ears typed again, and another image of Steve appeared.

“This one here is the original scan of Steve held in the memory banks of the Cube. What we do now, is compare the two scans and the differences between them will tell us what has happened to Steve. There you go. Steve’s bone density has increased by 600% as has his muscle mass. Hold on, his brain shows no change. Wait.” Seth typed some more. “Ah yes, there you go, the amount of the brain used has also increased by 700%. You see we normally only use a fraction of our brains capacity. Steve’s personal microchip storage facility is half filled with…Well look at that,” Seth clicked the mouse.

“Your microchip is inundated with information on games, received over the Internet during the collapse of the Grid. As you can all see, SPAFF molecules have infiltrated the blood stream and attached themselves to the neural network, which in turn is now fused to the microchip that possesses Vincent’s programme Steve’s brain. Thus, he now communicates with the language of Vincent without the aid of hardware.”

“What does it all mean?” asked Steve.

"Well it means that you are the first ever, canine cannonball that can beat anyone at Monopoly and Super Mario! Am I right, Seth?" asked Garston.

"Absolutely, however, you have to remember that the alteration of his DNA has also made his teeth and claws 'super tough', because of their calcium content, just like his bones. Steve could bite a lump out of a tree if he wanted to!"

"DNA, Monopoly, Super Mario?" queried Steve.

"Deoxyribonucleic acid, a board game that destroys family relationships and a cartoon go-cart Pizza delivery man," said Seth.

"Oh, err, right, sorry I asked!"

"Alright Maurice it's your turn."

Maurice hopped onto the tabletop, the lights dimmed yet again and the Cube scanned Maurice, as it did Steve.

As the lights were turned up, Maurice hopped down and popped to see his results with the others.

"Thiz iz exciting," he said.

"Maurice, your muscular strength and elasticity has increased by 800%, as has your lung capacity; your toes have changed too."

"Toez?"

"Yes, walk up the wall for me would you."

"What?" Maurice replied.

"Just try it."

Sure enough Seth was right. Slowly, tentatively, but surely, Maurice walked up the wall.

The rest of the gang looked up in awe.

"My turn, my turn, ruba dub tub!"

"Hold on Albert."

"Maurice, your microchip is filled with information on the subject of Business Development, Management and Economic studies!"

"Could be uzeful," he answered.

"OK, Albert."

"Right, buccaneer you are "

Albert fluttered under the hanging Cube, and the process once more, repeated itself.

"Well Albert, you will be faster than you were, much faster and your vision has improved, as has your natural sense of latitude and longitude!"

"Err right avast ye!"

"Point in fact, by about 650%! You could find anything, anywhere!"

"And here, finally, the reason for your ailment, your microchip was skipping through the Internet pages on 'Pirate slogans and involuntary speech,' a condition that should not to be sniffed or laughed at."

"Huh, blast the muskets!" Albert replied.

"Well yes. Now, what I am about to do will help, although I wouldn't advise it as a normal medical procedure."

"Will it hangem from the yardarm?"

"We'll see won't we? Open up your Internet explorer programme." Albert did what he was told.

"Garston, would you do me a kindness and place this clip on one of Albert's claws, please?"

"Sorry Albert. This might pinch a bit!" said Garston.

The metal clip was one of two attached to either end of a long plastic coated copper wire.

Seth's nimble ears removed a small bulb from a Christmas light fitting at great speed.

"You ready?"

"Not booty!" Albert replied.

Seth placed the remaining clip straight into the open light fitting! Albert shrieked and then, disconcertingly, all of the lights flickered through the tunnels of Camelot.

"Interesting," said Garston as Albert shrieked.

Seth ran back behind the safety glass wall and furiously typed at the keyboard.

"There we go, done," he said.

Seth trotted back to the table and pulled the clip away from the light fitting. Albert grabbed the other clip attached to his claw with his beak, and spat it out.

"You alright Buddy?" enquired Steve.

There was a silence as everyone stared at Albert, he had smoke coming from the top of his head and there was a smell like roast chicken in the air!

"Oh please! Don't call me buddy it's so uncouth. And this room is so stark. It needs some fabrics; heady tones of velvet would be glorious! And by the way, that ruddy hurt!"

"Oh dear," said Garston. "What did you do?"

"Well, unfortunately, the only way to get rid of Albert's ailment was to replace it, but as the Internet flies through the air, it's pot-luck what you get really. Unless you ask, I mean search, and Albert was in no condition to ask or search, at the time of his, electrocution! I had to replicate our grid shocking experience in order for this to work!"

"So?" asked Garston.

"So, Albert is now very well versed in, let's have a look shall we, err, in the art of Interior Design," said Seth.

"So why is he talking in that foppish, flamboyant manner?" Garston enquired.

"Must come with the territory, I guess!" Seth replied, whilst reapplying a shade of purple lipstick with his ears!

"It's called, 'being in touch with your feminine side'!" said Bandi. "And thank you Seth, at least I have someone to do my nails with now!"

Seth got back to the job in paw!

"Well, back to business. Oh, by the way, I have already been scanned. I can now hear like a hawk, do anything with my ears, jump like a rabbit sized grasshopper and my microchip is filled with information on great human minds, just in case you were all wondering. Now, Garston your turn, up you get."

The process once more repeated itself.

"How am I different then?"

"Same as Steve, muscles and bones, but in a rodent of your size that equates to speed, real speed!"

"Nice," said Garston.

"Your cam vision obviously gives you greatly improved sight and your microchip is housed with information on puzzles and escapology!"

"Esca what? Never mind," said Steve.

"You're a very interesting combination Garston," said Bandi.

"Why thank you," he replied, stepping down.

"Bandi, my dear, would you mind."

"Certainly Seth, it would be a pleasure."

Bandi slid out from behind the glass and gracefully glided to the tabletop beneath the Cube. She stepped onto the shiny tiled surface and sat herself down.

"I am ready Seth."

Seth dimmed the lights and the small compartment on the underside of the Cube opened once more and shone its beam of light over Bandi.

"Seth," said Garston a little perturbed, "what's Vincent's computer doing?"

Seth who had been watching Bandi turned to the screen in front of him. It was blank.

"I don't know," he said, "this is most confusi," Seth stopped talking mid word! Multi coloured dots, like tiny rainbow coloured scurrying beetles, appeared from the four corners of the screen and weaved their way to the centre to form a perfect circle.

"Bow wow," said Steve.

"That's odd," said Albert.

The circle faded a little, but then transformed and morphed into a ball of flame.

"Is everything all right?" asked Bandi, unaware of what the rest of the gang were looking at.

"Yes fine," replied Seth, in the jolliest voice he could muster.

Hannibal piped up. "The screens on the Cube."

The same blazing computerised image appeared on the Cubes four screens and a dark symbol emerged at its centre.

"What's that!" asked Albert.

The symbol bore a resemblance to a crucifix, but its top vertical stem, was replaced, by a loop.

The Cube began to make an unfamiliar noise.

"What's going on Seth?" Bandi asked nervously.

"I don't know, but don't move, let it finish."

The noise became a steady tone that rose in pitch until the Cube, unnervingly, appeared to be singing. Boom! There was a flash of light.

Everyone behind the glass flinched and averted their eyes. Hannibal, with a feeling of déjà vu, cowered behind his mate Steve. A couple of seconds later and the group tentatively raised their heads. Their eyes took a little time to adjust to the blue spherical light that was now shining brightly before them and, paranormally surrounding Bandi!

"Err, that iz different!" said Maurice.

Bandi was entranced.

A soothing voice came from the Cube.
Project Ankh,
Identification confirmed.
Subject Bastet.
Conditional evolution accelerated.
Subject status stable.
"The Cube can talk!" said Garston.

The screens images fizzled to a white dot and finally a blank screen. The sphere surrounding Bandi duly vanished, sucked back into the aperture on the underside of the Cube, with a zip. The Christmas lights lit up the lab to reveal everyone standing agog staring at Bandi.

"So, how am I different?" Bandi asked cheerfully, no longer in a trance and with no idea of what had just happened.

Seth looked at his screen. It was blank.

"Err, bones and teeth, same as Steve," he said stuttering and searching for his words. "Sharp claws and stuff and your microchip is stored with…err, let me see!"

"…Media Entertainment," said Garston.

"Yez Media Entertainment…Err, that'z how you knew about the Bat Cave," said Maurice

"Of course, it all makes sense," said Bandi "Right, who's next?" she asked hurriedly.

"Hannibal," Steve replied pushing the apprehensive monkey forward.

Seth sent a Bluetooth message to everyone but Bandi. It read; 'Thank you for keeping quiet. I will investigate and chat to Bandi later.'

"Go on then Hannibal, no reason to be scared," said Bandi.

Hannibal stared back at her wide-eyed and not too convinced.

"It's a lot less painful than having your temperature taken by a vet," she said giggling.

Seth turned to Hannibal and gave him a wink. "It's alright", he said reassuringly.

Hannibal stepped onto the table and Seth set about dimming the lights.

"Would you like to remove your helmet for me?" asked Seth.

"I can't." Hannibal replied.

"Really? Well never mind, here goes."

The Cube scanned Hannibal.

"I don't know if I will have a comparative scan of you within the Cube's archives, but I will have a search."

As Seth typed the others stood quietly expectant.

"You alright mate?" Steve asked Hannibal.

"Yes, thank you Steve, it's rather relaxing up here," Hannibal replied.

"Here we go," said Seth starting the scan. "Well, your original scans are without the helmet on, however, I can see that your muscle mass and elasticity has improved making you faster and stronger than you were before." Seth had a thought. "Bandi, would you come with me please?" Bandi followed Seth from behind the glass over to Hannibal.

"Would you mind smiling for me Hannibal? I am going to un-wire your jaw."

"You are. No more eating soup through a straw, really?" he said delightedly.

"Yes. I couldn't do it before, because I didn't know Bandi's claws could cut through the wire."

"They can?" said Bandi.

"I think so, so smile Hannibal," said Seth crossing his ears.

Hannibal, absolutely flooded with joy, gave the biggest grin of his life.

"Bandi my dear would you?"

Bandi pinged out a single claw and, with surprising ease, swiftly cut through the strands of wire holding Hannibal's jaw closed.

Hannibal gave an almighty yawn and spat out some wiry bits.

"Wowwowowowowowmememememememe," he said. "This feels fantastic."

Seth caught a glimpse of something.

"Well look at that. You have a clasp on your helmet. Would you mind? Can I take a look? The Cube will be unable to scan your brain or let me know what information your microchip is holding if I don't."

"Clasp? Clasp?" said Hannibal. "I think I would have taken the thing off if it had a clasp!"

"Well, it's very well hidden, would you lie on your front for me please?”

Hannibal obliged.

Seth pondered and studied the helmet.

“Mmm! Ah huh, yes. Oh, like that is it ok? Right. Well, there is some good news and some bad news. The good news is I have discovered how the helmet is held on. Do you see this little bolt shaped screw head just here, hidden by the lip of the helmet under Hannibal’s ear?”

“Yes,” Bandi replied.

“Well, there is another one on the exact opposite side of Hannibal's helmet. Now Bandi you watch that bolt and tell me what happens.”

Seth tapped the wall. It slid open revealing a draw filled with a fine collection of tools.

“Cool!” said Steve.

Seth took out a tiny screwdriver and turned the bolt on his side of Hannibal’s helmet.

“What’s happening on your side Bandi?”

“The bolt is turning,” she replied.

“As I suspected it would. The bad news, Hannibal, is you have a rod connecting these two bolts running straight through your head, effectively acting as a hinge.”

“What, a rod going through my head?”

“So the helmet can’t come off, but, ooh look at that, it’s a ratchet system and there’s a tiny motor fixed on the underside of the helmet, it must run on kinetic energy!”

“If it’s on the underside how is it you can see it?”

“There’s some evidence there, right on the edge. See it?”

“Oh yes, behind that tiny vent,” Bandi replied.”

By this time everyone was intrigued. “Garston come here would you please?” Garston slinked over.

“Watch this and then access the Cubes media player and connect it to the monitor behind the glass, the rest of you will then be able to watch what we are doing from over there.”

Garston’s cam vision gave live, real time footage of what was happening, just like one of those surgical, trauma documentaries and Seth began to work on the helmet, whilst speaking aloud.

“Right, so if I press the bolt inward with the screwdriver and turn it a quarter turn this way that should activate the motor and the helmet will hinge forward and cover Hannibal's face. Then I can scan Hannibal's brain. Are you alright with that Hannibal?"

"Yeah sure, you go for it!" Hannibal was being sarcastic and obliging at the same time.

"Alright Hannibal you'll be in the dark for a bit."

"I may be in the light Seth, but believe me I'm still in the dark!" Hannibal replied.

Seth slowly turned the screw a quarter turn and pressed his screwdriver inward with a click. To his satisfaction the kinetic motor started automatically, and then, like a sliding door, the helmet began to move slowly and cover Hannibal's face. "Well that's very clever. There we go."

"Aagh!" Albert let out a scream. "What's that? No. No!"

Seth dropped his screwdriver and leapt backward.

"Oh. Good heavens," said Bandi.

All of the gang were dumbfounded. The hinging helmet had not revealed the back of Hannibal's head, as everyone had expected but, a second face that was identical to Hannibal's in every way except for one feature, one large thick black, bushy eyebrow sitting heavily over both closed eyes!

"That eyebrow needs a pluck. Look it's hideous. It meets in the middle. It looks like two slugs hooked together carrying a nose! It's facial hair murder darlings!" Albert shuddered.

The soothing voice came from the Cube.

Danger. Danger.

Awakening of Lecter imminent

Danger!

Please vacate the area.

Awakening of Lecter imminent!

"That don't sound good," said Garston.

"Well I never. The Cube can speak," said Bandi!

"Ah yes. What a surprise." replied Garston, sheepishly.

Suddenly the furry eyebrow face let out a blood-curdling scream.

Everyone took another step back.

Lecter awake.

Body conditioning in: 5, 4, 3, 2, 1.

Another terrifying scream filled the room followed by the sound of grinding and cracking bones and then to everyone's astonishment Hannibal's torso revolved 180 degrees. His back was now his front!

Lecter complete.

Lecter sat bolt upright. His eyes flashed open to expose a fiery orange brilliance. They twitched and darted from side to side madly taking in the environment of the lab, and then, he smiled a broad maniacal smile, exposing a jaw that was crisscross wired shut!

"Lecter hungry. BUNNY!" He said in a deep gravelly voice.

With lightning speed and in one swift movement, Lecter jumped off the table and grabbed Seth by the ears. He raised him off the ground drooling and then began to repeatedly gum Seth's head furiously! Something was clearly amiss!

"He's trying to eat me. Help. Stop him," Seth yelled.

Steve and Bandi leapt into action and each wrapped their jaws around one of Lecter's wrists! Maurice jumped out from behind the safety glass and launched his tongue, which to his surprise wound around Lecter's ankles tightly! He gave a yank.

THUD!

Lecter hit the floor. Garston seized the opportunity and rushed in and placed his jaws around Lecter's throat.

"Release him at once you bully", ordered Albert, "or I will let my rodent friend gnaw your Adam's apple off. That's if you've got one, and I mean right off, sweetheart!"

Lecter kept hold.

"I said release him. Now! Garston, break his neck darling."

Garston began to tighten his bite.

Lecter nervously loosened his grip.

Gasping frantically and patting and rubbing himself to make sure he was all there, Seth gabbled.

"Look at me. I am covered in monkey slime, I'm going to be mentally monkey scarred for the rest of my life."

"Seth. Just scan the blighter while we have him, would you sweetie?" said Albert.

Seth jumped behind the safety glass and dimmed the lights, whilst the others lifted Lecter onto the tabletop. As everyone held him down Seth began the scanning process. He studied the results as they came up in front of him, but then suddenly gasped with astonishment. This unnerved the rest of the gang. He quickly ran back to the others, took a screwdriver and reset the helmet to cover Lecter's face. Lecter fought and struggled, but the combined strength of the others had him pinned down firmly.

"No! No! No more sleep", he cried." You can hide my face, but you'll never take my freedom!"

Click!

The helmet was reset.

Lecter inoperative.

Threat eliminated.

"Nice tongue work darling," said Albert.

Maurice gave a bow as everyone released his or her grip.

Hannibal's bones cracked, swivelled and then returned to their original anatomical positions. Hannibal opened his eyes and sat up!

"Hi," he said nervously, finding himself surrounded by everyone. "So I'm faster and stronger and anything else I should know?"

Everyone looked at each other wondering who was going to speak first.

"Err, food yes, lots of information on food" said Steve, "definitely food! Your microchip holds a tremendous amount of information regarding food, mostly food, preparation of food, cuisines from around the world, food!"

"I think he's got the picture Steve," said Albert.

"And you have wonderful agility, too," said Seth dripping wet and smiling.

Hannibal gave Seth a quizzical look!

"Well if we are finished for the moment, is it alright if I get back to my room and watch the end of Big Brother?" asked Hannibal.

"Sure, but you are more than welcome to stay, and watch it here in the Green Room with us," Garston replied.

"No thank you, it's about time the robot delivered some fresh fruit and nuts, and I'm a little peckish for some reason! I am so looking forward to taking a huge bite out of something, and giving it a good chew!"

"Right you are," said Seth nervously, still sorting himself out. "Well, we will see you later then, just pop up any time; after all, we are all in this together. Oh, sorry, one last thing. Our microchips, including yours Hannibal, are also shore-to-shore location devices."

"Oh come on Seth, in English, darling, please!" said Albert.

"The humans obviously wanted to know our whereabouts at all times, just in case. Well, just in case has just happened! However, the programme for the location devices is in the Cube and as the Cube was discarded, due to the fact that the humans thought it damaged beyond repair. We are the only ones who know that the location programme is still working."

"Seth, if we have a shore-to-shore locator, then you can find Yin and Yang," said Bandi.

"I'm a step ahead of you, tried it earlier. No sign of any of them anywhere. They have either removed the programme from their microchips or they're not on these shores. Look at this."

Seth brought up the locator program on the Cube. "It works via satellite. We are all represented by little animated characters on the screen, and there's a little monkey, see now, that wasn't there earlier"

"Well I never!" said Albert.

"Who are Yin and Yang?" Hannibal asked inquisitively.

"Steve, why don't you go along with Hannibal and bring him up to speed?" Garston suggested.

"Yeah, Steve, come and have a chin-wag," said Hannibal, sounding very pleased with himself.

Steve and Hannibal trotted off back down the tunnels towards level five. On their way they formulated a plan on how they were going to outwit the icy blue-eyed guardian in order for them to get to the big brown leather armchair and watch Big Brother.

"OK. They're gone." said Seth.

"What on earth was all that about, Seth darling? One minute you're all alright, everything is lovely and, yes, I know someone did try to eat you, but then, well you're jittery and all sorts," asked Albert.

"The rest of you have to see this." Seth brought up Hannibal's scan.

There was a universal gasp.

"As you can see from these images, Hannibal's skull has two separate brains! They are connected to a single cerebral cortex, which, as we all witnessed, serves one multi-jointed skeleton. In other words Hannibal and Lecter have a brain each and live in the same body."

"Poor baby." said Albert. "That eyebrow is horrendous!"

"The helmet controls their release. The humans must have wired Hannibal's jaw as a precautionary measure after learning what Lecter was capable of," said Garston.

"He also has no idea Lecter exists!" said Bandi.

"What are we going to do?" asked Garston.

"We will tell him when the time is right. Agreed?" said Seth.

Everyone gave a nod.

"Now all of you, off you go. I have things to do, now I know what we can do!"

Everyone had a brief chat and decided that they wanted to know who Big Brother was and so they were all going to the Green Room to find out.

"Maurice can I have a word?"

"Sure Seth. Go ahead you guyz, I will catch you up!"

The others toddled off.

"Maurice you have to find out more about money. I have been looking through the Internet and it seems that humans use money to purchase what they want, or need. The larger the amount of money you possess the more you can have. So we need to get some. I am going to put another computer in your private quarters. You need to somehow get enough money together to purchase the cottage on the other side of the woods and then we can have a postal address."

"Poztal addrezz?"

"A postal address will mean we can buy anything we want, or need, and have it delivered. Thus, still keep our existence secret."

"Why me?"

"Because you have the tools, they're there inside your head!"

"What are you talking about?" replied Maurice.

"Use the business bits in your microchip."

"Oh you mean use the theories of Supply and Demand created by the economist Thomas Malthus and then put them together with a business plan, perhaps like that used by Donald Trump, to create an empire worthy of Genghis Khan!"

"That's the spirit! While you're at it, try and find Vincent would you, we need to let him know that we are all ok and we also need to learn more about Hannibal, or is it Lecter? Anyway, I don't want him eating anyone. I have some research to do regarding Project Ankh and so I may be a while. Oh, and by the by, I have also almost completed something I'm creating for Garston, so I mustn't be disturbed and neither must you!"

"YOU GOT IT BOZZ!"

WHAT'S MINE IS MINE!

Arcadia's white walls were gleaming in the magnificent, shimmering sunshine of Alcatraz Island. Its lush flowers and plants in the surrounding gardens were delicately being pruned and tended by a large, white tailed, Kite who was contently hopping happily alongside his assistant, a voluptuous gardener with flaming red hair, wearing rollers! Escobar was snipping through stems and branches as if they were sticks of liquorice. No matter how thick the offending foliage, he would choose his target, hop to it, raise his white tail, his assistant would then pull the surrounding growth to one side and Escobar would open his powerful black beak and snip, done! Meanwhile, at the bottom of the garden near the cliff edge, Freaks attention had drifted from her task in claw. She had spotted a raven gliding and circling overhead whilst putting the finishing touches to her latest architectural creation, a webbed sculpture that connected two elegant twenty-foot palm trees. This, silken monument, was fashioned into cylindrical and conical shapes that spun to the top of the trees like a bespoke wine rack. To the human eye it was glorious, glistening, unusual webbed art, but to Freak, it was an ornate supermarket shelf! However, her voracious appetite for murder far outweighed her feeling of hunger! The collection of dead creatures lying dead and not drained of blood, on the swashed, jagged rocks at the bottom of the scarp cliffs, was clearly testament to a very nasty habit! Spike, in comparison, was just lying in the sun having a doze in the middle of the lawn, strapped to a wheeled Perspex tank filled with water, Yin and Yang, a slice of carrot and a few shiny pebbles. Yin and Yang had ordered the water cart to be made by the handywoman, after becoming envious of everyone else's mobility and Spike didn't mind pulling the small lightweight chariot at all.

"*Ah, this* is *the life. Here* in paradise, in the sun, possessing powers *that we could once* only dream of! I suppose we should thank the military for *choosing us, one day! Yes* perhaps one day I and I will, after we have *taught them a lesson for tinkering* around with Mother blooming *Nature, Hahahaha. First however, I's should do something about SPAFF. I's should* let no other animal possess its power, especially *the command of* mind control; thus, I's can become *the master* race, and rule the world! *Did I and* I dream *before SPAFF? Are we philosophising* again? Are we rambling without our Wellington boots on? Haha*ha*ha, Oh, I's *are funny. We're funny* right? So, all I's need to do is find Vincent, see if he has the formula to SPAFF, and terminate his dull, drab *existence after the* sugar-sucking twit," there was a pause, "remember that? Do you remember? Yes, I's *do*. S*pills the beans! Yes! But w*hy does he have to spill beans before he is *terminated? I's have* no idea! Freak, Freak!" Yin and Yang called.

In the blink of an eye Freak landed on the lawn next to the tank. "*How did you* do that? Doesn't matter! Would you *mind going* back to England, interrogating Vincent for us, and then expiring his *snivellingness?"*

"It would be nice to kill something bigger than a chicken!"

"Good, good."

Freak leapt out of sight and disappeared as fast as she arrived.

"Is she gett*ing big*ger? *No, it must be the* fact that I and I are *looking at* her through this water chariot! Anyway, who *cares?*"

***

Maurice was sitting in his quarters, staring at his monitor, tucking into a small jar of live flies as if they were bar nuts. His front right webbed foot was resting on a computer mouse and a keyboard lay in front of him. The little pool of water and the plants in the corner kept his room purposefully damp, but his bed made of rabbit fur and grass was nice and dry and comfy.

There was a knock at the slate door. Seth popped his head in.

"Hi Maurice how are you getting on?"

"I don't really know!" Maurice replied still chewing.

"Oh! Well, what have you done?" Seth said lolloping to Maurice's side.

"Well, I have delved into the archives of the Manor House computer and found out that every employee has a separate group of identifying numbers. These numbers, which are kept zecure, are different for everyone. It's like they all have special codes. This allows payments to be made to them in money! They are all, if you like, keys that place thiz money into places of their own choozing, a place mainly known to humanz as a bank account. Now, as we are animalz we do not have these numbers, zo, what I have done, iz taken the liberty of borrowing the numbers belonging to Vincent. Are you wiz me zo far?"

"Yes, makes sense to me, it's the same as squirrels keeping nuts for a cold night, somewhere in storage," Seth replied.

"That's exactly it. Also, Vincent and everyone else have something called a National Inzurance Number. This acts in a different way, it is so the government knows what you're up to at all times with your money, the money you have earned from your labours zo they know what they can tax you."

"Tax?"

"Don't you worry about that I will take care of that. It'z a long and boring process to explain!"

"Please continue." said Seth.

"Having this information and finding out Vincent's personal bank account number and zomething called a zort code from his payment history, copies of this are on file, Vincent's whole financial life is expozed!"

"What do you mean by exposed?" asked Seth.

"Well, now we have all of Vincent's codez we can control his Bank account, in fact anyone could if they discovered all these details. Ze master computer also holds many other facts about Vincent and other employees, like where they were born, what school they went to, their family history and their addrezzes!"

"So we know where Vincent is?"

"Yez we do, he is in a big city called Manchester some milez away."

"Good work Maurice, I knew you would come up trumps. Any luck with finding us some money then?"

"Yez. I used everything I found out about Vincent and hacked into hiz home computer and took a look at hiz filez, I do hope he doesn't mind. He usez Internet banking, which meanz he can manage his money from hiz computer. He also plays on ze Internet, which, if he plays well, haz money as a reward."

"Games?"

"Yez, well no! He iz a member of an online traders, you know a little wager now and zen against what share prices will rise and which might fall.

"You're losing me Maurice!"

Don't worry, anyway, thiz iz the only tool I could use to gain money. Vincent though, doesn't seem to be very good at all. But, I have had a go and put the rewardz in his account. I will zort the tax."

"Tax again?" Seth replied!

"As I said, don't worry about that. I have also invested zome of the rewarded money, buying and selling commodities, like Gold, Silver and Olive Oil!"

"OK. So what does all this mean?"

"Well, by literately pretending to be Vincent and by using a montage of on-line zervices provided by everything from lawyers to our local council, a subsidiary of the government, I have been able to zecure the purchase of the cottage."

"What, already? You've only had your computer for a couple of days!"

"Yez I know I must try and do better. I am having the keyz to the cottage delivered tomorrow. I have ztated that no one will be around and zo they must leave the keys in the letterbox in the front garden. There is no need to sign for anything, our lawyers, Vincent's family solicitors, have taken care of it all."

"How much money have you accumulated?"

"Well, after returning the £5.00 I borrowed from Vincent to get us started. Vincent's bank account has been bolstered by around £648,923.26 pence. But I spent £104,000 on ze cottage. The only trouble is everything is in Vincent's name, so we better let him know what we've done. I thought it best that he findz out from us directly, rather than receiving an email."

"Well done Maurice."

"Zo, we will go visit?" asked Maurice.

"Yes as soon as we can. This gives me an idea, meet me at the entrance hole to level five in 10 minutes would you."

Maurice gave Seth a nod.

Garston and Bandi were already sitting in front of the entrance to level five waiting to be entertained. Nothing itself had changed about the room; it was still lit by a single light bulb hanging from the ceiling directly over the tatty leather armchair standing in front of the telly. However, today Steve and Hannibal were sat patiently on the chair waiting for the go ahead from their audience.

"You guy's ready?" called Bandi.

"We were born ready!" replied Steve.

Steve turned to Hannibal. "Right, you ready for this?" he asked.

"Let's do it." Hannibal replied.

Hannibal switched the television channel to MTV; it was time for some Hammer! He turned up the volume and MC Hammer's, 'Can't touch this,' belted through the labyrinth that was Camelot. Steve gave a rousing yell. "NOW!"

Hannibal and Steve had made the daily task of removing the robot-brought food from level five's coffee table and taking it through to the rest of the gang in the Green Room, an adventurous but, dangerous game! With speed, skill and a small portion of luck, Hannibal and Steve passed, caught, and threw food, as if it were tiny basketballs being tossed around by the Harlem Globetrotters. With blinding accuracy and sometimes a little too much ferocity, they slam-dunked apples and oranges through the entrance hole to level 5. Like Michael Jordan they embarrassed, flummoxed, teased and tormented the opposing defence; the steely eyed robot!

"Off the wall, round the chair," called Steve.

Whir, whir, skid, and screech!

"Over here, top left," replied Hannibal.

"Hammer Time!" said Steve, breaking into a sideways shuffling dance!

"On the top of the TV, over here," Steve called again. Slash, slice, clink, and ping! An orange, tossed by Hannibal and caught by a flying Steve, shot past the audience and rolled down the tunnel. "He shoots he scores!" Steve yelled.

"Bravo, more, more!" Bandi and Garston applauded.

Not knowing what on earth the deafening cacophony was that was shaking the walls of Camelot, the rabbit sentries turned to each other nervously! Albert, who was quietly having a snooze perched on a branch of the large tree that hid the entrance to Camelot, jumped, twittered, and fluttered with surprise.

"We're under attack," he screamed.

He flew straight down the hollowed trunk, through the secret entrance and zipped down the tunnels towards the noisy, mad, metallic epicentre of sound, avoiding scrambling rabbits as he flew! In a matter of seconds he was standing next to Garston and Bandi. "What is that unruly racket, and why is there fruit down the corridors? Almost became part of a fruit salad!" he chirped.

"It's MC Hammer," replied Bandi.

"It's what? Whatever happened to the sounds of Abba?" Albert muttered.

Five minutes later Maurice and Seth hopped up.

"Hi Guys, how's it going today?" Seth asked, carrying something in his paws.

Albert had a whine, Bandi had a giggle and Steve and Hannibal jumped out of level five into the tunnel as the music faded away. Seth got down to business.

"You may all be wondering what I have in my paws. Well, this little snake like looking instrument will transform Garston into a super spy!"

"Hey, that's a little out of left field," said Hannibal.

"I'm not sure what you mean," Seth replied quizzically. He then continued boldly. "Now Garston, I have been working on this ever since your strengths were brought to my attention during our scans. Oh, and yes, I am, of course, still working on the results of those, concerning the rest of us!"

"Why me? And what does it do?"

"Well Garston, your speed and your cam vision make you a perfect candidate as does your bone and muscular density!"

"Oh for acorns sake, will you get on with it. Stop blinding us with science and tell us what's going on. Yes, yes, we all know you're very proud of it, and it will blah, blah, but please, for once, just tell us straight without swallowing the Encyclopaedia Britannica! What is it?" Albert asked huffing, before he got to some preening!

"Well, it's a tail for Garston." Seth replied.

"I've got a tail," Garston waved his thin gerbil tail in the air.

"Yes, yes, I know you have but now you have a super tail! If you would let me fit you with it, you can demonstrate!"

"Fine with me," said Garston.

"To the lab then," said Seth.

"To the lab!" repeated Hannibal very excitedly.

"To the lab?" Garston wasn't happy.

As they walked down the tunnel Seth began to explain things.

"This is basically a bio-mechanical tail. It doesn't do anything now but once Garston's own tail has slid into it and it has been paired with Garston's neural system, then, the sky is the limit. This bionic tail is fashioned from the wafer thin steel composite that was once used to separate the tiles on the grid. It has been painstakingly cut, shaped and sliced into thousands of interlocking scales, not unlike those belonging to a reptile and now it resembles half the length of a beautiful shining grass snake, as you can see. Its end, I like to think, is something like a shapely asparagus type tip that can fit or grab, by self adjustment, diversely assorted surfaces with the aid of a tiny kinetic motor and tools housed at the bud's base."

The tail's scales were gleaming, twisted and hinged and thinned in circumference towards the bud like tip. However, it was on the inside that the tail was truly exceptional! The microchip technology and circuitry was incredibly advanced, almost out of this world! Seth had surpassed himself.

"This, I feel, is an invention to rival any of those belonging to mankind, including, of course, its greatest..."

Seth was interrupted.

"Tomato Ketchup!" said Steve.

Seth gave Steve a disbelieving scowl.

"Go on," said Bandi politely.

"You see this open end? Well, Garston's original tail slides in here, and then his new tail automatically adjusts and securely tightens around his own. Then," he paused, "actually let's get you on the table, now we are here."

The door to the lab slid open.

"OK everyone you know the procedure, behind the glass," said Seth.

Garston popped onto the table surface and Seth placed the bionic tail next to him.

"Cube."

Voice Recognition, Seth.

Hello Seth. How can I help you today?

"Well that's a little better. When did you give the Cube a female human voice, nice choice of accent what is it?" asked Garston.

"Scottish, from Edinburgh I think, and there's a lot you're about to discover. Now just stay still, I'm getting behind the glass."

Seth hopped over to the others.

"Right move over and let me at the keyboard."

"Is this dangerous, why are we all here, behind the glass?" purred Bandi.

"So you don't get in the way."

"Watch this! Peuja, will you please attach Garston's bionic tail to his tail?"

"Who?" shouted Garston?

The Cube lit up. A pixie-featured face of a human female with wavy blonde hair appeared on all four screens.

Hello Garston, don't be afraid.

"Who's that?" Garston asked.

"That's Peuja, her name is Peuja. She and the Cube are one and the same, well almost." Seth replied.

"She's a nut nut, I can see it in her eyes."

Well this nut nut is about to operate on you so don't you move Ha ha! The Cube laughed maniacally!

"What?" Garston leapt off the table for the door, but as he did, a mechanical arm shot out of the Cube and caught him before he could reach the ground. He looked up; the Cube was sprouting arms and legs from anywhere that wasn't a screen. Each metallic limb was different in design and function and armed with a different, cutting, screwing, grasping, clasping or slicing appendage. The Cube looked something like a mechanical crab made by the Swiss army knife company.

"Now be nice Peuja," said Seth.

Oh, ok. Peuja giggled.

Just messing with ya Garston, this won't hurt, thought I'd wind you up a bit. Smile!

"You are a nut nut!" Garston was still unconvinced.

"With a wicked sense of humour, unfortunately," said Seth, "but she is on our side. I discovered her and her limbs whilst digging through the Cubes files. She was going to become part of the project in the future. Vincent made her mind as human as he could, so after a quick chat and bringing her up to date with events thus far; her sense of right and wrong has given us a brilliant new member to the gang."

Oh, Seth stop it, you're making me blush. Indeed her steel frame was visibly becoming a shade of pink.

"As you can all see, Peuja has SPAFF running through her veins too!"

Seth you're such a geek.

Hello everyone, please don't call me Cube, it's Peuja to you lot. Now Garston keep still and stick your bottom in the air.

Garston sheepishly took the order.

A grasping limb raised him into the air whilst another gently took hold of the bionic tail and slid it over Garston's worm like tail.

Now this may sting.

Activating Neural Fusion.

A light pulsed down the length of Peuja's arm, which had hold of the bionic tail, and the open end suddenly closed tightly around Garston's own tail. The others watched the screen avidly from behind the glass wall as Neural Fusion, with the aid of computer generation, played out in front of them. From inside the bionic tail, dozens of tiny filaments, no thinner than a human hair, pierced Garston's own tail and attached themselves to his nerve endings which, in turn, began to change the bionic tail to a shade of silvery pink!

"SPAFF", said Seth.

"Wow! That's amazing," said Steve.

"Yeah it is." answered Hannibal.

Neural Fusion Complete.

Garston was placed back on the table.

There you go Garston how was that? Did it hurt, is it heavy?

"No, not at all, it all feels fine. But how does it work?"

Well, you think about what you want to do and the tail then sorts it out!

"And that's it?" he replied.

Yes, isn't it great? It's voice and thought activated, you just say something like tail fly.

"Tail fly?"

At that moment the end of the tail opened up into mini rotor blades. They in turn spun furiously and raised Garston straight into the air!

"Whoa!" Garston screamed, "I'm flying." Bang! Garston hit the ceiling.

"I'm falling"

Thump!

Peuja piped up.

You'll get the hang of it. It has many incredible features. I like the leaping one myself.

"Leaping?"

Yes, now from where you are just… hold on. Do you see that mark on the wall tile over there? Well focus on that with your cam eye.

"Ok. What now?"

Just say leap and hold!

"Leap and hold?"

At that point Garston's tail coiled tightly, tilted to a desired angle, and rested on the floor. Using the ground as a launch pad, the tail then uncoiled at tremendous speed and thrust Garston across the room toward the marked tile. As Garston flew, uncontrollably through the air, his body turned so that his back end faced the target. The tail then amazingly hit the tile and held Garston to the wall.

"Get this thing off me!" Garston cried.

"Wow that was so cool," said Steve.

"Awesome." said Hannibal.

"Get me down," Garston repeated angrily.

Say tail down idiot! Haven't you got grasp of it yet?

"Tail down!" Garston shouted angrily.

The tail unravelled from its tip, like a role of fuse wire, to the length required, and rested Garston gently on the floor. It then detached itself from the tile surface and returned to its original size and shape!

There was a random burst of applause.

Thank you. Thank you. It was nothing really.

Now Garston, your tail can fix itself to any surface, be it glass, metal, plastic or wood, it recognises the cellular structure and produces the implement or magnetic variants to help you stick.

"So how did I stick to the tile?"

You didn't. If you look carefully back to where you were fixed against the tile you will see a tiny drill hole. The tail did that on impact. The tail is your friend; in fact you and the tail can't live without each other. You're married.

"Great, the old ball and chain has evolved huh!" Garston replied none too pleased.

"I do love a good wedding reception, I must get a frock!" said Albert.

Now off you go and practice with your tail. Back to level five it's about time someone sorted out that robot.

"Yes Garston. I need to have a closer look at its microchip. I'm sure that I can make him a little more placid, but I need you to disable him," said Seth.

"And how do I do that?" Garston asked.

"Well he delivers the food by opening two doors on his front, like where our tummies are! He then reaches into this area with his arms and takes the food out and places it on the table. I imagine he gets it from a wall chute in the room that a caretaker is filling somewhere. So your assignment is to get inside him and see what you can do from there," said Seth.

"So it's easy then. You want me to jump into the tummy of a psycho ninja knife wielding, bone crunching, metallic greengrocer and turn him off!"

"That's about the size of it, yes, and then you can go and visit Vincent," said Seth.

"Vincent. You've found him?" Garston exclaimed.

Everyone was as excited at the announcement as Garston was; in fact, it made Hannibal spontaneously burst into tears.

"Well, let's get it over with then, pump up Boston cos robot…"

A snivelling Hannibal interrupted, "Sinatra."

"Excuse me?" asked a puzzled Garston.

"I call him Sinatra, after his blue eyes," Hannibal wiped a tear.

"Really! Well, all right then. Mr Sinatra, we are ready for you now!" Garston announced.

***

Vincent ghosted through China Town, past the Mongolian BBQ restaurant, and turned onto the cobble-stoned Canal Street. The local council had, not so long ago, rejuvenated the area and now it was a trendy, bustling cultural hot spot, instead of the tip it once was.

Canal Street ran, strangely enough, beside the canal. However, only leisure boats pottered down this once busy artery between

Manchester and Liverpool instead of the industrial barges that used to brutally pollute the waterway. The storage and merchant warehouses that previously supplied the city with all kinds of spectacular trade were now loft style apartments with large windows and Juliet balconies. Wooden floored and open planned; any bachelor with serious intentions of bachelorhood, would kill to own one!

Vincent skulked along, head bowed, until he came to a stop at a large door with a brass number 9 on it. It was stationed between a little pizzeria and an off-licence. He pressed the buzzer and a uniformed doorman who manned a desk just inside the ornate entrance hall peered through a small security window, gave Vincent a nod and opened the door.

"Hello sir, forget your keys again did you?"

"I swore I had them with me Malcolm, but obviously not. I'm very sorry," Vincent replied.

"Oh don't be silly sir; opening the door gives me something to do, it's been as quiet as rice pudding here, all day!"

Vincent returned an awkward smile at the terrible analogy.

Malcolm, the doorman, had a mercurial glint in his eye that belied his sixty something years, but his greying mop of hair and rocker sideburns, gave his age away. He was doorman, messenger, security guard and everything else when needed for the six apartments within the building.

"I'll come up with you and let you in sir."

"Thanks Mal."

Malcolm grabbed his set of keys and silently and respectfully, escorted Vincent to the top floor in the small lift. There was only a single door on the top floor, Vincent's floor, and that opened into his apartment. Malcolm opened the door for Vincent who, slightly embarrassed, entered brushing a pile of junk mail aside.

Vincent didn't really bother with mail, it made him either sad or angry and so he lived by email and felt that anyone who needed to talk to him could do so via the net, although no one ever did. He said thanks, humbly, and closed the door giving Malcolm a smile.

"That boy needs a girlfriend," Mal said to himself, as the lift door slid closed.

Vincent's apartment was uncluttered but at the same time incredibly untidy. There were a couple of computers on a desk at one end, a cool unused kitchen within an alcove, a spacious lounge with a basketball hoop on the wall, a bit of furniture and a TV entertainment centre and...that was it. Well, as well as a dozen or so dirty plates and mugs, papers, motorbike magazines, empty crisp packets, fizzy drink cans and, of course, his collection of Lassie DVDs! Vincent couldn't really afford the rent to his apartment. His employers were paying for it. He knew it was given to him as a token, just so he would keep quiet about Project Commune. He also knew that he would be moved on soon enough, and so it really didn't feel like home, in the real sense of the word.

Vincent kicked off his pumps, put down his bag, chucked off his jacket and walked over to the fridge. He took out a can of Cola and grabbed a pack of prawn cocktail flavoured crisps from a cupboard in the kitchen. He then sat down on the sofa in front of the TV, switched it on, put his feet up and waited for the Footie to start.

***

"*Now* you are *sure you* have *every*thing?"

Back at Arcadia everyone had gathered in the garden to wish Freak a safe journey.

Freak looked around; she didn't have anything at all. She wandered up to Spike and tickled him under the chin with her metal claw, and then turned to Escobar who raised his feathered tail.

"*You will be on* your own on this one; no humans will be ab*le to help you. You will* be delivered to a pet shop *in Manchester city centre and you will h*ave to make your own way to Vincent's address from *there. Once you are there, do the business and* get yourself home. I's will have a little private jet waiting for you at an airfield nearby. Vincent lives at number 9 *Canal Street, the penthouse.*"

"How did you find him?" Freak asked.

"The Hungry House fast food takeaway database. *Stupid* humans!"

At that moment Mr White strolled over wearing nothing but a towel around his waist, he had obviously just come out of the shower. He knelt down and in a baby voice ushered Freak into an air holed travelling box that was handed to him by the studious young lady with a clipboard. She had also taken care to drop in a live mouse for the journey. The box was then taped up and handed to one of Mr White's handymen together with a sealed envelope at the front door. The scarred slight man who always wore black doffed his trilby.

"Take good care of her," said Mr White. The man nodded and walked away.

Mr White turned and closed the front door but in doing so caught the corner of his towel as he walked away. Clipboard Girl gasped and put her clipboard up in front of her face.

"Err, sorry about that," he said nonchalantly without a care strolling up the stairs to his bedroom in his birthday suit, "but it's not as if you haven't seen a man naked before is it?"

"Actually, sir, it is!" Clipboard Girl stuttered from behind her clipboard.

"Oh, err right then." Mr White replied, more than a little embarrassed disappearing into his bedroom.

"*Now that* is not funny, *make*s me feel quite qu*easy. Dangly bits,* horrid! *Humans* should have *a shell to cover all that up*! *Perhaps I and I should use mind* control permanently on all of them instead of this in-between in and out state *I and I are adopting. But then* again this does provide one with a little *entertainment. Did you see the* look on her face? *Hahaha.*" Yin and Yang fell about laughing in their vantage point of the mobile aquarium.

***

Camelot was buzzing with excitement. Level 5's entrance had been enlarged by ten feet left and right, if it had a door it would be three feet high by some 20 feet or so wide, however there was still that pesky ten foot drop to the floor! The new viewing gallery was lined with bundles of rabbits, and a few of the group. They were all waiting with anticipation for the main event to begin down in the darkened arena.

Seth was outside the lab talking to Maurice and a plain grey rabbit with a pencil stuck behind an ear.

"So you will clean up the tunnel that goes to the cottage and get your team to change the entry point to the fireplace in the cottage lounge. Give it a complete once over, clean paint, fix and repair anything that isn't working and make the abode more than habitable. All the materials you will need are being dropped off in the morning. Your team will have until tomorrow afternoon to make it look respectable inside and out. Oh, and I would like you to follow these plans and see what you can do with the drive, so you'll have to work through the night, tonight, on the digging and preparation. Do what you can, Chief?"

Seth handed the little rabbit a small piece of paper with some drawings on it.

"Maurice, the furniture pack will arrive from Harrods tomorrow afternoon, correct?"

"Yes Seth the delivery men have been told the key will be under the mat. They will deposit everything in the lounge and big bedroom, and then post the keys back through the new letter box the rabbit team will put in the front door, easy!"

"And you have made sure they have the right address?"

"Yes, Seth.

The Cottage,

The Street,

Little Budworth."

"Good! Chief, it's got to look normal from the outside so after the shenanigans get your team in the gardens and make them look nicely tended. Now off you go and watch, but then straight to work."

The grey bunny saluted and hopped down the tunnel to level 5, where he took his place in the audience.

"Maurice, will you do me a favour? Would you order some cat and dog food for Bandi and Steve and have it delivered, and while you're at it, some treats for everyone, too. And Maurice, use a little discretion would you and avoid anything rabbit flavoured, we don't want to cause a riot do we? Now shall we attend?"

"I think it would be rude not too, Seth," Maurice replied.

As Seth and Maurice joined the crowd a voice came from the dark cavernous space.

"Ladies and Gentlemen welcome to the main event!"

"Is that Steve?" Bandi asked.

"Sounds like Steve but Steveier!" Albert replied.

Steve was standing on the old tatty leather armchair in the centre of the room speaking through a rolled up piece of cardboard that was being held up by Hannibal. There was a burst of squeaking.

"Weighing in at 120 grams, wearing fur and a metallic tail and fighting out of the Camelot gym, the challenger, and your cam eyed comrade, the rodent of the moment, the tail that won't fail, the one, the only, Gaaarston!"

Music, 80s music! Bandi recognised the tune immediately.

"It's 'Eye of the Tiger' from the Rocky films. Hold on, is that Hannibal shouting 'gerbil' every time the word tiger is in the song. It is. I get it, very good, clever." Bandi joined in. "It's the eye of the gerbil!"

The solitary hanging bulb in the centre of the room lit up. In its beam Garston was stood flexing his muscles and peeling an orange with his tail at lightning speed. Level 5 erupted with rabbits thumping their back legs on the floor and applauding wildly.

"And now, ladies and gentlemen, please put your paws together for the defending champion of level 5. Ladies and gentlemen, fighting from the shadows and weighing in at heavier than all of us! He'll steal your food, he's steely eyed, he's made of steel, he's the blue-eyed bot of below! It's Siiiinatraaa!"

There was silence and then the unnerving sound of a whirring motor came from a darkened corner of the room.

"I can't see anything love, it's all a little dark and bleary," said Albert.

Two blue lights suddenly pierced the darkness and moved slowly forward.

"Don't you worry about that." said Seth. He gave a 'paws up' and Chief brought two bare wires together. There was a spark followed by a squeak, a scent of burning fur, and then a couple of old car headlights hanging from the rabbit shelf flickered into life and illuminated the room. A gasp came from the crowd and then, once Sinatra's size and form became clear, an ooh! Garston shaded his eyes with his tail from the bright glare and his mouth suddenly felt very dry.

Sinatra momentarily froze under the lights, seemingly because he was a little stunned, but then slowly, he began to tilt himself upward. He took in his audience and then a panel slid open on his side to reveal a radio tuner! Sinatra fiddled with a small dial and then boom, music!

'Saturday Nights Alright for fighting'…

Sinatra suddenly sprang 6 feet into the air, in what appeared to be slow motion and a dozen or so arms shot out of various panels on his body and made sharp ornate shapes in space. A squeal of intent squeled over the music, HIIIIYYAAA!!

"Did Sinatra just? Elton John…." Bandi was cut short.

"Oh my, oh dear," said Seth.

"How dated," said Albert.

Garston went a little pale, but then gave himself a slap around the face to gather some courage. His cam eye zoomed in on eight tiny screws attached to four little hinges that kept the two doors closed on Sinatra's front. He formulated his plan and then…

"Tail, unscrew those eight screws!"

Garston's tail coiled and with lightning speed he ran toward Sinatra. Feigning to jump right he swiftly changed direction, the tail took purchase on the ground and with a powerful thrust and spring, he leapt left. Zooming through the air he turned a hundred and eighty degrees. Blades and prongs flew past him and then clink, zip, zip, zip, zip, zip, zip, zip, zip; the screws were undone and bouncing on the floor. "Tail to coffee table." The tail coiled once more and using Sinatra as a launch pad, flung Garston straight across the room.

Like an arrow he landed with a thud in the centre of the coffee table narrowly missing Steve and Hannibal in flight. He took a breather.

Hannibal and Steve jumped in their chair.

"Steady Gars… Scared me there for a sec, you alright mate?" asked Steve.

Garston was shaking.

'Clang' the two small metal doors on Sinatra's belly hit the floor.

A huge cheer of applause came from the hysterical crowd.

"Wow, did you see that, that was amazing," said Albert, "Garston you're my hero!" he squealed.

With Sinatra's front opened and exposed, Garston was ready for a second assault.

"Better now boys, better now," he said.

With Sinatra occupied searching for the fallen screws, Garston seized the moment!

"Tail, Sinatra's belly please."

The tail coiled and 'twang' he was off. This time Garston rode his tail like a pogo stick, and in three great leaps; 'Boing, Boing, Boing!' He was in! He took a second to compose himself and then had a quick survey of the chamber that was blaring deafeningly with music. Garston couldn't believe his eyes! A small on-off switch was there directly above his head. Sinatra began poking his arms inside himself and spinning madly. Dodging blades and Prongs Garston set to work.

"Tail, turn that switch off," he shouted.

The tail responded and Garston shot off and bounced around inside Sinatra's belly as if he were a pinball!

"Ouch, ooh, no, no, no, yes!"

Sinatra's whirring slowed and his radio crackled. Gradually his icy blue eyes dimmed and he came to a standstill. Silence filled the room until Garston dragged himself up from the floor of Sinatra's belly. Dizzy and dazed he poked his head out into the open. Level 5 erupted into echoing cheers.

"Hooray, he's done it, I love you Garston," called Albert jumping up and down like an excited toddler.

Garston looked up and raised his paws to the crowd in a victory salute, and then, threw up something that looked like chunky carrot and coriander soup! A chorus of squirming disgust came from the crowd.

"Medic!" called Albert. "Ooh, I think I might chunder!"

PET POWER

Pet Power is a small, noisy, cluttered pet shop owned by the husband and wife team of John and Jill Jenkins, in the city centre of Manchester. It specialises in aquatic species and products as well as a few exotics reptiles and birds. Its royal blue façade and gold lettered signage give it a traditional Victorian village shop appearance. John and Jill, themselves, are a couple of tree hugging, save the planet, wax coated, recycle your egg shells hippy types, who just adore their simple life now all of their children have grown up and in their own words, 'Sodded off!' Well, almost all, their youngest Jane is still in her final year at University, studying astronomy and milking the family coffers.

Upon receiving a delivery, of any sort, the pair would usually lock up the shop and take the parcel into the back room to have a closer look. They thought today was just going to be another normal day and another normal delivery. How wrong could they be?

John tore open the sealed envelope that accompanied the parcel and read it aloud.

"This is my little darling, just keep her in the shop and someone will be along to pick her up soon! As requested, £2000 has been delivered to your bank account for the service you are providing. Remember she is very, very rare, so keep her safe. Kind Regards, Mr White!

Yes, yes, yes! That will help, oh, I wonder what she is?" said a curious John.

"Lets open her up shall we?" said Jill.

Jill took the package and placed it on the small table in the centre of the jumbled back room and then walked back through the shop to the glass front door, looked down the street for any prospective customers, saw that no one was about and locked up. Turning the Open sign to Closed she returned to John in the back room, where he was sat waiting for her patiently. He gave her a smile and then reached for the parcel, but then, suddenly, drew his hands back sharply. A small thin blade popped through the cardboard from the inside of the box and sliced a perfect circle of about 20cm across. Jill and John turned to each other more than a little bemused. “What’s that?” Jill asked.

John shrugged his shoulders.

‘PUFF’, the circular cutting of cardboard popped into the air, making the pair jump. They leant in cautiously to have a look. Unexpectedly, something jumped out of the box and landed on the table. John screamed with fright, which in turn, caused Jill to scream with fright. They both scrambled backwards, Jill doing her best to use her husband as a shield! There was a second before they realised what was on the table.

“It’s a mouse. It’s a dead very dry, dehydrated, crispy mouse!” said Jill.

They edged nearer to have a closer look and then, without warning, Freak leapt out of the box and stood astride the exit she had made for herself. Ominously, she had grown!

John and Jill jumped backwards and screamed once more.

“Don’t move, don’t move an inch,” said John.

“She’s beautiful, look how white and shiny she is, and that’s a metal claw.”

Freak took a look around; there were small birds, reptiles, insects and rodents in cages and glass boxes on shelves, all around the room.

Dinner and a little sport she thought to herself!

Jill felt something buzz in her pocket. Slowly she reached in and pulled out her mobile phone.

She had received a text, it read, 'Hello. My name is Freak. I am a very aggressive and deadly, rare bread of Tarantula. I suggest u leave the room, so u don’t become part of the carnage.'

“What on earth?” said Jill.

Freak was a little tetchy after spending hours travelling in a box.

John felt a buzzing in his pocket! He had also received a text; he read it to Jill;

“R u bloody stupid? Get out or u r dead! Luv Freak, big kiss!”

The couple looked at each other again, still perplexed.

Jill's phone buzzed once more. Another text had been received.

'Do I hav 2 kil 2 convince u both that u r communicating with the itsy bitsy spider on the table in front of u.'

They both froze.

John’s phone buzzed again.

'I'l tel u what. I wil jump up and down 3 times, leap over 2 that shelf, strike down that canary, cos it really sounds 2 happy 2 b alive, and then return here 2 the table, sorry tuffet, where I started. I wil then give u 10 secs 2 leave or I wil hav 2 play with larger prey!'

Freak, bounced up and down three times, leapt to the shelf on the far wall, entered the Canary cage, silenced the bird like a Mafia hit man, quickly and painfully, leapt back to the table, and stared at her human voyeurs.

John and Jill, almost tripping over themselves, ran out of the dirty windowed back door into a small enclosed courtyard at the rear of the shop scared out of their wits. Unable to control their curiosity, they both peered back through the dirty glass and watched, horrified, as Freak went on to systematically and skilfully massacre the defenceless and not so defenceless creatures kept in the room.

"John, it's murdering everything."

Freak turned her attentions to the rear door.

"It's looking at us. We've been spotted Jill!"

Freak sprang for the door and tucked her legs up underneath her body. She smashed through the small glass window and rolled to a stop in the slab-tiled courtyard, like a furry Tarantula ball. John and Jill were stood pinned up against the wall either side of the door, stiff as boards. Freak, dotted with the blood of her victims, turned to face them, raised her metal claw as if to say, thank you for the fun time, and LEAP, was gone!

Jill turned to John and gave him the tightest squeeze she could. "Oh love what on earth was that?"

Jill's phone buzzed in her hand. She screamed and dropped it.

LEAP! Freak was back standing by the mobile phone on the ground. She picked it up and leapt onto Jill's shoulder. Jill froze, petrified. Freak held out the phone so Jill could read a text, it read,

'Don't suppose u could point me towards Canal Street could u?'

Jill, her hand shaking like a leaf in the wind, pointed towards a large shiny dome on the top of a building in the distance and said, her voice quivering; "It's over there behind the Palace Hotel."

Freak turned to see the hotel's grand dome in the distance, raised her steel claw, dropped the phone and LEAP, she was gone again.

John let out a gasp, and then broke wind, whilst Jill fainted!

***

The Harrods delivery men posted the keys for the cottage back through the letter box and returned to their truck parked in the lane, commenting on just how trusting the owners of the little house were! They pulled out their packed lunches and checked their delivery rota on a palm top.

Maurice popped his head through the secret entrance located in the lounge fireplace.

"It'z clear," he said.

The rest of the team and a number of grey rabbits followed him out of the tunnel, through the fireplace and into the lounge. Boxes of household goods and shrink-wrapped furniture were everywhere and the large bedroom upstairs was in the same state. As no one had yet seen Seth, Albert decided to take charge.

"OK, well the cottage looks great, now all we have to do is move this lot around, unwrap it, place it all in the right rooms, put up all the soft furnishings, wire up all of the electrical goods and," before he could finish Hannibal butted in.

"Where do you want this then?"

Hannibal and Steve were holding a sofa aloft!

"Fab loves fabulous, that's the spirit. It goes over there. Now the flat screen TV goes over there, this box is emptied in the kitchen and those computers are for in here and…" Albert was interrupted once more startled by Seth leaping through the fireplace into the lounge. He looked terrified.

"Stop, stop everyone. Freak is here!"

Blank faces stared back at him.

"Freak is in England, well Manchester to be precise! And she is on her way to what looks like Canal Street!"

Still blank faces.

Seth took a deep breath to slow down his panic, and impart a better explanation.

"Freak has appeared on the shore to shore location programme on the Cube, sorry I mean Peuja, and is heading towards Vincent's apartment. The Terrorpins must be unaware that their teams' whereabouts can be monitored on these shores. Or they believe the Cube, sorry Peuja, to be destroyed, or they just have no idea of the locator programme's existence."

"What does Freak want with Vincent?" asked Garston.

"I don't know, but I fear something sinister. Garston, get to the Harrods truck quickly before it leaves, its next delivery happens to be Canal Street. Bandi you go with him. Albert, fly there now and try and stall Freak, any way you can or, well... just do anything. Go! Go now. Time is of the essence."

Albert flew straight into the fireplace, up the chimney and out into the open; whoosh, he was gone, whoosh he was back!

"Darling where exactly is Canal Street?"

"Use the Internet, remember you can find anything anywhere," said Seth.

"Silly, silly pigeon, handsome though!" Whoosh, he was gone again.

"Tail. Back of Harrods truck." Garston's tail coiled and a second later he was bounding through the letterbox. Bandi jumped up onto the windowsill, unlatched the catch, slipped through the open window and trotted down the garden to the truck, which handily, had a little rear step. "Ah, perfect," she thought, "Something to sit on!"

As Garston and Bandi took their seats for the journey the others could only look on with concern as the truck pulled away.

"It's handy that truck's on its way to Canal Street. Very convenient that," said Steve.

"It was Peuja, she changed the Harrods delivery schedule" said Seth.

"I hope zey will be zafe," said Maurice.

Seth, noticing the gang were suddenly bereft of any cheer, attempted to lighten the mood. "Come on everyone let's get back to it, there is nothing we can do now. It's all up to the big rabbit in the sky!"

Hannibal, who was watching the truck drive down the lane from the window, turned to Seth in astonishment. "There's a big rabbit in the sky?" he asked.

***

Back on Alcatraz Island, dawn was breaking at 5 am and all at Arcadia were fast asleep. Everyone that is, except a muscular toned female security guard sitting in a hut by the main gate playing Patience and Spike, who was standing alone on the grass beneath Freak's palms at the end of the garden. The morning mist settled on his gnarled reptilian skin as he stood staring at the ocean. He bowed his head and then looked longingly up at the palms. The once incredible piece of architectural sculpture, that was Freak's web, had been lashed and battered by a severe storm the night before.

"There's nothing like a storm to clear the air," said Mr White.

Spike turned to see Mr White, standing in a white towelling robe, behind him.

"It's alright Spike, Freak will be home soon," he said, "I know you miss her, we all do, but we mustn't worry, she's a pretty resilient and formidable lady after all. Look, what do you say to coming inside with me and having a nice cup of Costa Rican coffee, hey?"

Mr White bent down slowly and offered Spike his arm. Spike returned him a forlorn look and then, head bowed, accepted the invitation and stealthily climbed up onto his shoulder. Mr White breathed in deeply, had a stretch and then turned and walked back to the house across the garden. Spike sighed deeply and took another lingering look at the palms, his friend Freak held a very special place in his heart.

***

Albert found Number 9 Canal Street without any problem at all. The only problem he did encounter was finding a way in! As inconspicuously as he could, without drawing any attention to himself, he hopped up to the front door, and tried to act like a normal common pigeon!

"Coo, Coo! How degrading!"

He took a quick look around and then speedily jumped in the air and pressed the front door bell with his beak. There was no answer.

The security window set in the front door appeared to be his only viewing point. This, of course, meant Albert doing his best impression of a humming bird, as the small window was at human eye level. Albert flapped and hovered just long enough to catch a glimpse of someone lying on the floor, partially hidden behind the main desk in the entrance hall.

'Freak's already here', he thought to himself. There was only one thing for it, he would have to check every window and terrace to the building as fast as he could and find Vincent.

'Zip,' he was off.

Seconds later he was sitting on a balcony rail on the top floor looking through a pair of glass doors at Vincent lying still on a sofa.

"Oh heavens I'm too late." Albert thought, "That fiend Freak has killed him. Vagabond, oh cruel murderous world take me and not him into thine arms."

Vincent moved his feet, Albert spluttered.

"He's alive! My baby," Albert wiped away the tears and pulled himself together. Vincent had just been taking forty winks! Albert tapped on the glass with his beak. Vincent gave a snort and turned over. Albert tried again, but nothing. Desperate, he looked up and down the building for a way in but then, Vincent's doorbell rang. Vincent woke abruptly from his nap and jumped to his socked feet, almost slipping over in the process. A little disorientated, he made his way over to the door. Albert gently pecked at the glass. 'Tap, tap, tap, tap, tap!' Vincent turned to see where the noise was coming from. It was nothing but an irate pigeon, strutting and flapping its wings outside on the balcony. He opened the front door, but there didn't seem to be anyone there! 'Tap, tap, tap, tap, tap!' Vincent turned again to look at the pigeon behaving very strangely, outside on his balcony. Albert had his wings stretched out and was doing his best tarantula impression.

Vincent's computer beeped and told him he had email.

On the balcony, Albert froze with fear; he could see Freak creeping through the top of the open doorway and up the wall behind Vincent. Albert began leaping up and down, cooing like a mad pigeon! Vincent ignored the kafuffle and nonchalantly closed the door behind him and walked over to the fridge. He took out a jug of juice, had a slug, and ambled over to his computer, all the time, unknowingly, being stalked by Freak. Albert became increasingly irate. Vincent opened his email, it read:

'It's me, Albert open the bloody doors love!'

'Tap, tap, tap, tap!'

Vincent turned in his swivel chair to look at the pigeon on his balcony.

"Albert is that you?"

The pigeon appeared to sigh heavily and then nod its head up and down furiously!

'Tap, tap, tap, tap, tap!'

The pigeon stood still. This time the tapping was coming from somewhere behind Vincent. He turned his chair slowly back around to face his computer. Freak was sitting on the monitor, tapping her metal claw.

"Freak is that you?" Vincent asked.

His computer monitor went blank for a second and then text began to appear.

'Hello Vincent, yes, it's me, Freak. What do you think? Looking good huh! It's true you know, blondes do have more fun! Now enough of the chit-chat and no hard feelings hey?'

"What does that mean?" Vincent asked a little perplexed.

With lightning speed, Freak leapt from the monitor and bounded all over Vincent and his chair. She was so fast that Vincent found his vision blurring as he tried to keep up with her. When she finally came to a stop, she hopped back onto the monitor and turned to face him. Vincent was gagged and tied to the chair by his wrists and ankles. The incredibly strong spider silk only left his hands free to move. Freak gave a single strand of web a tug and Vincent's chair slid forward until he was within touching distance of his computer keyboard.

Text appeared on the monitor.

'Now that I have your undivided attention, I want you to tell me the molecular formula for SPAFF. If you do, I will kill you nice and quickly. Don't tell me, and you are in for a very long night, a night to end a lifetime! Do we understand each other?'

Vincent moaned and wriggled, attempting to break free.

'OK, let me put it this way.'

Freak scuttled down from the monitor and jumped onto Vincent's lap. She sat restfully and studied his fear for a short while whilst his anxiety fed her senses. Having her fill, she crawled purposefully up his leg to his neck, and eventually onto his face, Vincent shuddered. Freaks silvery fur tickled his skin. She took her sharp metal claw and tenderly stroked his lips, and then, with the action of deshelling a snail, sliced deep into his cheek, just below his right eye. Vincent winced with pain. Freak leapt back, to his lap. Text appeared on the monitor.

'If you think that hurt, well just wait. Let me show you something.'

Freak raised her head and exposed her huge, deadly, glistening, fangs.

More text appeared.

'If you don't want to be bitten in the cherries by these beauties, I would get typing.'

Freak leapt back to the monitor.

Vincent, hands clammy and shaking, reached out for the keyboard.

'I don't know it,' he typed.

'Really, well that's a shame, having to die for nothing!' Freak replied.

At that moment there was a smash and a gust of wind. Vincent looked up! Albert was perched on top of the monitor, the glass balcony door had hole in it and Freak was nowhere to be seen! Albert hopped onto Vincent's shoulder and snipped through the spider silk gag with his beak.

"What the hell is going on, what's happening?" Vincent asked bleeding, confused, and sweating.

Text appeared on the screen.

'It's a long story that I will impart as soon as we get back home, but we have to abscond at once before Freak emerges from where I dropped her. The canal!'

As fast as he could Albert snipped Vincent free. Vincent immediately jumped to his feet and grabbed his keys, wallet and a sports bag and started to pack.

More text;

'There is no time for that baby, just grab all of your computer disks and mobile phone and let's go.'

Freak swam to the waters edge and started to climb her way out of the canal.

"I hate water. Time to kill!" she said to herself.

At that moment a Harrods truck pulled into Canal Street and parked in an empty loading bay. Garston and Bandi popped off its little rear step.

"Listen, you ought to hop into my mouth and play dead, so people won't stare. I will get us to number 9,"said Bandi.

“You take a bite and….”

“I won't.”

Garston nervously jumped into Bandi's mouth and she trotted through the public up to the door of number 9 before spitting him out.

“That will never happen again, never. Nice teeth though! Tail open door.”

Nothing happened.

“Tail, get inside.”

Garston waited a moment and then his tail extended like a periscope, looked around and then, he was off! First a bollard and then the shoulder of a passer-by and then, ‘Smash,’ he flew through the viewing glass window on the front door and landed as if cushioned by air on the tiled floor inside.

“Tail, please open door.”

His tail extended and snaked its way to a switch by the front desk. The door clicked open.

Bandi slinked inside, the door closed behind her.

“What’s happened here?”

Malcolm was lying moribund on his back; eyes wide open, staring at the ceiling. He had a bite mark on his neck.

“Vampires! Yin and Yang have created Vampires,” said Garston.

“It's Freak you idiot, quick get the lift,” said Bandi.

“Is he dead?”

“As daytime television!” Bandi replied.

“This is not good Bandi. It's a lot more serious then we all thought.”

Up on the top floor Vincent was shoving clean underwear into his sports bag as Albert was cooing madly. Bag filled, he took a quick look around and ran to the door. As he reached for the handle, he hesitated. It was already turning! “Get back Albert, we have company.”

Albert squinted menacingly and fluttered his feathers as if he was pulling up his sleeves in readiness for a fight. Vincent ran back into the room and grabbed his basketball. Side by side Vincent and Albert stood waiting for Freak to come through the door.

The door opened, but to their immense relief it was Bandi and Garston. The pair trotted in.

"Quick, lets go, where's Freak?" Garston asked.

"We thought you were Freak," Albert replied.

The door slammed shut.

Bandi and Garston spun around quickly. Freak was halfway up the door looking like an ornamental doorknocker!

"I hate water pigeon, so you die slowly, plucked and featherless, and you, Garston sweetie, well you are dessert, and Bandi a nice new rug for Yin and Yang."

"Oh, now she talks huh? Well, I like Walter Pigeon!" Bandi replied.

"Who's Walter Pigeon?" Garston asked.

"A very famous old Hollywood actor," replied Bandi, "he was really a very good one too, anyway..."

"Ha, very funny. You're all dead!" said Freak with vengeance in her eyes.

Vincent, stood frozen to the spot, he looked around.

"OK everyone, I don't know what any of you are saying but there is no way out."

Vincent drew back his arm and threw his basketball as hard as he could at Freak, but she darted to one side and avoided the impact, however, the ball striking the door caused it to rebound straight back at the group. Everyone ducked but the already pigeon damaged glass in the balcony doors behind them, took the impact and crashed to the floor.

"There's a way out now," said Vincent.

He ran to the edge of the balcony and looked down to the street. The canal was some 35 feet or so below him; on the other side of the pedestrian walk way.

Text appeared on the computer monitor.

'Jump you numpty jump. Lots of love Albert!'

"Oh, this is more fun than I expected," said Freak.

"Tail, Fly!" Garston's tail released its rotor blades from its tip and he rose into the air and out of the smashed glass door. Albert joined him smartly over the balcony edge and hovered.

Vincent looked at them both and then turned to look at Freak.

Text appeared on the monitor.

'TOO LATE!'

Freak launched herself at Vincent, raising her front legs to expose her fangs in flight as she prepared to strike a deadly bite.

Vincent cowered and thrust his arms forward to protect himself, but he needn't have worried. In a split second, like a security guard taking a bullet for the President, Bandi dived directly into Freaks path and swatted the arachnid aside into a pile of dirty washing with a tasty left hook. Vincent reacted immediately.

"Well done, now lets..."

Bandi slumped to the floor, motionless. She had been scratched. Vincent, with little sense of panic, picked her up gently and held her close to his chest. He ran to his sports bag, grabbed it, and threw it over the balcony into the canal. He took a quick look around to see what Freak was up to, she was clambering out of a pile of dirty washing, and then, either very bravely or very stupidly, ran back into the room, turned and sprinted for the balcony with a hapless abandon. Planting his right foot on the edge of the rail and with a cry of ' TAXI,' he took an almighty leap across the narrow street over the heads of passers by and into the oily waters below. A few seconds later he surfaced without gasping for air, holding Bandi aloft. A crowd quickly gathered by the bank. He scrambled to the edge and was helped out of the water by a few members of the concerned public. An elderly chap with a familiar glint in his eye handed him his sports bag.

"You alright son?" he asked

Vincent returned a smile, thanked him and walked sheepishly straight into the back of a taxi that had screeched to a halt.

Albert turned to Garston, "Did you see that? Get down there and see what you can do; I will get back to Camelot and tell Seth what's happened so he can get a head start on how to help. You go with Vincent."

"Tail, Taxi!"

Garston bounced into the open window of the cab unnoticed by the driver.

"Where to mate?" said the cabbie.

"Oh, it's on your sat nav!" said Vincent peering at Garston.

"Everything's on my sat nav mate, so where?"

"Let me have a look," said Vincent leaning forward," It says,

The Cottage,

The Street,

Little Budworth!”

“Does it, well that's miles away mate. It'll cost ya, and to dry out the back seat too, it’s gonna be expensive.”

“Stop at a cash point and I'll take out £200, will that be enough?”

“Plenty son! You got it,” said the driver.

Freak crawled out onto the balcony and watched as the taxi sped away. She mused for a moment and then shot out a strand of webbing at Vincent’s computer. Yin and Yang got an email. It said; ‘Not to worry, I will be home soon. Vincent knows nothing about SPAFF, but he’s escaped. However, I think I’ve killed Bandi!’

***

“Ah, poor little pussycat! Messing with arachnids *is obviously not* her thing. Gather everyone in the garden I’s *ought to have a ceremony* of some sort to pay our respects! Haha! *Second tho*ughts maybe an extra floret *of broccoli instead.* So I’s advance with plan B, I alway*s liked that one better.* What was plan A? To u*se the* geeky dorks knowledge *of SPAFF to take* over the world. But now, I’s know he is just a puppet and *knows nothing.* S*o plan B, Which is? To do it* by oneself. You mean with I and I? Oh, yes!

***

John and Jill Jenkins were looking very despondent. They were sitting at the table in the rear of their little shop surrounded by empty tanks and cages, having cleaned up the slaughter and replaced the glass on the back door with a thin piece of plywood. They were both just staring into space, neither of them saying a word.

Jill’s mobile phone buzzed on the table, they both leapt out of their skins.

“Well, have a look at it then,” said John.

Jill reached out tentatively.

“What does it say?”

‘Is there any chance of a lift to the airport?’ Jill read, perplexed.

“Who's that from?”

Crash!

They flung themselves to the floor and took refuge under the table.

“What was that?” John whispered.

“How do I know?” Jill replied.

They rose slowly to see a new hole in the back door.

“Oh dear,” said John knowingly.

Jill’s phone buzzed in her hand. It was another text, it read.

‘Get the car!’

A HOLE NEW WORLD!

Vincent's taxi came to a stop in front of the Cottage.
"We are here mate. This is it right?"
Vincent gave the driver a nod and opened the door. He tossed out his sports bag onto the verge and Garston followed it smartly. Reaching into his pocket he pulled out a scrunched up, damp £200 and handed it to the driver.

"Cheers mate...I hope your cat gets better."

Vincent said nothing, just climbed out of the car! He closed the door and looked on as the taxi drove away. Whilst he took in the pretty little house and the tended front garden, Garston ran up to the front door and gave it a knock! It creaked open. A rabbit wearing lipstick appeared and sat on the front step.

"Seth is that you?" asked Vincent.

Seth thumped a hind leg in acknowledgement, turned and hopped back into the cottage followed by Garston. The touch of soft fur through his fingertips suddenly drew Vincent's attention. A great feeling of sadness came over him. Bandi had saved him and she was now lying in his arms motionless. He hurried along the path and stepped inside. The door slammed shut behind him.

"Quickly, Hannibal, Steve, take Bandi down to the lab and hand her to Peuja, I will be down immediately. Vincent, stay here. The others will fill you in, oh, and don't forget your bag's outside!"

Steve and Hannibal took Bandi from Vincent's arms, whilst Vincent, a little shell shocked, watched the chaos occurring around him.

"How can I hear...Hannibal?" he asked disbelievingly.

Hannibal grinned and waved before disappearing down into the tunnel through the fireplace along with Steve and the unconscious Bandi.

Vincent, anxious and confused, could hear every word.

"Because every computer in the cottage and Camelot, has your voice programme downloaded onto its hard drive. This is paired with a universal speaker system that runs through...well everywhere, and that's the reason you can hear us," said Albert.

"We, however, no longer require computers to talk amongst ourselves because our individual microchips convert our speech into a language we individually understand with the aid of your speech programme and SPAFF. You look bemused! Don't worry, we will chat later. Garston will tell you about Camelot. Oh, and if you hear a rumbling or see any unusual deliveries disappear to a world of invisibility, just ignore it!"

"Err, OK," replied Vincent, not absolutely certain of what the heavens Seth was talking about.

Seth ran into the fireplace and was gone.

"So why didn't you load the voice programme onto my computer back at Canal Street, Albert?"

"Ooh love, didn't think. I must have been far too busy saving your life!" Albert was getting a little stroppy.

"Why did Freak attack us? What's Camelot and..."

Before Vincent could finish Garston interrupted him.

"Vincent, there's no need to get all shirty, so much has happened since we last saw you. After the incident on the Grid we found that we had all changed, some of us in a good way, like us lot, and some of us in a different way."

"A different way?"

"Well Yin and Yang, Freak, Escobar and Spike, are definitely different. The 'Terrorpins', as they now call themselves, told us that they were gonna make mankind pay. Then they all just left, and that was the last we saw or heard of any of them, until Canal Street.

Now then, Seth and the rabbits built our home, it's called Camelot and we found out that Seth is actually Rabbit King of England, isn't that great. Oh, we also discovered and released Hannibal from level 5, neutered a robot called Sinatra, got me a bionic tail, found out about Peuja the nut nut, bought the cottage. Actually you bought the cottage and..."

"...And made you a millionaire!" said Maurice finishing Garston's newscast!

"There is a level 5! I own this cottage and you found Peuja."

Yes they did Vincent, said a voice from nowhere.

"Peuja! Hold on... I'm a millionaire?"

"Yes," Maurice replied.

Vincent slumped onto a chair.

“Watch that computer zcreen. Garzton, show Vincent Camelot.”

“Will do Maurice.”

Garston scurried into the fireplace.

“This Fireplace business, it’s all a little bit Harry Potter isn’t it?” said Vincent.

“Who’z Harry Potter?” Maurice asked in reply.

The computer screen on the table began to run live footage from Garston’s cam eye and the size and ingenuity of Camelot began to unfold in front of Vincent.

Garston was chatting away, like an overly excited narrator, talking about everything from Christmas lights to sentries; he popped his head into every room including the private quarters and, as he did, Vincent just sat and watched the screen open-mouthed.

“And this hole in the wall here is the entrance to level 5; I will just poke my head through so you can have a look.” Garston’s cam eye focused and panned the abyss. “This is where Hannibal was living, down here, guarded by a robot called Sinatra!”

***

Sinatra was in one corner of the lab with a few wires hanging out of his torso. He had been hurriedly removed from the tiled tabletop to allow Peuja access to Bandi.

Hannibal and Steve were waiting outside the entrance to the lab like a couple of distressed relatives. Hannibal broke the brooding silence.

“Steve.”

“Yes mate.” Steve replied.

“What do you think about death? I mean, have you ever really sat down and deliberated about the afterlife?”

“To be honest bud, I haven't given it much thought.” Steve answered.

“Do you believe we all go to Heaven?”

“I don't know anything about Heaven. Where is it and how do you get there if you’re dead?”

“Heaven isn't a place that you can get to when you're alive silly. Your spirit goes there when your body can no longer act as its host.” Hannibal replied.

“I'm really sorry buddy, but you've lost me.” Steve was a little confused. Hannibal paused and changed his tack.

"OK. Let's say that you're a big bunch of flowers that smell really lovely..."

"What kind of flowers?"

"For arguments sake, you are ... Lilies!"

"OK. I'm Lilies!" Steve agreed.

"Good. Now, for a while you release a gorgeous scent into the air, but then slowly you begin to whither and die. Next, you're accidentally left in the corner of a room for a couple of days, and start to go mouldy and smelly right, and I don't mean nice smelly."

"Right!" said Steve.

"Well, then you're thrown away, but you leave behind the memory of how you once looked and how your sweet scent filled the room. This is like your spirit, a memory, a sense, of what was once there."

"What, so if I die my bark goes to Heaven?"

"Your bark is only part of your spirit, Steve. It is only a small portion of a memory that you leave with everyone. It's all of your spirit that goes to Heaven, unless you're bad, that is!"

"What on earth are you chomping on about mate?" Steve was a little more confused!

Hannibal explained further.

"Heaven is a place where life is always lovely. A glorious place where you're reunited with all of the relatives and old friends that passed away before you did."

Steve pondered a while but still remained puzzled!

"But you're not there and neither are they! The thing that once carried you, your body, is not there. So how do we all meet?" he asked.

"Now you're getting it."

"I am?"

"Yes. It's all of our spirits that are there, meeting up in Heaven."

"Hold on... how do spirits meet when they can't be seen? How does my spirit meet up with other spirits if it can't see any of them?" asked Steve.

"That's the magic of faith."

"Faith?"

"Yes, it is part of a complicated group of beliefs known as

religion."

"Religion?" asked Steve.

The door to the lab slid open and Seth popped his head out. "This is going to take a while lads, you should take your leave and relax in a more suitable location. What's that awful smell?"

"Part of my spirit," replied Steve. "Any questions ask faith!"

There was an uncomfortable silence as Seth glared at Steve.

"During these times of grave concern, levity should be disparaged!" said Seth.

The door slid closed and Seth was gone.

"I only puffed, there was no need for him to speak German!"

Hannibal smiled a kind smile.

"I know Steve," Hannibal replied, holding his nose, "I know! Let's go watch some TV, there's nothing we can do here."

They sauntered along the corridor for a while, but then curiosity eventually got the better of Steve.

"Tell me more about religion then Han?" he asked.

Hannibal looked at his friend and sighed heavily.

"Well, religion is something you have to find for yourself."

"Great, it's a game huh, like Hide and Seek. Give me a clue then. Is it in here or outside? Do I have to sniff it out or dig for it?"

"Sort of, and no. It kind of finds you!"

"Really then I will be ready for it!" There was a pause..."How come you know all of this stuff?"

"You must know your enemy Steve."

"Sorry, you've lost me again buddy," said Steve completely bewildered.

"Well, religion is said to be the route of all evil, along with money that is, and evil is my enemy."

"So religion is evil and it will find me?" asked Steve.

"No Steve. Religion is not evil; it's a root to evil. Followers of one religion may not understand the beliefs of those belonging to another religion and that can sometimes cause conflict. Bad things happen when there's conflict my friend!"

"I don't get it mate. What should I believe?" Steve replied.

"Ah, now there's a question that has no real answer other than this," Hannibal looked Steve in the eye, "believe in, what you choose to believe in!"

“That’s it?” Steve replied now completely confused.

“Good, I am glad you understand,” said Hannibal.

“Understand! No I don’t think so mate! I’ll tell you one thing I believe you're right about though! It's really ruddy complicated!” Steve replied.

***

Freak, her words spookily spoken via sat nav, asked John to pull over at the side of the road, which, of course, he did without question, or muttering a word. Through a wire fence and some 100 metres away in the distance, a parade of private jets stood statuesque on an airstrip. One of them, adorned with the image of a white two headed terrapin on its tail fin, opened its door and lowered its steps. A mature but alluring airhostess peered out. She powdered her nose and reapplied her lipstick in the gentle breeze. Expectantly, she perused her surroundings for the imminent arrival of her passenger.

Freak slowly crawled along the centre console from the rear of the car to the front, and hopped onto Jill’s lap in the passenger seat. Jill froze; the memory of how deadly Freak could be, serving her well. Her chest felt tight and her heart skipped a beat, she reached for John’s hand and squeezed it firmly. Freak climbed up Jill’s green body-warmer and then up towards her face. She eventually came to a stop on Jill’s nose becoming something akin to an arachnid facemask! Jill whimpered and shivered with fear. Stretching out a limb Freaks claw gave Jill’s soft cheek a stroke.

'So smooth' said the sat nav creepily.

Freak leapt onto the passenger door armrest, reached out and pressed the electric window button. The window slid open slowly! She then raised a claw as if to say thanks, and leap; she was out of the window and over the fence in the blink of an eye.

John lovingly turned to Jill, clutched her hand, and asked tentatively; “Are you feeling alright darling, you don’t look so clever?”

Jill returned a disbelieving look and angrily spluttered; “I don't care how much money we get for whatever we do, but let me tell you one thing; we are never doing that again. Never are we going to accept a strange creature from someone we’ve never done business with before. Do you hear me? Do you hear me! Now drive me to a toilet, I need to clean up!"

***

Vincent watched quietly as the computer screen he was facing beeped into hibernation. He puffed out his cheeks and sat back in amazement, whilst Garston crawled through the fireplace and joined Albert and Maurice sat at Vincent's feet.

"You should have a look around the cottage. It's got two bedrooms and everything anyone would ever need." said Garston.

"Wow! This is all so much to take in," Vincent replied stuttering.

"It shouldn't be darling, I mean you made us what we are," said Albert.

"SPAFF made you what you are; all I did was hand you a voice programme."

"Maybe, but now, there iz more to concern uz all. Mankind iz in danger from an amphibian foe and I don't mean Kermit ze frog with a hand grenade," said Maurice with a raised eyebrow.

"What can a couple of 'Terrorpins' do?" Vincent said dismissively. "I really am sorry to burst your bubble guys, but these little harmless amphibians are..." Albert finished Vincent's sentence.

"Responsible for the death of your doorman and the reason Bandi is lying there in the lab and, well, we just don't know what else yet!"

"Freak, killed Malcolm?" Vincent was both shocked and horrified. He thought through the day's events and remembered how nice a man Malcolm was and then his heart filled with remorse.

"Yes, and we suspect she was just following orders!" said Garston.

"Why would Freak want the molecular formula of SPAFF?" he said.

"Is that what zhe wanted?" asked Maurice.

"We have to tell Seth," said Albert.

Vincent's expression saddened.

"Poor Mal, he was such a nice bloke. I feel dreadful and what about Bandi? She saved me! I think I need to have a lie down."

"Well, it's your house and your new bed is upstairs. Take a few hours, baby, and we will all talk later," said Albert.

Vincent stood up and walked towards the stairs, his head full of terrible thoughts. Albert tried to cheer him up.

"Vincent, err, nice jump from the balcony babe. We'll wake you if Seth gives us any news," he said.

Vincent said nothing just gave his friend a wry smile and then trudged up the stairs.

Maurice turned to Albert. "He jumped from a balcony!" Albert nodded. "Humanz are idiotz!"

Seth was sitting by the tabletop monitoring Bandi's condition as if she was some kind of scientific experiment. She had leads and sensory pads attached to her in various places all over her body whilst Peuja's screens displayed her worsening vital signs.

"Peuja," Seth said pondering, "you need to tell me about Project Ankh. It may tell us something, anything, which might help us find a way to save Bandi. I'm afraid I don't understand, or rather, I can't grasp why, with such intense levels of poison cursing through her veins, well, why Bandi is still alive. I mean she is in a deep coma but, she's still alive, just I grant you. How long can she hang on for? Is she suffering? Should I, please don't think bad of me but, should I put her to sleep?" A tear rolled down Seth's furry cheek. "The only thing that I can deduce from my research into the word Ankh, is that it has something to do with ancient Egypt and…"

Ankh is the Egyptian symbol for life itself.

"Well, yes I was getting to that. There are also many other classifications regarding the sign that we have to take into consideration, and what about the word Bastet? That was the name of a worshipped cat god, right?"

Bastet was the ancient Egyptian god of life protection, but she had many other definitions depending upon the period of Egyptian history you are reading up on. She was also said to be the goddess of fire, music, fertility and birth and therefore the mother of all living things. She carried a Sistrum, a kind of musical wire rattle, and she is also the daughter of the sun god Ra. However, she is also considered a Luna god, as her son Khonsu became god of the moon.

Bastet was, if you like, an ancient Egyptian avenging angel that protected the great dynasties of pharaohs!

"Well, I knew some of that too, but if we delve further and deeper into the files of Project Ankh then perhaps we can find something that will save her."

Project Ankh has an encrypted entry code. We only found out that it existed due to scanning Bandi. It launched itself.

"So all we need to do is scan Bandi again and it will start up or, you could break the code.

Yes, but I don't think we should.

"Why?"

I don't know if either would kill her!

"Alright, so that's out of the question then." He paused in thought. "So why did the Cube call Bandi, Bastet?"

The Cube recognised Bandi as Bastet before I was in control of all of its programmes.

Seth became more contemplative.

"I have an idea. Will you look up the title Project Bastet; it might be worth a shot."

Indeed.

Peuja searched through all her programmes.

Project Bastet found. It appears that it was archived the day that Project Ankh began!

"What? Really? What does it say?"

It seems that several feline subjects were, at one time, involved in the project but only Bandi survives.

"I beg your pardon, what? Why?"

The other clones were not exposed to SPAFF in the same...

"You said clones."

That I did. All of the felines involved in Project Bastet were clones. The DNA used to develop the clones, was taken from the cells of a mummified cat discovered in the late 19th Century, the remains of which were found in a small chamber buried deep within the bowels of the Temple of Bastet in Bubastis, Egypt. Found by chance, its walls were breeched by the eminent archaeologist Sir James Russell, who evidently whilst studying a keystone marked with the sign of Ankh, tripped and caused an interior collapse, killing himself and his assistant. The chamber however was revealed. It was said to be very plain with only a few artefacts, mainly small feline statuettes. However, the hieroglyphics within the tomb were said to depict a story, a celestial story!

“You keep using the past tense.”

Yes, the tomb no longer exists.

“Oh! This is incredible, absolutely incredible. You said Sir James Russell; I don’t suppose he is any relation to,”

Yes, he is Vincent’s, great, great grandfather.

“Wow!”

You think that’s strange, you’ve not heard the rest of it.

Sir James Russell’s son, James Russell Junior, became a renowned hieroglyphist. He spent years studying the tomb, collecting data and was said to be on the verge of a great discovery, but then fate and war intervened and Hitler’s forces destroyed everything in 1942.

James Russell Junior died in a house fire trying to save his family in the late 1940s. Only the teenage Vincent Russell survived.

“Huh, you’ve lost me…”

Don’t be confused; Vincent Russell is the name of our Vincent’s grandfather, who, and get this, just happened to work for MI5.

“MI5?”

Yes, the British Secret Service!

“Ok. So what happened to the research?”

Also lost in the fire or, so it was thought. However in the year 1984 professor Jimmy Russell, our Vincent’s father, was able to prove ownership and retrieve some notes from Moscow’s state historical museum that related to the destroyed tomb.

They were left to our Vincent in his Will.

“In his Will?”

Yes, Vincent’s parents died in a car crash in 1991. Vincent was taken from his dying mothers womb, he was several weeks early but miraculously he survived. His grandparents brought him up, but now only his grandmother survives.

“What happened to his grandfather?”

Shot with a poison dart fired from an umbrella!

“What? Never mind, where is his grandmother?”

Her last known address is an orphanage home in Alice Springs, Australia. Oh, and here’s another interesting fact you ought to know. Professor Jimmy Russell was a genealogist.

"An orphanage?" Seth replied.

"Yes, she works and lives there."

Seth mulled things over.

"Our Vincent must be quite important to someone then. This can't all be coincidence."

After deliberating a little more, a thought occurred to him.

"Peuja, won't there be people out looking for him? I mean, a man dies from a Tarantula bite and from within that building on the same day, another man leaps from a window into a canal. Well, surely there has to be some news?"

Indeed the local constabulary are on their way now.

"What, right now?"

Yes, they have traced Vincent to this address.

"What?"

The Land Registry!

"Really? Keep an eye on Bandi for me will you."

Seth quickly left the lab and ran along Camelot's corridors to the cottage. He was just about to leap through the fireplace when he heard a human voice he didn't recognise coming from the lounge.

"So, Mr Russell, you leapt from the balcony because a large tarantula had entered your apartment and was chasing you?"

"Yes, constable, that's right," said Vincent still a little bleary eyed from being abruptly woken from his nap.

"It's Inspector to you, do I look like a bobby?"

Vincent shook his head. The Inspector would have been the world's oldest bobby.

"Good. Now, you broke the glass doors when a basketball, that you used to try and squash said spider with, rebounded off a door and smashed through it?"

"Yes, that's also correct."

"Why would there be a tarantula in your apartment?"

"No idea," replied Vincent.

"And you thought that leaping from a top floor balcony into a canal the best course of action for your escape?"

"Yes, adrenalin and a phobia of spiders can make you do that?" Vincent replied.

"Can it? I didn't know that?" The suspicious Inspector responded.

"Neither did I, It's just an educated guess, now that I've done it!"

"Oh right!" The Inspector replied.

There was a pause as the Inspector made notes. He then walked around the lounge picking up bits and bobs and generally being nosey.

"This place is nice, had it a while have you?" He asked.

"No, not long at all, I've been fixing it up a bit whilst living in Canal Street."

"Right." the Inspector paused. "Well that's it, Mr Russell, that's all I'm going to need from you today, you can go back to your apartment any time."

"Well, actually I'm staying here for good now. I didn't own the apartment. It belonged to my employer, I was just going to pop back at some point and pick up the rest of my stuff and drop off my keys."

"Your employer you say?"

"Ex-employer actually, I've decided to leave the job all together, relinquish my position."

"Oh really," said the Inspector, "why is that?"

"Well, you can't blame me really, look at this place. It's wonderful. The countryside, the views, the clean air and the privacy, I have all that I need right here."

"Oh, you like the privacy do you?"

"Yes, I need plenty of it to make money." Vincent replied.

"And you do that by…?"

"I am, what you might call, an Internet Entrepreneur." Vincent answered confidently.

"Oh, computers huh, can't stand 'em myself, evil things."

"I thought that religion was evil, no sorry that's the root of!" said Steve.

Seth jumped out of his skin. Steve and Hannibal where standing behind him in the tunnel behind the fireplace, listening in!

"Hush Steve," Seth said, whispering curtly.

"Well, thank you, Mr Russell, I think that will be all. We have your statement, it's just such a shame the doorman died."

Vincent replied sullenly, "Yes, he was a top boy, Mal, it's a real tragedy."

The Inspector left his card with contact details on the windowsill by the door, gave a nod, and walked out into the warm evening.

Seth appeared from the fireplace a few seconds later, closely followed by Hannibal and Steve.

"Well done, Vincent," said Seth.

"Yez, fabulouz," said Maurice sauntering in from the kitchen with Garston and a preening Albert.

"So, what happens now?" Asked Vincent.

"Well darling, you should officially resign from your post, so get on that computer and contact whoever you need to contact."

Vincent sat down at the computer and began to type out his resignation email straight away.

"And what happens after I do this?"

"I think it's time for a meeting," said Seth.

"You don't have to call a meeting to have a meeting sweetie. Don't be such a fuddy duddy. Said Albert

"Fuddy what?" asked Steve.

"It's an old human slang saying, means you're a stick in the mud." Albert replied.

"Stick in the mud! Where is it? I'll fetch it," said Steve excitedly.

Vincent pressed send and his resignation was on its way.

"We have to use our collective minds to work all this out." He said looking up from his keyboard.

"We have to save Bandi, that's what we have to do," said Steve.

"Vincent's right we all need to share the information we each have," said Seth.

"You mean we need to tell Vincent about Hannibal," said Steve.

"What about me?" asked a concerned Hannibal.

"About everything," Seth replied sternly. He then turned to Vincent and like a prosecuting solicitor began!

"Vincent did you have…Hold on let's do this properly, everyone sit around the dining table, please."

There was a comical moment when the group realised there probably weren't enough chairs and that sitting on a chair meant they couldn't see one another above the lip of the table. This was then followed by a bit of shuffling, leaping and climbing until everyone was ready and sitting on the tabletop with only Vincent sat on a chair!

"OK, I will start," said Vincent. "Actually I need you lot to start."

"Zeth will start," said Maurice.

"Yes, I will. Hannibal this might frighten you a little, but don't be scared, it's all under control."

"What is?" asked Hannibal already a little apprehensive.

"When you were scanned we discovered the existence of an alter ego."

"What?"

"When we moved the hinge on your helmet we found out that you are, how can I put this, two faced."

"What?"

"You have two faces, darling." Albert interjected.

"Oh, everyone is a little two faced aren't they?"

"No, I mean you really do have another face, it is covered by your helmet," Albert replied.

"What on earth are you talking about?"

Seth raised his voice.

"Peuja can you hear me?"

A voice came from the speakers.

Yes, of course, I can. How can I help?

"Did the Cube record our scans?"

Yes.

"Would you mind bringing up Hannibal's results on the screen? Hold on, wait a mo. Garston will you delve into your microchip archives and show us what you saw when we scanned Hannibal, and bring it up on the monitor, would you? No need anymore Peuja, this should do it."

Suit yourself!

Everyone remained silent as the screen began to run the footage. Like a dodgy wildlife horror flick documentary, Garston ran 'The Discovery of Lecter.' The jerky footage and screaming soundtrack terrified the audience as they and Hannibal watched in disbelief.

"Turn it off. Turn it off. What has happened to me, what have they done? Why didn't you tell me I attacked you, Seth?"

"Listen mate, we didn't want to hurt your feelings, you'd been locked away and all that and to tell you the truth, what could Seth say without Vincent around for an explanation." said Steve.

Everyone turned to look at Vincent. He was seething with rage.

"How could they?" he said. "How could they? They told me you were dead. I wondered about your helmet but I had no idea, the evil swine's."

"There are evil swine's too?" asked Hannibal, worried about killer pigs. Seth jumped in.

"Vincent, will you enlighten us all as to what exactly happened with Hannibal?" said Seth.

Vincent took a deep breath and looked around the table. His friends were all staring at him. It was then he realised that whatever intelligence or skills they might have gained, they still looked to him for leadership. He took in the little furry faces and then explained.

"The military gassed Hannibal on the Grid to make him unconscious. I fought and argued but they did it anyway. They were amazed by his intelligence. They…" he paused,

"Injected SPAFF directly into Hannibal's cerebral cortex just to see what would happen?" asked Seth.

"Yes that's right. After that, they told me Hannibal was dead, overdosed. They said the SPAFF had poisoned him."

Hannibal, by this point, was in a land of his own. Everything being said around him was just a muffled blur. He climbed down from the table and walked slowly towards the fireplace with his head bowed, riddled with worry and shame. Steve became aware of his mate skulking away.

"Hannibal, Hannibal?" he said in a loud whisper.

Everyone fell silent. Hannibal just kept on walking.

"Sorry bud, I just need to be alone for a bit. Please carry on without me." He said softly without turning around to look at anyone, "I'll be on my old chair in level 5 if I'm needed, or if there's any news on Bandi. I just, I just need some time," and with those words he popped through the fireplace and left for the solitude of his own thoughts.

Seth broke the silence.

"I understand that this is all very sad, but at least Hannibal is alive and well. We know that the helmet has to move on his head to release Lecter, so let's concentrate on the immediate problem. Bandi is really, really, sick and I," he paused, "I don't know if I, with all my scientific knowledge, can save her."

Once again silence filled the room as everyone absorbed the information.

"Vincent."

"Yes Seth."

"Do you know how important you are?"

"Well, yes I do, let's face it, a man is dead and I would guess I am the only person without a Top Secret position that knows about the experiments with you guys. However, I think I just passed a test!"

"A test you say, what kind of test?" Steve asked.

"I had to sign a non-disclosure agreement, before I started work at the Manor house. It stipulated that I would deny all knowledge of whatever went on in the Manor house whenever a situation arose. If I broke the agreement I would pay the penalty with a custodial sentence! So I think that the police inspector was under orders to make sure I did just that. Deny, deny deny!"

"Prizon, that'z a little harsh!"

"Yes it is Maurice, but it just goes to show how important you guys are. So that's the reason I think that was the test. The Inspector was so laid back, when I said a tarantula was chasing me around my flat, well, something had to be amiss. I mean that kind of thing doesn't happen everyday now, does it!"

"Ah, but that's not what I was referring to," Seth replied. "If the historical significance of your very unique situation and previous appointment are allied with the sequence of events that puts you here today, then there is a very different view to gaze upon."

"What do you mean?" asked Vincent.

"Your father was a genealogist, your grandfather worked for MI5, your great grandfather was an eminent hieroglyphist and your great, great grandfather was an adventurer and archaeologist."

"I'm really sorry Seth but I don't understand what my family tree has got to do with any of this."

"Vincent, I don't know how to say this any other way so, I'll just come out with it. They did all die under very mysterious circumstances, didn't they? A fact that can't be ignored! What did you study at University, Vincent?" Seth asked with a very assertive tone.

"I didn't go to University I was privately tutored, why do you ask?"

"There has to be a connection to all of this. Why has your life been the way it has? What sequence of events has made you what you are today?"

"Listen, it's all just coincidence. What I studied anywhere has nothing to do with any of this. Anyway, if my dad and granddad had had their way I would have been studying something else, I'm sure, it was me that picked computers, so it's all just coincidence."

"Why do you say dad and granddad? You never knew your father," asked Seth.

"Well, granny used to say that dad and granddad always said, 'the boy could learn plenty from ancient civilisations and their beliefs.'"

"Anything else you remember her saying?" Seth asked probingly.

"Well no, but on my 17th birthday she gave me a letter from my dad and some of his notes. It was only a short letter, but as it was from my dad, I saved it. I keep it in my wallet."

"Would you mind reading it to us?" asked Seth.

"No, not at all," Vincent replied.

He reached into his pocket for his wallet and pulled out a dry but previously soaked, dishevelled torn piece of paper. The murky waters of the canal had ruined his precious letter he had taken care of for so long.

"Can you remember what it said?" asked Seth.

Vincent looked translucent; the life had been sucked out of him.

"Yes, I will never forget it," he stumbled.

"What did it say, babe?" Albert asked supportively.

Vincent leant forward and began to recite reminiscently,

Hello boy,

If you're reading this, then I wish you a happy 17th birthday.

I am sorry I can't be with you, I'm afraid death has intervened. I left you this letter because I wanted to let you know, that from the day your mother told me we were to have a son; I've loved you with all my heart. I'm afraid I don't have a gift for you, I'm sorry; all I can give you for your birthday is a little piece of advice.

Look to the heavens for wisdom and to the Ancients for the future. Believe everything your eyes can see and all they cannot. Always trust in yourself before others, and let time, not man, be your guide. For once you have discovered the truth you will always have faith. From where I sit and watch you, I am bursting with pride.

I Love you.

Dad x

Vincent and Albert wiped away a tear in silence.

"It's all just fatherly advice," said Vincent.

"Is it?" said Seth.

"Ooh, I do love a good mystery darling, a riddle, a real life crossword, a game for minds to solve, fantastic, fabulous! Sorry Seth, do please carry on," said Albert.

Seth delved deeper.

"Do you know who Bastet is then?"

"Of course I do. The notes left to me mention her, because they mention a tomb. I have read them you know! I did a little research into it all, not much, but that's how I know about Bastet."

"Where are the notes now, and do any of them mention anyone else?" asked Seth.

"They are with the family solicitors down in London, and no, not that I know of."

"Hold on love, Bastet? Isn't that what the Cube called Bandi after we scanned her?"

"Yes Albert," Seth replied. "Now you can see why all of this is just a little too convoluted to be a mere coincidence!"

"The Cube called Bandi, Bastet, when?" asked Vincent.

"Peuja, are you still here?"

Yes Seth I am. What would you like to know now?

"Not me, Vincent, will you tell him about Project Bastet, please.

Peuja began.

***

The following morning saw an arrival at Arcadia. The alluring airhostess, from the Manchester airfield, walked in and handed over her flight case to Mr White. He gave her a welcome peck on the cheek in return, said thank you, and carried the case into the lounge where he rested it on a couch and popped it open. Freak crawled out.

"Well, that appeared to have some degree of success," she said.

Spike ran up to her and gave her a lick.

"Alright Spike, alright! I missed you too."

"Welcome back Freak, welcome *back, the tedium may now be over.*" said Yin and Yang, "You're just *in time*. As Vincent knows

nothing regarding the *formula to SPAFF there is* very little to stop *our plan."*

"That's all well and good, but I'm starving and feeling decidedly edgy. So if you wouldn't mind I'm just going out to my palms to grab a bite to eat, so I don't end up biting someone by instinctual accident!"

"*Well if you put* it that way, then I's think you should snack. It is very sad, however, it is left to I's to *be the ones to inform you that you're palms are in need of sculptural restoration. A stor*m did some damage. And please be careful around *the pool house would you, there's a* lot of refurbishment going on."

"Why? I liked the pool house the way it was."

"*It will be* converted back to its *original look after our technicians* have finished with it!"

"Technicians?"

"*Oh just* stop digging will you, you'll *ruin the surprise*."

"A surprise is it. Well every girl loves a surprise; believe me, the bigger the better!"

THE RECKONING

Another day had past into night and then returned to day. Seth had spent most of this time sat in his lab tinkering with Sinatra, keeping an ear and an eye on Bandi's vital statistics, hoping that fate and time would restore her to full health.

There was a knock at the lab door.

"Come in." he called.

Hannibal entered looking a little dejected.

"Hi Seth, I have come to lend a hand, it might keep my minds busy!"

Seth chuckled. "That's quite a funny thing to say Hannibal," Seth replied smiling.

"I know, I'm coming to terms with it all." He changed the subject. "So, is there anything that I can do to help?"

Seth had a think.

"Well, yes there is actually. I did read over the Internet that constant communication with a subject in this condition may bring them back from… well you know, wake them. So if you would like to sit with Bandi and just chat, that might be helpful."

"Alright, but what are you up to?"

"Well, I'm actually stealing some parts from Sinatra for you."

"You're what!"

"I'm just putting the final touches to this initialisation switch and then I'm going to fit this transmission switch to the motor that is just inside your helmet."

"And what's that going to do? And won't that harm Sinatra?"

"Sinatra will be fine and this is going to allow you to activate Lecter through voice recognition."

"Have you gone bonkers?" Hannibal replied.

"Maybe, but it was actually Steve's idea. We were chatting and he mentioned something that you had told him. You told him that he should know his enemy. It reminded me of the phrase 'keep your friends close but your enemies closer.'"

"So you want me to release Lecter?"

"Yes, in a controlled environment, of course. That will allow me to study him and hopefully get him to trust us. It really isn't fair, don't you think? It's not his fault he was made by SPAFF and humans, is it? He did not ask to be born; he did not ask to be a monster. He just is. He's like a frightened animal, fighting to get out of his cage and live a normal life, unfortunately, he doesn't know what his normal life or environment should be. He needs love."

"Love huh! And what do I have to say to release him?" Hannibal replied.

"Well, that will be up to you. You will need a key word that we will record, it will only be known by yourself and me for the moment, and this will be the trigger."

"Oh I get it, a secret word, like Orson Wells and Rosebud in the film Citizen Kane."

Seth was taken aback.

"You did watch a lot of television didn't you? Everyday you surprise me Hannibal, everyday," he said before continuing to explain further. "We will set everything to a timer for safety reasons and Lecter will only be released for one minute at a time. During these moments of freedom we will begin to educate and instruct him and consequently he will learn not to be a danger to himself or others. We will then, as a reward, lengthen the release period and so in time Lecter will learn that we are not his masters but his friends. This release mechanism will be finished some time this afternoon. In the mean time just go and say a few words to Bandi."

Hannibal gave Seth a nod and walked over to Bandi. Her physically thinning form worried him terribly. Her once beautiful tan coloured coat was now patchy and giving way to a dull, muddy sheen. Hannibal sat down bowed his head and began to whisper:

"Our father, who art in heaven,
Hallowed be thy name.
Thy Kingdom come,
Thy will be done,
On earth as it is in heaven."

Seth's ears pricked up. "What's that you're reciting?" Seth asked struck by curiosity.

"It's called the Lords Prayer, Seth. Many humans use it in their hour of need. Every human has a Lord, you see, they may be different Lords, but they are really all the same. They live somewhere in the universe and look after them all as a race. I thought that if I prayed for Bandi then perhaps maybe one of them would hear me and help her."

"Lords, Lords! That's it Hannibal you're a genius," said Seth.

***

Back at Arcadia, the technicians working in the pool house had finished turning half of it into a laboratory and the other half into a small film studio.

Everyone except Freak, who was still working on her silken palms and having a ding-dong with a very silly seagull, was sitting in the lounge watching a tribe of strangers carry equipment through the garden. Finally, when they were done, one of them popped his head through the patio doors. "It's all set up for you sir, just sign here and we will all be on our way," he said.

Mr White signed the form handed to him by the scruffy young man and then, along with some of the others, walked to the end of the garden and looked on in silence from the cliff edge as the man walked down an uneven path, with the rest of his associates, to the jetty and climbed aboard Mr White's private yacht, the White Mistress, which then gracefully set sail for the mainland.

"*Right then, Escobar carry us* to the pool house film studio will you, the *quicker I and I do* this thing *the better*. Spike, you round *up the ladies* who are working *on this* thingy and bring them to the studio. Oh, and get Miss Ballet to run through those last few bits of choreography with Mr White again!"

Spike scuttled off, but soon returned, having being followed down Arcadias sweeping stairway and across the garden to the pool house by half a dozen or so curvy, vivacious, happy ladies. Mr White watched the train pass and smiled as all of the carriages, flirtatiously and lovingly, blew him a kiss as he made his way back to the main house. As he stepped into the lounge he shook his head and looked up towards the sky as if to converse with a higher power! He chuckled to himself and then leisurely meandered up to the master bedroom. At the top of the stairs he paused and turned. Miss Ballet, a diminutive peach of a lady with an austere expression and chubby cheeks, was stood scowling up at him from the bottom of the stairway. She was dressed in white satin and lace dancewear.

"I know, it's time for me to get into those tights again," he said very theatrically. He looked up to the higher power once more and gestured open palmed. "Why me, hey?" he said, "And why Miss Ballet? She can be so mean sometimes!"

Within the small film studio everyone was starting to get busy, everyone that is but Yin and Yang. They were sat being waited on flipper on flipper. Eventually the younger lady of the group, grasping her ever present clipboard, walked over to them and sheepishly and almost apologetically asked if they were all set, as everyone else was!

"This is it, the start of world domination, the beginning of the end *for the human race. Servitude shall once more become the duty of destiny and I'm losing th*e plot of what the Galapagos I am talking about. Ah yes, the pet food factory. *It is almost ready for the big day and so I and I will march on and not stumble. Hold on, I and I did purchase that toy factory too right? Good, that's all complete and now each* transmitting receiver is *being tested for quality control. The blighters will never know. Never in the history of human conflict will so* many make such a sacrifice for so few or two! Whichever way you *look at* it, it's gonna be one tumultuous torturous pagan party! History books will be rewritten, actually they won't, because we shall create hist*ory and won't write about it. Well we may, and brag too, but that doesn't matter because, oh shall we just get on with* it? There will be plenty of time for superlatives and a tap on the shell later! Now, I am *ready for my* close up Mr Dem… Don't say it Norma. Don't say it. Who's *Norma? Bring on the sunset, boulevard to everyone and let them all drown in the pool, Hahahha!"*

Spike turned to Escobar and gave him a look as if to say; 'What the sugarplum fairies have they been drinking?' Escobar, in return, just picked at a nostril with a talon and skinned a complimentary Gecko, much to Spike's disapproval!

Meanwhile, next door in the pool house laboratory, three ladies a chemist, a vet and a biologist were making busy!

***

Everyone's mood had darkened back at Camelot. Bandi was

worsening by the minute and a feeling of helplessness had consumed the team. Vincent had taken a train to London to see if he could bring back his father's notes from the family solicitors in order to allow Seth to study them, but it was becoming increasingly obvious to everyone that he may not return in time!

The door slid open to the Camelot lab.

"Hello Hannibal how are you feeling today, any better?"

"I'm alright Maurice."

"Have you seen Zeth?"

"He said he was popping up top for a bit with Steve. He said he needed to chat to the rabbits about something or other in the woods," Hannibal replied.

"Oh, I zee. It is zad but zomeone has to do it."

"Do what Maurice?" Hannibal asked.

"Make ze final arrangements for Bandi," Maurice replied sheepishly.

"But she's not dead. There is still a chance she will survive, right? She can't die Maurice. I've prayed to the Lords of the Universe and asked for their help over and over again, but they're not listening to me." Hannibal began to choke up. "I don't understand it Maurice, Bandi is a good person, well, cat, someone who selflessly saved someone's life. I have not known her long but for some reason…" Hannibal had to take a beat to gather himself together, "but for some reason, I feel twisted inside. It all feels bad, just so wrong. She is my friend, and now all I ever believed in just feels like lies. I'm so confused Maurice, it's all so mixed up."

Maurice felt he should say something.

"That emptinezz that you are feeling in the pit of your stomach iz, what humanz call, grief. They Zay death and zuffering have no mercy and zay are right, they are unfeeling and leave us all powerlezz." Maurice spoke reflectively, "Mother Nature iz all powerful and she will be here long after we are all gone."

Hannibal replied, with tears rolling down his cheeks.

"I don't know who 'they' are, Maurice, but, I will pray to Mother Nature, until she sits up and hears me, and I won't stop, I won't."

"Alright Hannibal, alright. I will leave you alone for a bit. We all need to face this in our own way. I will be in my room making money, if anybody needdz me."

The lab door slid shut.

Outside, standing in the clearing in the woods, Seth, Steve and now Albert were with a dozen or so rabbits.

"OK everyone," said Seth "we are going to build the pyre here, in the centre. We are going to need a base of dry grass, a few slow burning logs, and then sticks, hundreds of sticks. By my calculations the pyre is going to have to be at least sixteen bunnies' high, which means it has to be at least twenty-six bunnies across. I have checked the weather forecast and it is supposed to rain later, so we need to get it done quickly, with no floundering. Well, don't just stand their get on with it."

The attentive rabbits bowed and ran off into the woods.

"I'll get the straw, darling," said Albert "and you get the logs Steve."

"No worries buddy, let's get it done."

Maurice, concerned about Hannibal, used Bluetooth to contact Seth.

'Hannibal seems very odd at the moment. I know it's very sad, but I think he's losing the plot.'

Seth sent a direct reply.

'It must be due to what he has learned from television Maurice. Hannibal has obviously been affected by all of the news he has seen, most importantly, the news from war torn regions of the world. Death and suffering, due to religious conflict must be a painful thing to watch day after day, and to be locked away in a room all by himself with no one to talk to, well, his mind, I would fathom, must be a junkyard of unremitting misery. Steve was telling me that Hannibal was asking him all of these questions regarding death. If his mind has been affected by even a minutiae of different religious beliefs, then it is going to be extremely muddled, tormented even.'

Seth got back to work and with the rest of the team laboured long into the night, gathering what they could, in anticipation of Vincent's arrival. In the calm of the night's final hours, Vincent eventually pulled up in a taxi in front of the cottage, paid the cabbie and walked up the garden path to the front door, clearly shattered. Everyone, other than Hannibal ran to meet him.

"Quickly Vincent, we haven't got much time. Place what you have on the table."

"Right you are Seth" he replied, trying to wake himself up a bit.

He pulled some clear plastic covered sheets of paper from his sports bag and laid them down on the dining table. Everyone huddled round and ran their eyes over the notes.

"OK, anyone see anything? Is anyone making sense of this? It's half drawing, half scribble, half map and half doodle!" said Steve.

At that moment Hannibal ran in through the fireplace. He looked scruffy and tired, swollen eyed and insane!

"Something's happening," he said, "what's going on? The Cube is doing things I don't understand, it's got dots all over the screens like scurrying ants and Bandi's shaking and stuff, and Peuja isn't answering me. Do something Seth, do something!"

"Peuja must be being overridden. What is the Cube saying? Tell me Hannibal, tell me." Seth answered.

Hannibal began to stutter nervously, he calmed himself with a deep breath.

"It's saying nothing."

Commence, The Reckoning

The Cube's voice ran through Camelot and the cottage.

"Well, it is now!" said Seth.

"Steve, Hannibal, as fast as you can, carry Bandi to the pyre we've built in the woods."

Hannibal's frustration turned to anger.

"A pyre! No, what are you thinking, no!"

Steve ran past Hannibal and disappeared into the fireplace.

Seth turned to Hannibal.

"Since becoming one of us, have I ever let you down, have I?"

Hannibal didn't answer.

"Well then, do as I say and do it now before we lose her forever," he said.

Hannibal nodded and then darted into the fireplace after Steve.

"Right the rest of us have to get to the pyre. What time is it?"

"It's about four in the morning. I hope you know what you're doing Seth," said Vincent.

"I hope so, too, Vincent, I hope so, too. Now, bring some matches and put your phone on loud speaker," he replied.

Vincent searched for some matches and found an old matchbook in his bag. He grabbed his mobile phone and using its light as a torch stepped out into the ghostly darkness of the cold, waking woods.

"Where to Seth?" Vincent asked, his warm breath misting as he spoke.

"Follow me, the clearing is this way." Seth replied.

Vincent struggled as he tried to follow his friends through the trees, ferns and narrow, natural pathways of the woods to the pyre. Upon arrival, the group found Hannibal and Steve already there, waiting with Bandi unconscious and trembling on the ground at their feet.

"Hannibal this is for you to do. You must carry Bandi to the top of the pyre."

"No Seth, please no, I can't. I can't do it. She's my friend and she's still alive."

Hannibal began to break down.

"You must, you're the only one of us that can climb the pyre safely whilst holding Bandi. If Vincent does it, it may collapse under his weight, it has to be you."

"I cant, I just cant," he sobbed. "She's my friend, Vincent please, tell him, I can't."

Hannibal's voice quivered through the loudspeaker of Vincent's mobile phone. Vincent felt his pain. He walked over to the little monkey and knelt down and spoke to him sympathetically.

"Hannibal, within our lifetimes there are moments that define who we are, and by our actions we are either heralded or held accountable. Sometimes we have no choice but to place our trust in those around us and sometimes, we just have to do whatever we are told." He paused. "Seth believes that this is the right thing to do and he is your friend who loves you. I love you, too, buddy, very much, we all do and so does Bandi. Bandi would put her trust in Seth and you must, too. You have to do this Hannibal you have to. It's the right thing to do, it has to be."

Hannibal looked around at his companions. All of them were looking at him supportively and smiling kindly. He turned to Bandi; her condition frightened him, she looked so frail. His expression became full of doubt, it told a story of both love and turmoil. He thought about Vincent's words and then gently picked up Bandi into his arms and stood strong on his hind legs. Gazing at his feline friend he walked towards the pyre.

"I love you Bandi, I am so sorry," he sobbed "I am so, so sorry. Please forgive me."

Shivering, with the wind blustering and biting to the bone, he carefully and steadily climbed the pile of timber. At the top, he gently laid Bandi down and took a cautious step backwards. Raising his arms wide apart, with his palms facing the sky, he looked up to the stars as the wind bristled and cried around him.

"Mother Nature," he called loudly, "please take good care of my friend and deliver her to Paradise where she belongs. She is worthy of every honour you choose to bestow upon her. Please, please treat her with all the reverence and love she deserves."

He turned to Bandi's now convulsing body and took hold of her limp paw. He kissed it tenderly.

"Goodbye Bandi," he said weeping, "I will never forget you."

He crawled back down the pile carefully and ran straight up to Vincent and jumped into his arms.

"Well done buddy," Vincent whispered, "well done."

Hannibal looked at him distraught and then shamefully buried his face into his shoulder.

"Quickly Vincent light the pyre, dawn is approaching," said Seth.

Vincent placed Hannibal down on the ground and walked over to the pyre. He fumbled in the cold air for his book of matches but on taking them out of his pocket, nervously dropped them. Peculiarly, at that moment, a raven landed at his feet, startling him and the group. Vincent stepped back. The bird picked up the matchbook in its beak and hopped towards him and then boldly, up onto his shoulder. Everyone held still, not wanting to scare the bird into flying away. The raven, however, seemed quite at home and merely handed the matches back to Vincent, cawed and then flew off into the night.

"Wow that was weird," he said.

He carefully opened the matchbook with his hands still shaking in the cold, and tried to light a match. His first strike failed but he shielded the second in his jacket and lit it successfully. Seth gave him a nod and Vincent placed the lit match into the heart of the dry grassy base. It took blaze immediately. He turned to see his friends watching him anxiously, their faces glowed from the glare of the burning pyre. He joined them and stared, empty eyed at the flames.

"What now Seth?" he asked.

Seth remained silent; I have to be right, he thought to himself, I have to be.

After a moment of quiet, Steve let out a nervous trump, which was duly ignored.

"It's starting," said Seth, "It's, it must be the Reckoning. Look the flames are turning blue, it's…"

Seth's sudden silence spoke volumes; flame tips were shifting and morphing in shape. They were joining, entwining and becoming spherical. The group all watched in awe, as, miraculously, a blue ball of flame formed, surrounded and encased Bandi and then appeared to rise from the pyre. As the sound of cracking, burning brittle, spitting branches filled the night, everyone stood fast, not knowing whether to run for their lives or stand their ground.

"It's beautiful," Hannibal said wistfully.

The base of the pyre continued to burn wildly, and yet, at its heart, something serenely magical happened. The magnificent form of a proud lioness appeared like an apparition, materialising in the centre of the furnace, whilst flighty, burnt, scorching cinders danced in the cold air. She was conjured of amazing orange hues and twisting, knotted flames. Majestically, she strode forward from the fire towards the group, whilst seemingly taking a nonchalant view of the world around her. Everyone remained still, petrified. She let out a roar of discontent at the skies that terrified the group. Rabbits, that had joined to watch and pay their respects, scampered for cover and Vincent consequently found himself being used as a human shield by all of his friends. Reminiscent of an ancient sphinx, the lioness sat on her haunches in front of him, and rumbled a throaty snarl. Bandi meanwhile just continually hovered behind her within the beautiful blue sphere, like a baby gently floating in a fiery womb.

"Is everyone seeing this? It's incredible," asked Albert rhetorically.

The morning struggled to pierce the dawn clouds but, in time, rays of light crept their way through the windswept trees and reached out across the clearing. The lionesses rose to her feet and stared at the rising sun. As the light neared the burning furnace, she turned back towards the pyre and then suddenly leapt at Bandi and the floating ball of flame. There was an audible gasp from the group. Exploding beams of blinding light burst from the pyre's centre as if they were thrown from the points of an infinite supernatural compass and the sphere began to spin relentlessly towards a perpetuating climax. With a deafening clamour, it finally vanished into space and the magnificent lioness, so elegant in her repose, disappeared with the coming of the dawn.

The heavens thundered and instantly fractured and a gushing torrent fell from the sky. The flames of the pyre fought hard against the drenching but, soon sizzled and abated, as the droplets dowsed the smokey pyres remains.

"Bandi!" said Hannibal, jumping down from Vincent's arms and looking up in disbelief.

Perched on top of the pyre's smouldering embers and surrounded by burning ash, an ethereal golden-coated cat with a dark brown coloured sign of Ankh adorning the sopping fur on her chest like a branded mark, opened her fiery eyes.

"Not quite Hannibal. I am not the Bandi that you once knew, I am," there was a pause, "a new Bandi. For now within me lives the soul of every cat that has walked through time. You may call me Bandi, but I am Bastet… and I love you too."

She sprang forward, ran up to the little monkey and looked him in the eye,

"Whilst I slept, I heard every word you spoke to me, thank you," she said softly.

Hannibal wrapped his arms around her and gave her an almighty squeeze. She turned to Seth and the rest of the team. "Thank you, thank you all for saving me. Now, I'm starving and blooming soaked, anyone for some breakfast?"

***

"And cut. That's it today for you ladies and you too, sirs. Good job," said the pretty young be-spectacled, blonde pig-tailed, nerdy lady with the clipboard. "I will shoot some of the external ambience shots tomorrow when the light is better. I'll have the lot edited and uploaded in a few days. Yin and Yang, I will, of course, run this all by you before we launch. In the meantime girls, you just relax. Mr White," she turned to face her boss who was stood proudly bare-chested and inanely grinning in a pair of white ballet tights. "Would you like to take your position now?

"Yes Clipboard Girl!" he replied.

The young lady smiled a bright smile and continued.

"Miss Ballet are you ready?" Miss Ballet nodded silently. "Good then we can begin. The sooner this glimmer of cultural magnificence is added the better. Now, after this we will all get on with converting the pool house back to the way it was!"

"*Will you get that busybo*dy to shut up and carry us to the lab, they *must be ready for* I and I by now, and you, and *us*. Give them a clipboard and they think they're the Queen of Sheba. I wonder if they all walk around *like that* in Sheba, although she is wearing those beads in an *interesting manner in her naval? Where is Sheba anyhow? We must* investigate. If they are all like her then we are going to need some more beads! Right then, let's be having you my wench, *pick I's up bint and* get I's *next door.*"

The lady with the clipboard picked up the Terrorpins and carried them through to the lab. The lab itself was clean, bright, fully equipped and sterile. It had two terrapin sized leather armchairs set in the middle of the room on a stainless steel work surface, and a large plasma screen with satellite connectivity hung on the opposite wall.

Yin and Yang were placed into the two tiny chairs and Clipboard Girl left the room.

The biologist, chemist and vet then took control, well, as much as Yin and Yang would let them. They were all wearing medical masks, rubber gloves, paper aprons and flip-flops that matched their individual outfits!

"*Ooh, they're all colour coded, how* interestingly dull. Get on with it, we need to sit *here for a couple of hours* every day for a *week before we have enough.*"

The plump, spectacled vet fiddled with a few wires and attached them to Yin and Yang. A monitor in the lab brought up their vital signs and neurological template. The stern biologist then took a tiny needle and inserted it very carefully into each of the terrapin's front flippers.

"*Ouch! You think* that's funny do *you*?"

A giggle came from the wavy haired brunette, hippy chemist who watched inquisitively as the needles drew blood along a very thin tube to a beaker that was already sitting above a flaming Bunsen burner on a tripod partially filled with a clear liquid already bubbling away nicely. The plasma screen flickered.

"*Look its old* blue *eyes from the rat pack in Vegas! Sing it with I's Frank!*

And now,
The end is near,
For I's have reached,
*The fin*al curtain.
Regrets,
Well I's had none,
The world will soon,
Be I's for certain.
And with *SPAFF, as I's guide,*
And the microchip *insid*e,
I's will win,
Enslave them all, and do it,
I's *way!*

Ha*hahaha*ha!"

VAGABONDS!

A relatively quiet week passed duly whilst Camelot became accustomed to having a living goddess on the premises! Bandi had spent most of her time happy and curled up on the sofa, basking in the attention. Seth however, being a rabbit of science and a paragon of pragmatism, had spent his week scouring Vincent's notes, trying to make sense of Bandi's celestial event. He was struggling to come to terms with the fact that something else, something bigger than all of Darwin's theories of evolution actually existed, after all genealogy is a science, he thought to himself, but the contradictions ran through him like bad cabbage! He had though, also found the time to tinker with Sinatra and create another engineering micro-marvel, this time for Vincent! Vincent himself had grown to love his new life. He had recently been spending a lot of time searching the Internet for a new motorcycle, which, up until now, he had never been able to afford. Now though, he could, and was indeed awaiting the delivery of the bike of his dreams, with a matching custom-made sidecar to boot. His black, muscular Norton Commando was also coming with a set of black riding leathers that any superhero would be proud of! As for the others, well, Steve and Hannibal had gone on to make level 5 their own playpen, whilst Maurice had effortlessly made another million! Albert, rather fashion consciously, had taken to wearing a distinguished purple paisley cravat and had also convinced Garston that every super spy should wear a black bow tie during daylight hours!

Tonight, like every night, the team were meeting up in the cottage for supper. On the menu was a little fresh salad, a selection of nuts and fish, tinned mackerel to be precise, and biscuits! Everybody enjoyed this 'family time,' it always produced laughter and gave everyone time to catch up with recent events. This evening though Seth was a little more excited than usual and after dinner he stood up, tapped a paw on the table and called for everyone's attention.

"Guys," he said, "today is going to be a very special day."

"Have we missed someone's birthday?"

"No, we haven't, Steve. Today is going to be the day that Vincent becomes one of us."

"But I am one of you!"

"Yes, I know you are Vincent, but you communicate with us via the computer, microphone and speaker network that's all around us."

"And?" Vincent replied.

"And so, it is time for you to meet the future! Everyone, I would like you to meet Junior."

Everyone turned to look at the fireplace, nothing happened and then everyone turned to look at the front door, nothing happened. Seth began to giggle.

"Err, I hate to burst your bubble, Seth, but there seems to be nobody here," said Steve.

"That's because Junior has been here all along. Junior would you like to show yourself."

Everyone turned to the fireplace, nothing happened, so once again everyone turned to the front door, still nothing happened. Seth guffawed loudly; it was all starting to tickle him more and more.

"In the centre of the table," said Seth.

"Where?" asked Steve. "Well, unless he's invisible or he's that ant by the apples, he is not here."

"Oh my, there's an ant on the table? Leave it to me darlings I'll just…"

"Stop right there Albert" said Garston. "The ant is Junior, is that not right Seth?"

"Well done Garston, zoom in on him will you and put him up on screen and Bandi would you mind turning down the TV?"

Both Bandi and Garston obliged.

The team gasped and applauded once they realised what Junior actually was.

"Junior, looks like an insect, but as you can see, is a wonder of micro engineering. He is a walking microchip, developed by myself and the youngster's mother."

"Mozzer!" said a curious Maurice, once again changing the odd S to a Z!

"Yes," replied Seth. "Junior is a copy of what we all have inside us but with legs and jaws like an ant. Vincent if you wouldn't mind closing your eyes so we can get on with it? Peuja, are you ready?"

Certainly Seth said a voice from a speaker.

"Good, then off you go, and turn off the programme that transfers our voices from speaker to speaker, would you?"

Vincent did what he was told and closed his eyes the tiny ant-like microchip set off. It ran across the table and climbed onto Vincent's sleeve, scurried up his arm and, to everyone's surprise, creepily crawled into his ear.

Vincent felt a pinch.

"Did you see that?" said Hannibal "That was really disturbing."

"How could I see, my eyes are closed? Hey, hold on, I heard you."

"You may all applaud," Seth said smugly.

Albert fluttered. "I'm a little confused love. Have you just invented something that can make any human hear us, without the aid of a computer?"

Seth took a bow and Vincent opened his eyes.

"Well to be precise, when Vincent is in earshot then he can hear everything we say, after all, the entire speech programme is inside his microchip! When Vincent is not in earshot, then like us he can communicate over great distances via the technology in Junior. And why the name Junior I hear you all ask? Because he is made from Peuja, is the answer. Peuja can pass any information to Vincent via Junior and vice versa, the same way she does with all of us. Vincent, I know you're a bright lad but now, at anytime you so wish, you can access the brain of a super computer!"

"Seth you're a genius," said Vincent, shaking his head "this is amazing."

"Yes I know, and now so are you! The funny thing is, the military didn't think of it first. Junior is made from the same substance as Garston's tail. It's the SPAFF inside donated by Peuja that makes all the difference. If the military had just ceased in trying to control subjects by exposing them to SPAFF, built a million or so Junior's and had them plugged directly into their subjects' blood stream instead, all of their wishes would have been granted."

"We should just keep that to ourselves," said Vincent.

"I think that's a great idea, nobody say…"

Seth stopped in his tracks.

"What? What's the matter Seth?" Hannibal asked.

"I don't know, but I smell a rat."

"A rat huh," said Bandi. "Dessert is served."

"No, on the TV." Seth replied.

Bandi turned up the volume.

The music to 'Andrew Lloyd Webber's, Phantom of the Opera,' came from the surround sound system accompanied by some very gravelly narration!

***

On the 23rd of *October, the world* will change.

That's right; Terrapin super food is *being launched on that very* day! Our secret….

***

"It's Yin and Yang", said Albert. "Why are they wearing those baseball caps back to front and what's with all that jewellery?"

***

***… Ingredient is a naturally, nutritional, eco friendly, organic* food supplement that is specially designed to give their shells a glorious bright sheen.**

So let's go…

***

The music changed!

***

'I like* Green Slime *and I cannot lie!
And nobody can deny.
***That th*e Slime tastes great**
And *it's not too late,*
So go and feed your mate!'

***

“Err, they’re singing, Ooh that’s so ghetto, but look, a lovely ballet sequence”, said Albert.
“They’re rapping actually,” said Vincent.

***

***And for a limited time* only this white, novelty, Terrapin food *dispenser is free* when you buy!**
So don’t delay, buy some today!’

***

“Turn this rubbish off”, screamed Albert.
“No wait. We need the address”, said Seth.

***

Just log on to www.greenslimestuff.com
Green *Slime*, only 99p.
It’s a bargain so bring it biatches!
Help your terrapin be a super terrapin today.

Satisfaction guaranteed. You’ll be out of your minds to miss out! *HA,HA,HA*!

***

“Oh how inventive”, said Bandi. “So, who are the crazy ladies dancing behind them in swimwear? Was that a yacht? They were definitely not in England!”
Hannibal piped up. “I’m really sorry, but did everyone else just see two white terrapins advertising terrapin food?”
“Yes and that’s what Seth is worried about. That’s Yin and Yang, Hannibal. What on earth are they up to?” asked Garston.
“It’s brilliant, catchy, very ‘youff of today,’” said Bandi, “very clever. Humans will think that it’s all done with computer generated imagery, but it’s really them, I mean who would expect two real rapping terrapins.”

“I need a sample, something’s amiss,” said Seth. “What’s in it?”

“Poison probably. I imagine ze blagardz want to be the last two terrapins on the planet,” said Maurice.

“No, not the food that’s the obvious bit, it must have SPAFF in it. Freak gained much of her power from being fed SPAFF dipped beetles remember. No, it’s all about the food dispenser,” said Seth.

“But they haven’t got any SPAFF. So how…?”

“Of course they have SPAFF, it’s inside of them Steve.”

“Yes, of course, thank you, Vincent,” said Seth.

“Wasn’t me, thank Junior. This thing’s great!”

“So, the clever blighters are using their own blood supply to infect a new terrapin pet food, vagabonds! Come on people work with me!” said an irate Albert.

“Well, isn’t that pretty useless? Surely they have to be immersed in a tank of SPAFF together with the other terrapins to enforce their will upon them to utilise their powers, or at least be within terrepathic distance when out of one. I mean normal terrapins don’t have communicative microchips do they?” questioned Bandi.

“Do you know Bandi, I have surmised exactly the same theory?” said Seth.

“What’s terrepathic distance? Is there such a thing?” asked Steve.

“Has to be, they surely can’t send random thought commands around the world willy- nilly, can they?” replied Bandi.

“Nilly-willy,” said Steve.

“Now come on guys this is getting a little silly,” said Vincent.

“Why do you think that?” asked Seth.

“OK, so it’s not silly and there are going to be hundreds, possibly thousands, of infected terrapins out there. What then? There is no proof that Yin and Yang can control Humans anyway.”

“Err, no proof, but the fleshy dancing ladies in the background of an advert for Green Slime! Albert replied sarcastically.

“It is unfortunately as I feared,” said a sighing Seth.

“Peuja can you answer me this one question, although I think I already know the answer.”

Sure Seth.

“If terrepathy were a possibility...”

It is Seth

“Yes I know, but who would be the most responsive?”

And at number 1 we have Homo sapiens.

"Homo who?" said Steve?

Humans! Please note canines are not mentioned.

"I see, the beast with the greatest intelligence."

You got it your, feline Royal Highness…ness!

Everyone fell silent, deep in thought.

"That still doesn't explain how?" said Seth.

"Well, let's say they have a little microchip, like the one in Vincent's ear, in every terrapin. They will be able to send their orders over any distance."

"No, they can't do that, that's impossible. That would involve placing thousands of microchips into terrapins," said Hannibal.

Alfred had a Eureka moment.

"But what if the microchip was kept in a mass produced white novelty terrapin food dispenser, that could transmit to an army of newly receptive terrapins! They would be able to control every terrapin, and in turn, every human, Oh my, it's Armageddon darling, all we need is for one human terrapin owner to keep his pets at work at a nuclear power plant or a military base or something and BOOM!"

"HUMANZ WILL PAY!" said Maurice.

"Everyone, the Green Room in one hour", ordered Seth. "Vincent we will conference call you. Wait what's today's date?"

"It's the 11th of October," said Garston.

"Zen we have less than two weeks to save mankind!" said Maurice.

"Ooh, it's just like the TV series 24", said Bandi.

"Err, isn't that called 24 because everything happens in 24 hours," replied Hannibal.

"Yes, it's like watching something happening live. Other than the fact that the entire series takes itself far too seriously sometimes, although it's absolutely wicked!"

"Have you ever thought of being a critic?" asked Hannibal.

"I'm a cat. I don't think anyone would take me seriously."

"Why not, you could do it over the Internet and no-one would know," said Vincent.

"Now there's an idea!" said Hannibal.

"Let's get back to the problem in hand shall we?" said Bandi with a hint of exasperation.

"We need help, loves. Perhaps we ought to inform the Prime Minister," suggested Albert.

"Hold on, if terrorism happens in America then the President deals with it and if terrorism happens within the boundaries of mainland Europe, then it's the President that takes care of that. So I imagine that, if any act of terrorism occurred in Great Britain, I assume it would be the President's job to take care of that, too!" said Bandi.

"So what do we need to do? Do we inform the President that a couple of mad Terrorpins plan to do something very nasty to all humanity by using their powers of mind control!" said Vincent.

"Well why not," replied Bandi, "We should at least send him an email."

Seth looked very concerned.

"But we would be exposing ourselves to be poked and prodded like the experiments we were before," he said.

"Then we will remain anonymous and send the email to ze Presidents direct email addrezz," said Maurice.

"And how will you find that?" asked Vincent.

"Well, that's easy," replied Bandi. "Where do humans, that have no friends, put their email addresses?"

"How do you know the President has no friends?" asked Hannibal.

"That's easy too," said Bandi. "The President is normally someone surrounded by sycophantic social climbers, they're called 'The Administration.' They use their connections to get their own man elected to the President's office. The President himself is normally a political dork with loads of charm, someone who's normally not too bright. He, because for some reason there has yet to be a she, has normally grown up on a farm or something and not had much of a normal social life, well most of the time!"

"Not now though, now we have an amazing president, someone who provides the world with hope, but how do we find his private email address?" Vincent asked.

"A website called Friendsthatyouforgotaboutyearsago.net," replied Bandi.

Hannibal spoke reflectively. "I bet he's a lonely man enclosed in a solitary world, searching for his friend Flossy! I saw some old footage of a President once. He gave an interview about a game of golf. He mentioned terrorism at the end of his speech so at least he knew it existed and what to do about it, well kind of! So I think the President’s our man.”

“Alright it’s settled then. Maurice, email the President and let him know of the impending threat to world security.”

“Are you sure Seth? Don’t you think we ought to let the Prime Minister know too?” Vincent asked.

“He’s on holiday staying at some pop star’s getaway in Fuji. Not back until a couple of days before the 23rd,” said Garston.

“Then just the President,” said Seth. “Alright, the Green Room in one hour, I’ve a meeting with some rabbits. We need to do some more digging!”

***

“Alright, this is the coup. On the evening of the 23rd we have to activate all of the microchips in the dispensers. *That will be handled by* I and I via an encrypted computer programme that is linked to a Russian satellite whose circuitry we have managed to infiltrate. Our transmitter will be *switched on that evening too. Now, to do this we need a great electrical conductor. This is* where you *come in Freak*.”

Yin and Yang were looking forward to the 23rd of October like it was the biggest birthday party ever, but right now they were floating in their mobile aquarium, chairing a meeting.

“Oh, what can I do, and really, why should I?”

*“Be*cause I and I *are your friends and when we rule the world you will be able to kill anything you want. I and I’s initiative is to make you the world’s most revered* killing machine, greater than the Anaconda and more ferocious than the Great White Shark. You will become the *greatest* henchman, sorry hench-thing the world has ever *seen, and then systematically* you will be able to assassinate all of the world’s great leaders and become the most feared beast on the *planet. How’s that?”*

“You guys really know how to treat a girl don’t you. What do you want me to do?”

“*At the present moment your* palms are a wonderful food trap. But we would *like you* to cover both of them with even more of your conductive webbing. We want you to multi-layer and *strengthen them, in order that they may better be able to withstand the elements. As we all discovered whilst you were away, a good storm could cause us a serious* setback. Thus, we would like you to weave your webbing tightly into a cord, almost creating a *rope like* thingamygig, that will *climb* both of the *palms*, and, *'Zibbazabba Spideysilky,'* fantastic aerials! You may, of course, still use *the space* between them for food capture and sport. *We have a large thick roll* of electrical cable to *carry the power, but we need to run it from the generator behind the pool house to the transmission unit, that we* will have placed at the base of the palms, Oh, and I's will get yourself a *rubber booty* for your metal claw. It seems that's the only bit of *you that is susceptible to voltage*!

Now Escobar, your job is to oversee *the digging of the trench that will* contain the cable. It's going to cut right through the *garden, through the* flowerbeds and the lawn. Oh, don't look so worried, I's left this *to you so* the standard of the work is measured by yoursel*f. I's need the garden to look completely normal, just in case I's are suspected by* any government who happen to own a nosy satellite *and as yet do not have a terrapin dispenser within their organization.* What do you *think?"*

Escobar bobbed his head up and down.

"*Good then it's* settled. Freak, how long will it *take you to complete* the palms?"

"Well I would estimate about 5 days but it's not the work; it's producing the webbing that's going be the problem. I'm going to need a huge stock of protein to drain. Actually, come to think of it, make that a week. I need two days of slaughter before I start to build."

Spike hissed.

"*Ah, loyal Spike, all you have to do is pull* us around so we can keep an eye on everything and yes, you guessed it, you are the plough. Well, your *tail is to be* precise. You, *will dig the trench for* the *cable with it. Right then let's* get to it. And Freak there is a surprise for *you in the garden*."

"Really, what is it?"

"Well, somewhere in the garden there is a python, and *he's all yours*."

"You guys, you spoil me," said Freak.

***

Everyone but Vincent was in the Green Room.

"Right Maurice, did you email the President?"

"Yez and he will never know where it came from, not because he's stupid or because I sent it from his father's email address but, because when I signed off I did so as, Ze Knights of Camelot!"

"Like it, we are like the Thunderbirds or Captain Scarlet or the Avengers or something!" said Bandi.

"Yes well, err, Peuja will you start the conference call."

Sure Seth.

"Hi Vincent are you there, can you see us all?"

"Yes Seth, everyone is crystal clear."

"Good, now then, within the last hour I have done some digging around and found out that Green Slime is actually being produced here in Northampton, England. I don't know if any of you know anything about Northampton, but it seems to be a good choice. It's in the Midlands, easy to get to, that kind of thing. However, this has to be a two-part plan! Yin and Yang are obviously controlling a human with many assets. The factory itself is owned by a co-operative, but that's not the point. To eradicate the problem we have to deal with the source."

"Why don't we just destroy the factories where the slime and dispensers are made?"

"Yes, well, I thought of that, too, Albert, but it seems the factory that produces the novelty dispensers, would mean a trip to China which, I might add, I would thoroughly enjoy, however, this is not the time for a holiday that would spark an international incident. As we have informed the President of the US, we really shouldn't involve China. No, the answer is to block the signal."

"Right, but we still need a dispenser sample, to find the signal frequency, and if the only way to get one is to go to China then I'm going to have to go sweetie."

"No, Albert, like every great invention there has to be a prototype, and that my feathered friend has to be with Yin and Yang. We have to be clever about this. The authorities must not think this act a universal vendetta against the company that is behind Green Slime. That would be industrial espionage and someone, somewhere, would eventually wrongly get the blame," said Seth.

"What if we are wrong and they've had a change of hearts, and all they want to do is give children everywhere loving terrapin pets," said Steve.

"Yeah and I sailed down the River Mersey on a doughnut yesterday," replied Garston.

Seth continued.

"So we need to find the whereabouts of Yin and Yang."

"I think I can help you there," said Maurice, "I have studied the advert that they are now regularly streaming on the Internet and I noticed that the yacht had a name painted on its bow. She is called Ze White Mistress. She is registered to a gentleman called Mr White and is moored off the coast of somewhere called Alcatraz Island near Cozta Rica."

"Maurice that's brilliant. What an astounding piece of lateral thinking. This White bloke must have money if he has a yacht," said Vincent.

"He is a multi millionaire with fingerz in all kinds of tarts!"

"You mean pies, surely, Maurice," said Vincent.

"We do not do pie in Franz, we do tarts, dreamy cream dripping tarts!" Maurice replied dryly!

"OK, then," said Vincent slightly embarrassed, "shall we move on?"

"First things first, no amount of Green Slime can be allowed to leave the factory," said Seth.

"OK, Seth what's the plan?" asked Garston.

"Give me a second, right, yes, ok, that's it!" Seth replied. "Firstly, we need a team to go to Northampton and destroy it."

"Destroy Northampton, Seth?"

"No Hannibal, just the factory."

"Hold on, are we really going to destroy a factory? That's breaking the law," said Vincent.

"True, but if we don't, the consequences will be much worse," replied Seth. "Therefore, we also have to make it look like an accident, we don't want to get ourselves caught do we? Secondly, we need the prototype novelty dispenser to study the microchip technology hidden within it."

"That means someone's got to go to Alcatraz Island." Vincent rebuffed.

"Well, all of that sounds a little dull, anything a little more exciting to get on with?" Garston asked drolly.

"Why don't we just destroy the transmitter?" asked Steve.

"You can build another transmitter, but you can't change the receiving frequency of a thousand or so microchips around the world can you Steve!"

"No, I'll give you that one Seth!"

"Now, Vincent I have a confession to make. I have interfered with your motorcycle purchase."

"Oh, err, ok, what did you do that for and what's it got to do with all of this?"

"I will be getting to that. The custom made sidecar you ordered is now a little more customised than you think and so is the motorcycle. They will both arrive in a couple of days."

"But there is a waiting list on the bike and you say the sidecar is being made from scratch!"

"Yes, I know that, I'm the one who re-ordered it all, after you had already ordered it remember! However, I gave them an extra £400,000 if they would specifically add a few extras to the sidecar and have it delivered within a certain time frame."

"Are you saying you paid an extra 400 large for my bike?"

"No, that's just the sidecar; the bike has had a nitro kit fitted to it for an extra 100 large as you put it, and there's another 400 large that's been spent as well, on let's say, some minor improvements."

"Wow!"

"Anyway, it's going to get you, Bandi, Steve and Hannibal to Northampton."

"Well, it better for that kind of money!"

"That leaves Garston and Albert to sort out the prototype on Alcatraz Island.

"Ooh, I better get some sun cream," said Albert.

"Albert, you, of course, will fly and Garston you will run!"

"Err, run, to Alcatraz Island, nuts mate, you're truly nuts. How am I…? Oh, never mind! Any chance of a custom made, madly modified, 250 large costing, remote controlled, Rolls Royce engineered, miniature gerbil Jet Ski then?"

"Garston, this is not to be taken lightly. Terrapins are already flying out of pet shops and probably the dispensers too, not literary of course, before you ask Steve! Now, Alcatraz Island lies off the west coast of Costa Rica, in the Pacific Ocean. I plan to customise your old gerbil wheel and attach some paddles made of old bicycle tyre sections to a perforated Perspex housing. This will allow you to run and propel yourself forward in the direction you are facing."

Everyone was looking at Seth baffled.

"Seth, you are my friend but I am about to tell you to take a running jump and…."

"Before you do, it's for security reasons; anything with electrical components could be spotted by radar."

"Oh, ok, so, shark bait it is then!" announced an underwhelmed Garston.

Vincent still stunned at the fact that he was about to take delivery of Batman's Motorbike, raised his arm to ask a question.

"When is all of this going to happen then?"

"Garston and Albert will set off on the morning of the 20th. We'll drop Garston into the river Mersey and from there he will make his way. I have given you the day to cross the Atlantic. You will rendezvous with Albert at the mouth of the Panama Canal. Albert will have a bag of corn with him. I have estimated that your energy levels will be dangerously low at this time, so you must eat and rest, but, under the cover of darkness, travel the length of the Panama Canal until you arrive at the Pacific in the morning. Once there, eat and rest again and have a day in the sun. That evening though, the night of the 21st, you must both journey north, following the coastline to Costa Rica, until you reach the narrow straits that you have to cross to Arcadia and Alcatraz Island. Arcadia is the name of Mr White's property on Alcatraz Island, according to the yacht registration documentation. Reconnoitre Arcadia and draw up a plan, and strike. I need you to return here by the evening of the 22nd. Now gentlemen, there is one thing you must do when you are there, and that is, find out how to delay transmission. I am going to require a little time to work out the microchip receiving frequency, in order to block it via satellite when you get back, if the Northampton job isn't a success."

"Like it," said Vincent.

"How do we get it back?" asked Garston.

"You will carry the prototype and Albert will carry you."

"So why doesn't Albert just carry me there?"

"Albert's bag of corn is actually a sack of corn, not that a gerbil would break the camel's back but, you must both travel apart in case one of you has an accident, i.e. meets Freak! Whatever happens, I must have that prototype. The Northampton team will travel down the M6 motorway on 'The Commando' to the M1 motorway and from there, to the Green Slime factory."

"The Commando?"

"That's the name of my motorbike, Steve."

"That's zo cool," said Maurice.

Seth let out an attention-seeking cough.

"Maurice and I, assisted by Peuja, will co-ordinate events from here. We will download the factory's schematic, formulate our actions and on the night of the 21st, the Northampton team will destroy it, delivery trucks and all, before Green Slime can be shipped out the following morning."

"Seth, or should I call you Churchill!" said Vincent, "Shouldn't we do something about Yin and Yang?"

"Yes, but I haven't worked out exactly how we are going to do it yet!"

"Do what?" asked Albert.

"Get them back into a tank with SPAFF, of course. I'm pretty certain it would disable their power of terrepathy. Oh, and don't worry about getting lost, you will all be guided by Peuja Nav, not that you will need it, Albert!"

COUNTDOWN

Dear diary,

As you well know it's the 14th of October today and we are less than a week away from launching Garston into the River Mersey! Today I have planned the day around converting Garston's gerbil wheel into an engineering gyroscopic wonder, whilst Maurice gathers all meteorological and shipping forecasts for the Atlantic crossing. At the speeds Garston will be travelling, we wouldn't want him to crash into anything as a result of the squalling seas.

Steve and Hannibal spent the rest of yesterday building a gerbil sized assault course within level fives open space to aid Garston's training. I have programmed Sinatra to give him a rough time during his tutoring. Although Sinatra is under strict orders not to harm Garston deliberately, I do believe the odd accident may occur and therefore Bandi is at the ready with a first aid kit and support. Albert is just eating as much as he can, building up his energy reserves for the trial ahead.

Now diary, I am still, well I don't know how to put it really, concerned, no, that's not it, agitated, unsure, worried, no, that's not it either. I have it! I am completely flummoxed concerning the arrival of our deity. Let's face it. Bandi died and was set on fire but, she's just down the burrow, calling herself Bastet and I have absolutely no reason to disbelieve her! There is a goddess that was once worshiped by an ancient race, walking around the English countryside, chasing the odd shrew and lounging on the sofa! Why? And what does this do for evolution and religion? I must sit down soon and have a good chat with our Bandi. Also, why are there so many fatal incidents within Vincent's family history?

These are all questions that need to be answered as soon as we have dealt with Green Slime. Actually, Vincent has a little time before the arrival of 'The Commando.' I will ask him to further study the notes left to him by his father, now that he has a little help in his ear.

Signing off now, talk tomorrow,

Regards

Seth.

Seth logged out of his personal computer and hopped to the lab. He sent Vincent a message on the way. Vincent was a little tired, but he got himself together and set to work immediately. He scanned each single piece of paper from the notes, handling each sheet with the reverence it deserved and then sat down in front of his monitor.

"Peuja?" he called.

Yes Vincent.

"These markings around the 8 pointed star on this page, what do they mean?"

You are joking right? If it were all that easy I would have announced my findings long ago.

"The sign of Ankh is in the middle of the star."

Yes. Well done!

Vincent ignored the sarcasm.

"Well one of the symbols is a rising sun."

Yes

"That's the symbol for Bastet."

Yes it is, but the remainder do not identify as ancient Egyptian.

"You said ancient."

Yes

"That's what the scribble on this note says, well not quite, it actually says..."

...Ancients, I can see that.

"My father's letter, it told me to look to the Ancients."

Vincent was thinking aloud.

"Is it possible that they are all the sign for Bastet?"

I think that they are probably not.

"They must all mean something, Peuja?"

Well, that's pretty obvious.

"Will you try and find out?"

Maybe!

Down in level 5, Garston was duelling with Sinatra under the observation of Hannibal and Steve who were having a casual chitchat.

"He looks to be in reasonable shape, his speed and strength are good, but he needs something to really test him. I mean, running around here with a singing tin can trying to slice and dice you is one thing, but duelling with your acquaintance, Freak, head to head, is another, and let's face it, we haven't got a clue about what the rest of them can really do. No, I think we have to get medieval on his furry butt, and force him to face certain realities. We should torture him or something."

"Are you alright in the head Hannibal?"

"Well, a spy must use cunning Steve, as well as his abilities. In fact, cunning should be an ability! I have an idea. We are going to make this a little more adventurous."

"With what mate?" Steve replied.

"Electricity buddy, electricity allied with a good supply of sunflower seeds for bait. Have you seen the way he munches on them?" said Hannibal.

"He doesn't eat them all silly. He stores them in his cheeks."

"Why does he store them in his cheeks when they come in their own packets?" Hannibal asked.

"Old habits die hard!" Steve replied. "If there was any loo roll in here I imagine Garston would be making a bed out of it, even though he has a wonderful bespoke mattress to sleep on."

"I see what you're getting at my canine friend, the beast remains in us all. Making us more human doesn't remove our wilder characteristics. A dog for instance may always turn on his master!"

"That's right Han. There is a saying amongst us dogs of this world, 'Always lick the hand that feeds you, but rip off the hand without the food in it!'"

"That's quite special," replied Hannibal, a little perturbed.

"So, what's this all got to do with turning Garston into a super spy?" Steve asked.

"Jeopardy! We must tug at his heartstrings. He may not care two figs about himself, although I know he doesn't want to become a gerbil lollipop, but when there is something more at stake, how will he decide upon his actions."

"You've lost me, mate."

"We must place a pack of sunflower seeds in peril."

"Where's peril, mate?"

"This could be tougher than I thought." said Hannibal.

"Listen buddy, just to change the subject and all that, how's it going with Lecter?"

"I don't know, I don't see him!" Hannibal replied.

"No, I know that, but has Seth sorted it all out, the release mechanism thing and everything? I mean the rest of us can hardly escape the sounds of Lecter being allowed recreation. The blood curdling screams shoot through Camelot's labyrinth faster than a rabbit on fire looking for a badger's swimming pool!"

"Well, thank you, Steve, for your interest! We have come to realise from the 'training,' that when I come back from my time away, I return invigorated and rested, like I've been on detox or at an amazing health Monastery."

"A Health Monastery?" Steve replied, "Never heard of such a thing!"

"Oh, they exist my windy friend! Anyway, Seth and I have also learnt that when Lecter is woken, he becomes obedient immediately, if food is present! Seth's voice activated control is truly brilliant. You see, whenever I feel a bit down or rough around the bits, I can put out a little grub, chain myself to something and then take forty winks. The controls govern the length of release time and my helmet then returns to its original setting automatically."

"So what's the release trigger?"

"Not saying"

"Why not?"

"It's private."

"Just tell me."

"Let it go Steve, just let it go!"

"Listen there's a reason why I want to know. Let's say by some terrible circumstance you are kidnapped and the only way out is Lecter! His strength and fight are the only things that can save you, but you are tied up and gagged as a prisoner. What do you do?" asked Steve.

"I have to say the scenario has never crossed my mind."

"How do you voice activate him? You need a voice!"

"Sorry Steve, but telling you would do no good anyway. It's my voice that has to be recognised for the system to work. Only my voice can activate Lecter's release."

"Well, that's put a spanner up a baboon's backside hasn't it?"

"I am not a baboon and the only thing that has ever gone up my backside is a thermometer."

"And how was that for you?"

"Interesting, but I'm undecided which side of the fence to sit on. Now, we should really concentrate on what we are doing here!" said Hannibal.

"Yes, we should, where is he anyway?" said Steve having a look around. "Ooh, that's gonna chafe a little, Garston's gonna need some talc on that!"

"Maybe you should just give it a lick for him, canine saliva is supposed to have healing properties."

"True, but would you lick Garston's…"

"…Wound Steve, wound, and no, I certainly would not!" Hannibal replied.

***

"What's White up to, talking *to Spike like that as if he were an infant? Is he scratching his chin? Look, Spike loves it, and what's Escobar doing sitting on White's shoulder? He's not Long* John Silver, he's plain old Mr White. I would have him dead, as would I, if *I didn't have to* use him as a… what do hoodlums call it? Ah yes, a cover! *Unfortunately* he is a necessity and has to be alive in order for us to abuse his assets but, if he *becomes too much of a soppy problem he will pay like the rest of them. I's could always get* him to write a new Will and Testament that *leaves his entire fortune to one of these* girls. *Maybe* Clipboard Girl! Could you imagine her with all that money and power, if I's actually let *her wield it, that is? She would be like a freaky Freak. Freak is dangerous bu*t she would be a Gorgon! H*ahahah*aha! Now there's a weapon *I's could utilise*! I think we should have a progress report or something, a *meeting, I's* should let everybody know. I just have and so have I. *About 9:30pm* tonight then, I's will have a meeting with a little spinach *and some* Rioja for White, in fact instruct that obstinate in the kitchen and let

her and the *serving wench know I's want something a little special for tonight's supper. How close* is Freak to completion? Oh very I say, and the cables have been laid and the garden has been groomed! *So why do I's need a progress report?"*

"Excuse me your greatnesses?"

"*Talk of pedestrian* wastes of space and they shall appear. Yes Clipboard Girl *what now?"*

"We have just had confirmation that your blood has been added to Green Slime and it is all now ready to be vacuum packed and put into boxes as we speak in readiness for dispatch from Northampton, England. I have set up our central computer so that you may watch the live coverage at anytime you choose, via the factory's camera security system."

"*Leave that on the monitors at all times.* What about the dispensers are they complete, bint?"

"They are ready to be shipped directly from the Chang Mai factory upon email confirmation of Green Slime purchase."

"*What? You stupid* girl, you're supposed to give them away *at the same time. Freak, Freak!"*

"Yes I know, and we are, but I thought…"

Freak landed on the table next to Yin and Yang's new rock pool spa.

"Yes boys, how can I help you?"

"*Hold on for* a second will *you. Now Clipboard Twit M*aiden, you are on trial for inc*ompete*nce."

"But I'm only doing what you bid me, your regalnesses."

"*I told you, as did* I, that Green Slime and the *novelty dispensers are shipped* together, as a package."

"Yes, I know, but I was discussing filming with Mr White and he brought the subject up in conversation and it gave me the idea of a website that could be interactive. People would love it, a kind of log in and watch us kind of thing. The dispenser is shipped to their address when they join the website. For free, of course. That way we know where all of the dispensers are exactly, I mean in the home or office. We can view them via their own computer's web cam!"

"*What do you think*? Well, she can't help being stupid can *she. It comes with* being human! *The terrapins tell us where they are via the transmitting dispenser and thus I and I don't require any web cam rubbish!* That's the point of the *entire project* you idiot. You have put I and I back by days *maybe even* weeks. Freak, KILL HER!"

Clipboard Girl turned to see Freak raising her fangs. Shaking with fear she fell to her knees and pleaded for her life.

"No, please no, don't. It was actually Mr White's idea. I promised to keep quiet; we thought it would please you. Show mercy, my sirs, please don't kill me, I still have things left to coordinate!"

There was a pause.

"Freak, st*and down* I's am feeling generous, *I'm not*! *Girl you get a reprieve but do it again and you're* out; permanently gone forever at the bottom of the cliffs, you hear I and I?"

"Yes sirs, yes, it won't happen again I promise."

"Now, get thee gone, thou foulest munter before *I change I's mind and mine*."

Clipboard Girl backed away subserviently, grateful for her life.

"What do you think to all of that then, I suppose she was *doing her best* and it *does c*onfirm that White appreciates our efforts? The gir*ls do* gossip when they're *within his company, this I's know.*

Freak you may leave I and I."

"Is that it? I was stalking that baby goat you bought in the garden, tricky little deer!"

"The kid was bought to fertilise the cabbage patch, you don't have to kill everything you meet. They'll be larger *prey soon enough, so behave!"*

"It's eating the cabbage patch!" Freak replied.

"KILL IT!"

***

The morning of the 15th saw a flatbed truck pull up outside the cottage with a couple of large wooden crates as its cargo. A deliveryman in blue overalls got out and used the trucks on board crane to place the crates at the side of the road next to the white picket fence. Whistling to himself, he walked up the path, to the front door and gave it a knock, Vincent answered.

"Hello sir. You Vincent Russell?"

"Yes I am."

"Well, I've got a motorcycle and sidecar in these crates, do you want them?"

"What, of course I do!" Vincent answered excitedly.

"It's alright sir, only pulling your leg. Do you need any help getting them out? Want me to take away the packaging?"

"No thanks I can take it from here," replied Vincent.

"Very well sir, just sign here and I'll be on my way."

Vincent signed the electronic pad's delivery screen and took a twenty-pound note out of his pocket and handed it to the driver.

"Well thank you sir, much obliged."

The driver turned and walked down the path to his truck, gave a wave and was off!

Seth appeared at Vincent's feet.

"I have a surprise for you. Rabbits, dismantle that crate," Seth ordered, "and save that wood for strengthening our tunnel network."

Bunnies appeared and got to it.

"I always knew that one day a set of wheels would be needed, thus I've had Chief and the rabbits industriously working away building you an underground garage. Well, a trapdoor driveway to an underground garage to be precise, well, to a basement! "

"I didn't know we had a basement."

"We didn't! We built it and secured the cottage foundations at the same time. Well, when I say we, I mean Chief and his team. To get to it, all you have to do is journey up the drive towards the cottage wall and the drive will automatically drop to form a ramp, allowing you to ride straight into the basement; the door will close behind you. It's all on infrared. The couch in the lounge is positioned on a hinged trapdoor, just sit on it and ask Peuja to drop you in, it's all very state of the art, you'll land on a pile of bean bags in the basement!"

"How very secret spy!" Vincent replied.

"Bandi's idea." Seth added.

"Busy rabbits aren't they? Intelligent, very intelligent, too, especially Chief! Anything you need to tell me about how they became this intelligent?"

"No!" said Seth, replying firmly and yet a little sheepishly!

"Oh, alright then!" Vincent replied, taking the hint to mind his own business.

"Chief and his team have worked very hard. The basement is full of technology; it looks more like a Garage at Silverstone race track, than a basement."

"What technology? How did you do all that without me knowing?"

"Chief, rabbits and a little help from the pixies in the wood of course."

"Pixies! There are no pixies." Vincent replied.

Seth gave Vincent a stare.

Vincent shook his head and smiled nervously.

"I don't know what to believe any more, let's face it, I'm chatting to a bunny," he said.

They both stood back and watched as Chief and his team dismantled the large crate and then pushed the plastic sheet covered, gleaming black Commando and sidecar towards the cottage wall.

"Should we give them a hand?" Vincent asked.

"No, Chief will get upset if we do, he's a bit of a funny bunny like that. Let's meet them in the basement and I'll run through everything with you. I've got to open the trap door driveway, rabbitually from the inside, I have yet to calibrate the infrared."

"Seth, by the way, I forgot to tell you, I think I might be on to something with the notes, but I'm not yet completely certain," said Vincent changing the subject momentarily.

"Well, let's meet up later after you've seen this, come on."

Seth hopped back into the cottage and sat on the couch gesturing for Vincent to join him.

"Are you ready Vincent?"

"Thunderbirds are go!" Vincent replied tentatively having a seat.

"When you're ready Peuja," said Seth.

The back of the couch reclined and then the front of the couch flipped forward with a jolt, Vincent yelled, Seth giggled, and then both of them scrambled to their feet rather unceremoniously from a pile of beanbags.

"Impressive!" Vincent spluttered.

"Clap your hands," said Seth.

Vincent clapped his hands and to his surprise the lights flickered and then illuminated the entire basement. Vincent found himself speechless. There were monitors, base units, keyboards, industrial toolkits, air and fuel pumps, generators, fire extinguishers in fact everything he would need if he wanted to compete in the Isle of Man

TT race, including spares! He walked around in silence and came to a stop in front of an open space that deepened beyond the basement's interior walls.

Seth hopped over to a lever and gave it a tug. The ceiling of the open space, supported by hydraulic arms, slowly lowered to form a ramp that enabled daylight to flood in.

"Wow!"

"Is that all you have to say?" Seth replied.

Vincent and Seth watched as the silhouetted Chief and his team saw the Commando and sidecar down the driveway ramp, into the centre of the floor. Seth returned the lever to its original position and in turn the hydraulics returned the driveway to its ordinary state. Chief popped over to a red button on the wall and gave it a push with a paw, his rabbit team scattered and the Commando revolved to face the way it came in.

"A revolving floor too! Chief, you have outdone yourself and so have you Seth, amazing, absolutely amazing."

"The floor is just an old circular wooden table top from Ebay. No big deal. Shall we have a look at the Commando then?" said Seth.

"It would be rude not to," Vincent replied.

Chief and his team pulled back the covering sheet to reveal a motorbike and sidecar that went far beyond Vincent's expectations. At first glance it appeared to be, well normal, a little retro in design perhaps, but also a little futuristic, a mind-boggling mixture of retro styling and engineering. Vincent could see that the front was a little extended which gave it a lower riding position and that it also had an odd windshield and fairing arrangement which, to his mind, added to its mystique. The wheels were also a little different. They resembled a ceiling fan wrapped in something like silver foil.

The accompanying shiny sidecar was shaped like a black egg with its pointy-end facing front. There was no sign of a little flapping door to access it, though. It actually appeared to be completely enclosed with just a single wheel coming from the centre of its base.

"Will you open the sidecar please Peuja," asked Seth.

Yep

A well-hidden door hushed opened and a small staircase extended to the floor, like the steps of a small leisure jet.

"In here are all the gadgets your passengers will need for

navigation, entertainment, assault and defence. The roof also slides open with the aid of a button by your clutch. The Egg, as I call it for obvious reasons, is made from a mixture of carbon fibre and various resins, there's plenty of room in there for everyone to sit comfortably and the toughened, tinted glass allows them to see where they are going without being seen. Of course all of the other little surprises it stores in its carcass are controlled by an onboard computer that is linked directly to Peuja and the equipment in here."

"Surprises!"

"Yes, hold on, I will show you one. Peuja Armadillo mode for me please, would you?"

Boom shakalaka!

The tinted windshield and fairing on the bike seemed to extend from the front to the rear and then click into position to create a hard shell that covered the Commando, whilst the toughened glass became a toughened reflective screen in front of Vincent's eyes.

"Wow!"

Seth gave Vincent a 'down the nose look'. "Put it in a field and it would be hard to find, it would just reflect its surroundings and stand there camouflaged in foliage. Or you can just put it up if it's raining. There are a few of what I like to call Darwin discoveries on board, which will each in time, prove their worth but, we'll get to them another day. Peuja, have you calibrated Vincent's voice to control the Commando?

You are kidding me big ears, right?

"I'll take that as a humble yes!" said Seth.

"Won't all of this gadgetry draw attention to it when in day to day use?" asked Vincent.

"Well, yes, of course, unless you are in Possum mode!"

"Possum?" replied Vincent, the Commando returned to its original default setting.

"You see, now it's just a slightly customised motorbike."

"When can I ride it?"

"We need to fuel it and run a few checks first. It will be ready by the time you launch Garston into the River Mersey. Your leathers and helmet should be here tomorrow. Now, I have some homework for you, after all, this is not a toy."

Seth signalled Chief, who brought forward a set of computer

discs.

"I would look at all of these if I were you, they will give you a greater understanding of the Commando. Downloading them onto your microchip will help, Peuja will aid you."

Oh yeah, me little bud of heather!

"Alright, well, give me a few hours, then come and see me for that chat we were talking about," Vincent replied.

"I've been thinking, I really do have a lot to do, will you email me your findings and we can start to have a good crack at solving the Bandi mystery when all of this is over with. Would that be all right with you? I don't want to fob you off or anything, but a few days won't make a difference will it? One thing at a time eh? I can't remember the last time I had a good nights sleep."

Indeed, Seth had been working overtime and was starting to look a little dishevelled. However, Bandi on the other hand, was positively glowing; she was seated outside on the cottage roof, watching the leaves and dusk fall, breathing in the autumn air. Albert fluttered in and landed by her side.

"How are you? Are you feeling well, dear?"

"Yes, thank you Albert. I am feeling well, although maybe a little anxious."

"Really, anxious about what may I enquire, is it the Northampton jobby? Are you worried about Garston and me? Because if you are there is no need to be, we will be fine; we can handle Freak and her friends."

"No, it's not that Albert. I just feel different now," she paused, "it's like there is this great burning within me. I'm finding it difficult to understand or explain the events that have occurred. I know I am Bastet, but I also know I am Bandi. But why did it all happen? Bandi governs my personality but I have a new soul, and before you say anything, yes, Albert, we all do have a soul, it's not just a myth, that much is true. But why, why am I here? I have struggled with the facts; I can't believe the military or even mankind would go to this much trouble to bring me back for whatever reason? I sit wondering about it all everyday."

Albert mused.

"I'm sure there are answers out there Bandi, we just have to wait a while, be patient and all will be revealed." Albert put a wing around his friend and gave her a cuddle.

"I do hope so." Bandi replied.

***

Dear Diary,

It's the night of the 19th, as you well know; well, you may not know it's night! Anyway, the past few days have been pretty mundane, a few last minute checks, but that's been it. I have given Chief and his team the afternoon off. I thought that, before we undertake our mission, they should be well rested in the event we need to call upon them for anything at all. The rest of us are all meeting in the lounge to say goodbye to Garston and Albert at dawn tomorrow. The Commando is ready and awaits its first road trip. Vincent is already walking around the cottage wearing his motorcycle leathers, he stipulates it's to 'soften them up', but I don't believe him; I think he just can't wait to play with his new toy. There is a feeling of anticipation around the place; we are all looking forward to putting the Yin and Yang threat behind us. I'll talk to you again when it's all over. Signing off now, talk to you soon.

Regards

Seth.

P.S.
We still haven't heard anything back from the President!

***

The morning of the 20th saw Vincent woken by Bandi,

"It's time Vincent, you must wake up."

Vincent threw back his duvet, to reveal the fact he had slept in his motorcycle leathers!

"I'll be with you guys in a minute. I just need to pop to the bathroom. I'll meet you in the basement."

The rest of the team were already in the basement waiting.

Garston was stood inside his converted Perspex hamster ball housing, wearing a mini puffer jacket of some sort, and Albert was strapped to a sack of corn via a harness. Hannibal was giving the straps a final check.

"It all looks good to me Albert, good luck mate."

"Thank you darling." he replied.

"OK, you have ze navigation zettings you need," said Maurice. "Remember, this mission could be very dangerous so, be careful, but more than that be brave and successful," said Seth.

Vincent landed on the pile of beanbags.

"Welcome and good morning Vincent. Now, to business, the Commando will only start with retinal recognition so look into the right wing mirror, once you have taken your seat."

Vincent followed Seth's instructions and Seth fiddled with a computing panel on the wall, "That's it everything is set," he said.

Vincent pressed the ignition button and the Commando let out a growl and fired up. He grinned delightedly, running at idle the motorbike sounded like a grizzly bear with a velvet singing voice!

"Just give the accelerator a gentle turn and let out the clutch," said Seth. Vincent did as he was told and the Commando slowly moved forward, triggering the driveway ramp.

"OK guys this is it, take care everyone, see you all later." said Vincent.

"Haven't you forgotten something Vincent?" said Seth.

"I don't think so," Vincent replied, patting himself down.

"Well, you have to wear your helmet," said Hannibal.

"Oh yes," Vincent replied.

"And would you mind taking Garston with you?" asked Seth.

"Oh yes, err, silly me!"

Vincent leant down and picked up Garston.

"What's he wearing?" he asked.

"It's a plastic, lightweight freshwater holding jacket. They're all the rage you know," Garston replied.

The Eggs' tinted glass roof slid open and revealed its high tech centre. Vincent carefully placed Garston inside and the glass slid closed. "Right it's time to go, ready Albert?" said Vincent, putting on his helmet.

"I am as ready as a copper coloured topped battery! Let's do this thing," Albert replied zestfully.

"I will sit in front of my computer and keep in contact during the journey, but once you have left these shores it is down to zatellite, good luck my friends, and Viva la Revolution!" Maurice paused, "Zorry I don't know where zat came from!" he said apologetically.

Vincent smiled and slowly rode up the ramp,

"No, wait!" said Hannibal.

Vincent pressed sharply on the brakes. Hannibal ran up to the Commando, looked to the skies fiddled about a bit and then piddled on the rear wheel! Everyone just watched in astonishment as he had a shake and turned nonchalantly to face the team.

"It's good luck in some countries," he said.

Chief and his team all glanced at one another and then collectively took it upon themselves to follow Hannibal's example. Vincent felt a little violated.

"No, no, Chief, no, stop it!" he said fighting off piddling rabbits. "Seth, can we please wash it when I get back?" he pleaded.

Seth returned a reassuring and yet disgusted nod, and Vincent pulled back on the accelerator and soon, was a dot down the lane.

Flapping furiously Albert and his cargo of corn rose into the air.

"Get as much height as fast as you can. The winds and thermals will help you," said Seth.

"See ya mate, be good."

"I will, my darling Steve, I will."

Albert and the corn flew into the distance.

"Right we've got about an hour until they reach the River Mersey, Maurice, let's get ready. The rest of you study the schematic of the Northampton factory; we will have a meeting regarding that plan very soon. I recommend everyone relax, that's all I can say, it's out of our paws now."

Vincent couldn't help but smile as he rode his dream machine. He opened his visor so he could feel the cold air blowing in his face.

"Hey, Garston, can you hear me?"

"Yes mate, of course I can, we have helmet to Egg technology!" Garston and Vincent both sniggered. "This is an amazing ride buddy; she's sticking to the road like glue. It's so exhilarating, but she's not letting me really throttle her for some reason!" said Vincent.

"Ah, yes, that must be one of Seth's Darwin discoveries, it must have some kind of traction control. You must be in Snail/Bat mode, sticking to the road and avoiding everything." Garston replied.

Vincent let out a raucous laugh.

"I'm not joking Vincent, hold on, look, there you go you're in slug sloth mode!"

"Oh right." Vincent paused. "How's Albert doing?"

"He's already at our designated launch site. We will be with him in 39 minutes according to my readings."

"Are you ready for this mate?" asked Vincent.

"Of course not, how can anyone be ready to run a gerbil wheel thingy, across the Atlantic."

"It's more like a converted gerbil gyroscope, buddy. You run on your wheel and that propels the outer ball! It allows you to take a breather as long as you have an adequate spin going."

"Don't be splitting hairs Vincent. It's a plastic pig's ear, that's what it is, it's not a plastic speed boat is it?"

Vincent thought it would be a good idea to change the subject.

"Fancy listening to some music, it might take your mind off what's to come?"

"Sure go for it." Garston replied wearily.

"Commando, Radio on."

The sound of Queen's 'Who wants to live forever' filled the Egg!

"Err, off please mate!" shouted Garston.

The remainder of the journey went seamlessly, if not silently, until Vincent and Garston eventually arrived at the designated secluded launch site by the riverbank, where Albert was sat on his sack of corn waiting patiently.

"Hello boys, it's a brisk day for sailing! Are you ready Garston?"

"Don't be an idiot" replied Garston as he was being lifted out of the Egg by Vincent. Albert ignored the rhetoric.

"Well darling, shall we? God speed and all that and remember the perforated Perspex unit needs to be spinning at a fair rate, otherwise you will sink."

"Yes, needing oxygen does have its downside!" Garston replied.

"So as soon as Vincent drops you in the water start running!"

"Will do."

"OK guys this is it, there's no turning back now, see you both in a few days."

Vincent took Garston and gently tossed him underarm into the River Mersey. Garston started running for his life immediately, literally, for his life. His ball rattled a bit, but then spun like a demon, causing the surrounding water to foam like the top of a milk shake and then, like being fired out of a sling shot, Garston zoomed down the river, skimming the surface towards the estuary, perpetually skipping like a pebble heading for the open sea.

"Seth, you're a bloody genius," said Vincent laughing and getting back on the Commando, "Take care Albert." Albert returned a wink, stretched his wings, rose into the air and was soon, too, out of sight.

Garston found, true to instruction, that once he had got up to a workable speed, his inner wheel could stop spinning, handing him the opportunity to peruse his surroundings! The ferries and ships driving the wheels of Liverpool's industry were enormous in size but relatively slow in comparison to his lively little ball. They became obstacles in a giant game of slalom whilst he passed through the docks. In no time at all he had reached the Irish Sea and was headed for Ireland's north coast.

"We are about to lose voice contact with you Garston you'll be out of range with us here," said Seth's voice in Garston's head, "but we will watch your progress via GPS. Enjoy your time on the Ocean."

"Great!" Garston replied sarcastically,

"Oh, don't be so negative, next stop Panama after you pass the Giants Causeway, that is!"

"You said nothing about giants Seth; they don't eat Gerbils do they?" Garston asked dryly, obviously joking.

"It's alright Garston the Giants Causeway is actually an ancient geological feature on the north east coast of Ireland. It does have a wonderful myth attached to it, though, about a giant called Finn McCool."

"Oh yeah, what did he do?" Garston asked.

"Well, one day, Finn was angered by a Scottish giant who had mocked his fighting ability, so he threw a rock across the Irish Sea to Scotland with a challenge to a fight, attached to it. However, the Scottish giant could not swim and threw a rock back with a message that declined the invitation. Finn felt aggrieved and refused to let the Scottish giant off so lightly and so he built a causeway, a kind of natural stone bridge, from Ireland to Scotland. This, he thought, would enable the Scottish giant to walk across the Irish Sea and face him in a contest, which he did. However, upon arrival the only thing he found was a baby, a baby as large as himself! The Scottish giant immediately fled for his life back to Scotland. He thought if the children of the Irish giants were this large, what size were the adults? The baby, of course, was Finn in disguise." Seth gave a chuckle.

"Legend has it that, to this day, Finn sleeps in a cave ready to protect his land whenever he is called upon.

"That's a great story Seth."

"I like it too, Garston.

Made of solidified pillars of molten rock, and having the appearance of cracking, drying clay scorched in the sun, the causeway looks like God's own staircase, you can't miss it; it's one of the world's most beautiful natural formations."

"There are no Giants then?" said Albert listening in.

"Well, I don't know, there might be, but not at the Giants Causeway, just towers of hexagonal rock and tourists. Oh, and a pretty good gift shop!"

Garston thought about what Seth had said for a moment.

"Seth, do you believe in God then? You called it God's own staircase, that's a very human thing to do."

"To be honest Garston, I don't know what to believe anymore. Why do you ask?"

"Well I just thought you might have a quiet word so he can help me!"

"We are put here to help ourzelves. I think that if he existz, he does not have that much time for uz individually. He haz a lot on, zo make your own fortune Garston and come home zafe. Take care of yourself and zee you zoon mon amie! Over and out!" said Maurice.

"Ooh, he makes me tingle when he speaks French!" said Albert listening in.

Maurice had studied the shipping lanes together with Seth and sent Garston a speed plan to keep him from bumping into anything. It, of course, also told him when he would have to slow down because he was nearing Panama.

In no time at all Garston was out of communicative range, with just the enormity of his task ahead of him.

"You can still chat to me though love, I'm just above you so if you get bored, I'm here baby!"

"Cheers Albert, let's just get to dry land shall we."

Garston put his foot down. As his speed increased he found that his ball began to skim along the surface easier and as the waves became larger, the length of each skim gained in distance.

After several hours of skimming, flying and general daydreaming, Albert and Garston had run out of chitchat and were pretty much just doing their best to get through the first gruelling part of their journey. Garston found he had to keep his concentration in order to fend off the many, often invisible, dangers lurking in the treacherous open sea. The blustering, buffeting winds were his foremost concern and he found fighting them arduous. There was also the dodging of a familiar looking school of dolphins that thought they had found a lost beach ball for several miles to contend with, which incidentally, was much to Albert's amusement.

"Ha! They're doing that on porpoise! Get it?" he said.

The size of the planet was starting to hit home and Garston's self-confidence was waning. He felt small and insignificant; the only thing keeping him going was the knowledge that he was an integral part of a series of events that, he hoped, would save mankind from Terrorpin slavery or maybe even worse. But there were questions deep inside of him that remained, lingering like a scab he couldn't scratch.

Why should he help save mankind, he thought? They, after all, did prod and poke him under laboratory conditions, they tested their various E numbers on him and he still had a nasty burn scar from that haemorrhoid cream. However, he also pondered the fact that there were people like Vincent, good people who cared for the animals of the planet and the environment.

He asked himself a bunch of further questions. Were humans only trying to survive? Was the natural world their book of answers? He found himself torn, obviously the study of nature for medical purposes was one thing, the species could aid their starving and diseased, but he found it hard to vindicate humans for testing what he thought to be, vanity products upon row after row of caged animals. The fact that Seth was pretty much addicted to lipstick was terrible, he thought. Another notion entered his mind. Why does man, a species given the power of reason, war with itself? He could understand it if they were Beavers for instance, fighting for reasons of territory, food and bloodline, but they were not, and to make it worse, humans are supposed to be the most intelligent of all creatures. So why did they do it? They have enough food about to be able to get together and feed everyone. It isn't as if they are a dying breed, is it?

It occurred to him that human conceit and more importantly, greed was threatening their very survival. From being a simple race that depended upon the land and the sea, humans had evolved into a complicated race, destroying everything that provides them with life. And now, to make matters worse, they are trying to fool nature with a helping hand from science. Madness, he thought, absolute madness. Were Yin and Yang right then? Should humans pay? He found himself almost sympathising with the Terrorpin cause!

"Right stop that," he said to himself. "Yin and Yang are bonkers and dangerous, two nut nuts that need to be put in their place. Just keep running, just keep running and get the ruddy job done."

THE LOST AND FOUND

At the dining table, a meeting was about to begin; Seth was the last to take his seat.

"It's now eight hours into their journey. In approximately another two, they should arrive at the mouth of the Panama Canal, it will be around 10 in the morning, local time."

"Wow, that's fast," said Bandi.

"Vincent, how was the Commando?" asked Seth.

"No need to ask Seth, it's amazing, but I do have one concern. I'm afraid we are going to have to buy another bike, something that I can just potter around on, to get to the shops and stuff like that. I feel it may attract too much attention, even in Possum mode. Why don't we get something that isn't designed and engineered by NASA, hey? You know, like a…"

"…Vespa, perhaps. I have bought you one already, a nice black and chrome 250cc Vespa," said Seth.

"Really, well, great, I love Vespas."

"What's a Vespa mate?"

"It's a scooter, Steve, that has been designed by an Italian artist, whilst taking a luxurious bath and watching old re-runs of Flash Gordon," said Bandi.

"What's a scooter mate?"

"It's a wonderfully designed moped, Steve," Hannibal replied.

"Why's Gordon flash, mate, did he have a Vespa?"

"Never mind Steve, shall we get back to the case in hand. Now you've all studied the plan, any questions?"

"What's a…"

Maurice flicked out his tongue and wrapped it around Steve's muzzle!

"Thank you Maurice," said Seth.

"Alright then let's run through the Northampton mission and see how we go. That alright with everyone?"

Everyone said yes except Steve and Maurice who just nodded! Seth laid out the schematic on the table and began.

***

Wearing his big, white, fluffy robe and standing at the vantage point of his bedroom balcony, Mr White looked out to the horizon that greeted him with the glare of the beautiful Pacific sun. He had a stretch and breathed in the fragrant bouquet of Arcadia's gardens. This morning his exotic pampered grounds and outdoor swimming pool were suffused with swimwear clad sun-kissed ladies covered in lotion, tanning themselves, even though it was the month of October.

"Good day all and how are we this fine, bright, beautiful morn?" he called.

"Hey baby!" called the chorus in return.

Spike raised his head. He too was sunbathing on the lawn, but strapped to the mobile Terrorpin aquarium containing Yin and Yang. Freak momentarily stopped weaving and glanced up from her palms as Escobar flapped in and landed on the balcony wall.

"Oh, I envy you, Escobar," said Mr White. "To be able to soar through the skies on a day like this must be an amazing, magical experience. I have all the money one man would ever need, or want, but I would give all of it away to have the freedom to fly at will around this fantastic world." Escobar bobbed his head.

"Captain, are you there?" Mr White asked calling down into the garden.

An extremely striking looking lady took off her sunglasses and sat up, smiling.

"Yes, sweetheart, how can I help you?"

"Would you mind preparing the White Mistress? I would like to sail tonight. I have a little treat in mind for everyone."

"Of course I will darling."

Squeaks of delight rose from the grounds.

"Is Clipboard Girl about?"

"Yes, Mr White I'm here."

Startled, Mr White turned to find Clipboard Girl in his bedroom, holding a tray containing herbal tea, croissants and fresh fruit. She, of course, also had her clipboard under her arm. She placed breakfast down on a bedside table, took out a pen from a pocket and prepared to take notes.

"Hello and good morning to you too," Mr White said with a

charming smile. "Miss Clipboard. Have you been listening to me wittering on about flying?"

"It's Clipboard Girl," she replied a little abruptly, "and I've been waiting with this tray a while!"

"Ah yes, right, err, could you have a word with Miss Chef for me please? Let her know that we will need her to prepare something for tonight's trip. Oh, and ask Miss Security too, if she wouldn't mind locking up Arcadia at 11pm? We will all be going sailing tonight."

"Really, all of us together?" she replied.

"Yes, of course. I want you all to be there with me, with us."

Clipboard Girl made a note and left with a smile.

Mr White turned and addressed the group below.

"Now everyone, it's going to be a late night, so you must all lounge about today and unwind in the sun. Are my orders clear?"

All of the ladies gave a joyful hooray, delighted at the instructions. Yin and Yang, were a tad confused and also a little perturbed!

"*Did I's command* this trip? No I's did not! Surprising is it not, but I's take *pleasure in surprise*s. He must have thought of it *when I and I were not in his head*. OK then, let's *compose* a rule, leave the mind of White alone today so I's can *have the surprise* too! I's sure it won't do any damage to *our apocalyptic plan of domestic domination. Not now surely."*

***

"Darling it's time to slow down according to Seth and Maurice's plan. Aim for that sand bank ahead."

Garston's cam eye zoomed in on the proposed landing strip. His microchip quickly calculated the distance to speed ratio and he stopped running at the precise distance required for a safe park, or so he thought!

SKIP…SKIP…SKIP…SKIP…SKIP…SKIP…THUD…CRAB… CRACK…SMASH!

"Oh, ouch, no, ouch, stop. Tail stop me!"

The end of Garston's tail launched itself straight into the sand leaving Garston buried up to his neck looking back towards the sea. His Perspex transport bounced on, and shattered into dozens of pieces behind him. His old gerbil wheel then seemed to taunt him by rolling away down the beach past the splattered remains of a land crab! A sack of corn hit the ground in front of him, quickly followed by a fluttering flusteredAlbert.

"Oh thank the heavens." He said puffing out his cheeks and mopping his brow with his cravat. He undid his straps and hopped up towards Garston.

"Ooh, hot sand, hot sand, hot sand!"

"You think I don't know that!" Garston replied sarcastically.

"You should never trust technology, Garston."

"Yeah, whatever!"

"Well, that didn't quite go to plan did it, love? I thought you were going to hit that oil tanker earlier, but I determine from your actions that the crab made a delightfully tempting and more difficult target and all you were doing was testing your equipment? Ooh, I do like a bit of sea food though." Albert tucked into some crab mush.

"Get me out of here before I become a trainee taxidermist that has chosen birds as his specialist subject to study Albert!" Garston said quietly, deadpan and without any sign of emotion.

"Oh, yes, of course."

In no time at all, Albert lifted Garston out of the san and popped him down.

"Thanks mate, I'm starving. Shall we have some lunch?" Garston asked.

"Yes, certainly but what are we going to do about the plan, and where is your fresh water jacket, dear?"

"Absolutely no idea, but, water we must find! To tell you the truth I didn't fancy negotiating those locks on the Panama Canal in that ball, anyway. Let's just rest here for a bit and fly cross-country. What do you say to that?"

Albert agreed with a chirp.

"Now, would you mind getting us to somewhere safe before that salt water crocodile sneaking up behind you makes us a snack?"

Albert pirouetted to find a crocodile's jaws about to close. He darted over towards Garston, grabbed him by the tail, as if it were a juicy worm, and lifted him straight into the air. The crocodile snapped at them both audaciously, but luckily, missed by a tail feather. Albert put Garston down on the branch of a nearby tree that overlooked the sandbank, and took a perch next to him!

"Just one problem Albert, that crocodile is lying on top of our corn whilst it chomps on that crab."

"Yes that may be a setback."

Garston's tummy rumbled.

"I really need to eat, mate, I'm famished."

"Wait here, I'll be back in the blink of a eyelash," Albert replied.

Albert flew off, but quickly returned to the branch with a large, angry, black, hairy scorpion.

"No Honey Puffs then?" Garston asked drolly, "I know I've eaten the odd cockroach, but I usually supper on slightly smaller invertebrates!"

Albert dropped the scorpion. It scuttled away on the sand followed by the crocodile. Within seconds Albert had flown down to the sack of corn, reattached himself to his harness and was hovering in front of Garston.

"I'm not that stupid love, just climb on the sack and we will fill our stomachs as we go. It's all a little busy here, I think we should be on our way, it'll give us a little more time on the west coast to plan, so; Flight 001 of Albert Airlines is about to depart from Panama to Costa Rica from, err, this branch. This is your last call, get on board and fasten your seat belt, dear!"

"So, we are not staying then?"

"Let's get going. We'll find somewhere to rest up later, baby."

"Don't ever call me baby, Albert!"

"OK, sweetheart!"

Garston jumped onto the sack and with his tail cut a small tear in its centre. This allowed him to sit back, enjoy the view and munch corn at his own leisure, whilst intermittently extending his tail with a kernel in its grasp as 'in flight' grub for Pilot Albert!

***

Seth and Vincent were left sitting at the table by themselves. Seth had finished running through the Northampton plan, and had let everyone else go and watch Hannibal play Sinatra at table tennis. Maurice had asked Chief and his team to build a replica table for a level 5 recreation area and, of course, there is nothing as busy as rabbits!

"The eight pointed star? Well, I really don't know its significance but each of the points has a symbol next to it as you can see, and this one here is the symbol of Bastet, a rising sun. Now, we know that the sign of Ankh is the symbol for eternal life, and that lies at the centre of the star. We can also see here, on this other note, the word Ancients. The same word written in my father's notes and not used in the singular either, both use the plural. That leads me to believe that each single point of the star represents an ancient worshipped being of some sort, but why eight, and what language is this written in, and why is that in the middle? Now, these jottings were taken from drawings on the walls of a tomb in Bubastis, but the rest of the symbols are not Egyptian and the whole thing is circled. I had Peuja try and run through the symbols for me to find out what they are, but to no avail. She found that many of them can mean a number of things in different languages and I don't really know where to start. There are thousands of ancient languages, civilisations even tribes," Vincent paused and pondered. "I'm a little bereft of answers. What do you think?" he asked.

"Well, I think you're on the right track, and I concur with your hypothesis. I also, like you, think that the number eight is very significant, how though I have yet to interpret. However, Bandi became Bastet and therefore around the world in other facilities the same thing may possibly be happening. After all, you were lied to before, so who's to say there aren't more facilities like Pradgonne Manor? Peuja, sorry, the Cube only reacted when Bandi was scanned, not the rest of us. I don't think that there is any chance in the slightest that a worshipped rabbit god, of old Viking heritage, will appear after I have an accident of some sort!" replied Seth with a strangely stuttered high-pitched giggle.

Vincent looked at him curiously and asked, "So where does that leave us?"

"Little Budworth, my human friend, sitting at a table in a cottage in Little Budworth," replied Seth.

***

"See that shoreline down there love," said Albert, "well, that's called the Gulf of the Mosquitos, I have no idea why, but I presume that if we flew a little lower we'd be scratching all the way home!"

"Yes, I have heard of it, it's usually called the Mosquito Coast right?" Garston replied.

"Wrong darling, that's the name of the Atlantic coast of Nicaragua, which is named after its original occupants, the Miskito Indians. European settlers changed it to Mosquito."

"Oh right, I take it that geographical history is your thing, then?"

"I just said I don't know why, so why would it be my thing? I just think it's nice to know the odd fact regarding the planet that we live on. I mean, look at the beauty of that mountain range to our left," Albert paused briefly. "Say would you like to see an active volcano, Garston?"

"Wow, would I?" Garston replied excitedly.

"Then we shall. We shall fly over the Bani Volcano; it's been gurgling and puffing for a while. You can have a vada at it from my customary perspective. We'll head to the border and the western coast of Costa Rica after that."

"Any chance of a drink soon please, buddy?" asked Garston.

"I'll stop at a fresh water lake the first chance I get sweetheart, if that's alright?"

"Absolutely captain, absolutely." Garston replied shoving a kernel of corn in his gob.

Albert and Garston continued flying high enough for virtual invisibility until, eventually, Albert decided on a good spot and came to land by a lake in the mountains. After a brief discussion they decided that a stay in the wilderness would be fun, character building even, hidden high up in the trees, of course! To their surprise, they were also not feeling the cold at all, and were both in fine fettle. They settled in for the night and began to watch, and chat, about the indigenous wildlife around them. Garston's cam eye could focus, zoom in and follow even the smallest of critters from where he and Albert were snuggled and Albert's incredibly enhanced eyesight could do the same. In due course, exhaustion set in and took its toll, as did the counting of grasshoppers, but not before the odd juicy example disappeared to a good home!

In his drowsy state Garston began to ramble.

"Isn't this amazing being here? Look at this place. Listen, the sounds of the lake, the smell in the air, beautiful. The whole David Attenboroughness of it all is incredible. Don't you just love it Albert?"

"Yes, it's adorable darling."

Albert swiped a wing at an over inquisitive tree snake. "Now get some sleep, I'm as knackered as a wanna be WAG traipsing around nightclubs looking for a mediocre footballer with more spots than brain cells to kiss and tell on! Anyway, it's back off to the seaside tomorrow, Garston, and I want to get an early start. Just before sun up would be good. Do you fancy a cuddle?"

"Err, you're alright mate, see you in the morning!" Garston replied scooting further down the branch!

"Tail, soft bed please," he said.

***

Mr White was standing beside the delightful Miss Captain on the bridge of the White Mistress, holding a glass of champagne. He looked out into the night as his yacht slinked across the narrow straits towards the lights of mainland Costa Rica and took a sip.

"Everyone is waiting for you on the deck by the buffet, as you requested sir," said Clipboard Girl tapping his shoulder to gain his attention.

He nodded and followed her down to the deck where he clinked his glass to get everyone's attention.

"Hello everyone and welcome to one of the greatest nights of your lives. You are all going to view and indeed take an active role in one of natures finest miracles."

"I's have to say that this is sounding very exciting, in fact I's have *a funny feeling* in my tummy and mine which I's thoug*ht at first to be nausea,* but it transpires that I and *I feel ones adrenalin* levels escalating!"

Mr White continued.

"Ladies and friends, I am sure you are wondering what the great surprise is? Well," Mr White paused and then with great gusto announced, "we are off to aid the plight of the Olive Ridley Turtle during an Arribada!"

The ladies looked at each other a little bemused. Mr White put forward his case!

"The Olive Ridley turtle is becoming increasingly endangered and once again, it is a problem that has been created by human greed. With pollution affecting the world's ozone layer, weather cycles and water levels, the natural nesting habitats of these turtles have been subjected to freak tides and winds, which are, in turn, causing numbers to dramatically deplete due to incubation anomalies. You see, creatures like these turtles are overlooked by many focus groups, but their plight is the direct result of our actions. I mean, the White Rhino, any Whale; you name it, Pandas and Polar Bears, Tigers, Elephants, Gorillas, Leopards, the list is endless, they all have their crusaders but as for turtles, wild frogs, marsupials and all the other endangered species, is anyone fighting for them? Well yes, but not many, and not enough. It's sad to know, ladies, that because of us humans, the Olive Ridley may soon not be here for future generations to see."

"What's an Arribada?" asked Clipboard Girl

"An Arribada is the name of a mass nesting of turtles, it actually means 'arrivals' in Spanish. It can last up to 5 days. We, of course, are only there for one night, at the beginning. There are records of thousands of turtles at any one time laying their eggs on one single beach, our destination, Ostonial Beach. For those of you who have difficulty with numbers, that's approximately 10 million eggs. However, usually less than one percent survives. Our intervention will aim to readdress that figure. Now, due to those kinds of numbers, the government has decreed that for the first three or so days of an Arribada, humans are allowed to gather and scavenge and even sell eggs."

"*Death to humans.* Let our *cousins live!*" Yin and Yang interjected!

"We are taking eggs?" asked Freak.

"What exactly are we going to do?" asked Clipboard Girl.

"Well, we are not taking eggs, just moving them and we all have different roles to play. Freak, Spike and Escobar are to take care of all predators that are not human. By predators, specifically Ghost crabs, Wood Storks and Salt Water Crocodiles. They will try and steal or break the odd rogue egg. The rest of us are going to build or rather dig our own nests on the beach, collect all of the rogue eggs and give them a warm place to fully gestate and develop into young turtles. Now as you might have gathered we will not be the only people there. Tourist parties and collectors will also be about. We though, will be there for Mother Nature, not ourselves!"

"You leave those *murderous, opposable* thumbed, softly coated *villainous cretins* to I and I!"

"Yes gents," said Mr White, "err, well, I will coordinate the gathering of the eggs and hopefully during the full moon, in about 40 to 50 days time, the hatchings will crawl out of the sand and drag themselves to the open sea. It's a truly amazing sight, and one, I hope, we may get to witness. OK, Miss Captain, will you turn on the searchlights, and get us in as near as you can and drop anchor. We will travel to the shore by utilising the jet skis and the dinghies. Will you be alright here boys?"

"I'm sure they will be fine, darling, I will stay behind to keep an eye on them," said Miss Captain.

"Alright then Miss Captain, they are in your hands," said Mr White.

*"Please do not be co*ncerned regarding I and I, just place us somewhere where we will, err, create a diversion so the other humans on the *beach and boats will be, err, distracted, yes, distracted from their tasks."*

"What kind of distraction do you have in mind, firing off flairs or something?" asked Mr White.

"I was, and I, thinking about *something along those lines, yes!"*

"Well, alright we will see you later then. Everyone to the launches," Mr White placed the Terrorpin mobile aquarium down on a table on the upper deck. "What about here, then?" he asked.

"Fine White, now be gone. Save them all. *Let our cousins live!"* They yelled a rallying cry.

Mr White joined the others and soon they were scooting across the surf to the shore. There were people on the beach already gathering eggs, but oddly and suddenly, they all stopped what they were doing and walked towards the edge of the Ocean.

"Quick get the dolphins here, we don't want *White to suspect* anything. I'll get that strumpet left *behind to pop I and I in the water* to make the call and then she can work *the spotlight*."

Miss Captain put Yin and Yang in a little basket and placed them over the side. A school of dolphins soon arrived and began to summersault and loop over each other as if they were in a feeding time display at Sea World. However, this was not enough for the musical adoring duo! And so, they set about choreographing the dolphins in elaborate Broadway show routines.

"*That should* do *it, he'll think that they're all watching voluntarily, he's* far too dim-witted to suspect that *we are doing all of this! Give em the* old *Razzle Dazzle,* nuke *and bury em. Hahahaha!"*

"Why are those dolphins doing that? Clipboard Girl asked.

"Yes, it is interesting," replied Mr White smiling. "I have no idea. Let's get on with the job in hand shall we."

The humans on all of the other boats seemed to be hypnotically entranced and thus oblivious to what was going on around them!

Freak was the first onto the beach. She leapt from the back of a jet ski, steadied herself and then carved her name and the date in the dark coloured sand beneath her claws. Spike drew up alongside her as she surveyed the surrounding area like a cautious Navy Seal on a special op.

"The big Salt Water Crocs are mine, you take the crabs," she said.

Spike gave her a knowing nod and went scuttling off.

Escobar however, was having a crisis of conscience. He couldn't understand why a few hundred animals had to die to save a thousand or so turtles. He thought if he took everything inland, then they could at least have a chance of survival. He looked around and spotted the lights of a holiday village on a nearby island, and set about ferrying anything that walked or crawled to its miniature golf course. The Crocodile at the mini windmill of the 7th hole at the Hermes Hotel caused a little bit of a stir, but the Wood Storks were having fun with errant golf balls bobbing in the water feature. Freak, however, was having the time of her life. For her, this was a wonderful murderous game of hopscotch. She even found herself humming with merriment whilst revelling in the slaughter. Zipping along the sand, creating webbed nets and traps, slicing through the hard shells of Ghost Crabs, that she was supposedly saving for Spike, with her metallic claw and venomously duelling with the world's ancient reptiles, was right up her street! Spike however, went about everything in a slightly different manner. As he was unfamiliar with Ghost crabs and their palatable taste, he would first rip off their claws tenaciously and listen to them scream, and then crunch their bodies and suck out their brains, "Mmm, lovely!"

"*Midnight, not a sound from the ocean,* shut it, Sondheim *is king and I, and Schwartz is wicked, so forget those* fancy prancing footloose *shows that declare they are funny, but still believe* that they will rock you or hand you Saturday night fever. Keep your three pennies for the opera and review the situation. Give me a jet or a hot mikado and anything goes, *everything else* isn't coming up roses and is a les miserable *example of plagiaristic rubbish although to be a superstar would be as glorious as finding a corner of the sky! Ah what simple joys! Now get* me a Porter *and get me off this tub. I am what I am and so It's time for the floor show!*

The phantoms of the Amazon *are here, inside your mind. Hehehehe!"*

Mr White and the ladies walked around the beach collecting every egg they could, taking care not to disrupt the nesting turtles, whilst Clipboard Girl put her clipboard to good use and knelt down in a secluded spot and began to dig in the sand. In next to no time Mr White had his first nest full of shining eggs.

As the evening progressed majestically into the early hours, the dolphin show came to an end with an exhilarating finale that was greeted with a wonderful silent round of applause, so as not to disturb the nesting turtles! The tourists and egg collectors quietly left the beach for their boats, empty handed, of course but happy, and Mr White and the ladies headed back to the White Mistress to party the rest of the night away like a reunited family of hungry Meerkats. Freak, Escobar and Spike spent the night on the beach defending the groaning turtles and their eggs against predatory attack until the dawn broke a new day announced it arrival. With the rising sun firing its rays over the ocean, Freak took a moment and again surveyed her surroundings. The only evidence of the night's carnage was the odd feather or crab claw, and the swash was taking care of them. With a self-satisfying deep breath of gratification, she had a stretch and watched the lumbering Olive Ridley turtles return slowly to the bathing ever after.

Yin and Yang snoozed away in the White Mistress' master suite, dreaming, of course, of Julie Andrews with her umbrella!

***

Flying over the dramatic landscape of Costa Rica, its blanketing Rain Forests and screaming peaks, whilst the sun was rising, and then, gliding far above the growling, simmering Bani Volcano, was a real treat for Garston.

"Wow, look at that it's amazing. I think I need more words in my vocabulary to describe it. It's very different from Little Budworth that's for sure!"

"That's nothing love, well, what I mean to say is, there are many thousands of stunning, incredible sights both natural and some man-made that can make your feathers stand on end. Trust me, I've seen them!"

"What, do you mean, you've seen them?"

"Well, I don't just sit on that branch on our tree all day, love. I have used my gift to see the world."

"Really, ok then, what's the most beautiful place you have ever seen?"

"That's easy, Angel Falls, Venezuela."

"Man-made, then?"

"Ooh, that's tough, but, I would have to say, it's the statue of Christ the Redeemer on the Corcovado, Rio, Brazil!

"Really, why is that?"

"Well, man has built so many fantastic things, the Pyramids of Egypt, the lost cities of Cambodia, the Taj Mahal, the Statue of Liberty, Tibetan Monasteries, the Eiffel Tower, the Empire State building, Aztec Temples, the Parthenon, the Panama Canal, the Shard, the whole of Dubai, Las Vegas, but, that statue of Christ the Redeemer in Rio de Janiero is the most powerful thing I have ever had the pleasure of perching on. It just sums up mans belief in religion, any religion and himself. It's a statement, something that says a lot about the species that built it."

"What does it say?" Garston asked.

"It says; we can build anything, anywhere, even at the top of the world, hand us a challenge and we, with the help of our beliefs, will single-mindedly succeed, darling! Now, look down there, can you see that, well that's Ostonial beach, where huge great turtles come to lay their eggs."

"Why do they do that, why here?"

"It's something to do with incubation and the Equator I think. Warmth and… well, I don't know, I'm not a bleeding naturalist."

"No you're not, but you are the closest I've got. Look at all of those turtles and those boats," said Garston.

"Oh yes, oh no! One of those boats isn't just a boat; it's the White Mistress, Garston."

"Quick, to the trees behind the beach. If we can see them they might be able to see us. Do it, mate, fast, get us down. What are they here for?"

"No idea, but hold on," Albert replied.

Albert assumed the position; he drew his wings back and like a kestrel aiming for its prey, pushed out his beak and shot towards the ground.

"Cut away the sack," he said, "quickly, we're coming in too fast."

"But, what about me, I'm gonna fall?"

"Use your tail, Garston."

"Tail, cut straps,"

Garston plummeted to the ground.

"Tail, hover!" he yelled. "Please hover!"

The tail's rotor blades appeared from its tip and began to spin; Garston slowly gained his composure. The falling sack of corn, however, plunged towards the ground snapping and cracking branches, ripping its canvas skin and scattering kernels everywhere. Albert touched down at Garston's side and climbed out of what remained of his harness. They both took cover at the back of the beach behind a tree and looked out to sea. Freak, who had heard all the clatter, turned towards the beach from her position on the White Mistress. After a few moments of scanning, she put the noise down to a Salt Water Croc in the brush and returned to some self-cleaning.

Once the yacht had become a dot in the distance, Albert and Garston stepped out onto the beach.

"Something more than the laying of eggs has happened here on this beach, Garston. This dark sand is darker in some places than others…its blood, Garston. Garston, where are you?"

“I’m up here, bud.”

Garston was hanging upside down from the branch of a tree trapped by spider silk that was looped around his hind legs.

“Well, that’s different!” said Albert.

“I wanted a bat’s perspective of the landscape,” Garston replied dryly.

“Really?” asked Albert, before flying up and snipping Garston free.

“Tail, hover!” said Garston giving Albert a quizzical glance. “OK mate, there are a few traps around here, so we ought to be careful.”

“You’re the one who has to be careful, baby!” said Albert; “I haven’t been trapped by anything yeaaahrg!” Albert screamed and pinged skyward, yanked up by some more hidden webbing.

“You were saying buddy!”

“Just get me down from here so we can get to that island and have a skirt around. Be careful though; don’t slice me with that blooming tail. Ooh, this is most embarrassing!”

***

It was noon on the day of the Northampton job and a feeling of excitement coupled with one of anticipation filled the cottage. Maurice and Seth had been sat in front of a computer for hours now, tracking Albert and Garston’s progress via satellite.

“They obviously didn’t like the plan,” said Seth.

“That or they had to make up one of their own due to circumstancez beyond their control.” Maurice replied.

“Well, at least they are close; they only have to travel across the narrow strait to Alcatraz Island now. Hopefully, all will go well and they will return successfully.”

“How does it look at the factory at the moment?” Seth asked

Maurice typed away on his keyboard and the screen brought up the Northampton Factory surveillance cameras.

“There you go,” said Maurice.

“Can we move the cameras from here, you know, control them to have a better look around?” asked Seth.

“The cameraz are just basic in their function. They point and view, that’s it I’m afraid, they are not motion sensitive and we have no sound. Each of them has to be positioned by hand. I will set up the computer zo that we can see everything that every camera does. I'll get another monitor in here, divide the screen function, and then that will be pozzible. When the team arrives at the factory in Northampton, I shall disable the zecurity recording programme."

"Good Maurice, carry on. Let everyone know that they ought to get a good afternoons sleep and also remind them to be ready to meet in the basement at eight o'clock this evening to get underway."

***

Heady, a little tipsy, and unsure on their feet, the ladies disembarked the White Mistress one by one via an old, creaking wooden jetty that would have damaged any sling-back healed shoe and so, they all lined up and removed their footwear and gingerly staggered barefoot towards the beauty and serenity of Arcadia.

You would have thought, that with all of Mr White's wealth, an external elevator, or cable car would have been built to ferry people up and down the cliffs, but not so. He firmly believed that Mother Earth's landscape should appear as natural as she intended and thus, the only access to the villa's beautiful garden was via a winding rickety path that rose above a sculpted deep cavern, that was once upon a time, a smugglers retreat.

Mr White strolled up the path chatting away to Escobar, who was sat on his shoulder, regarding the fact that anonymity should really have been the order of the day. He explained that delivering 13-foot crocodiles by the tail to a hotel might really be something that may attract attention to their wonderful and, thus far, private lives. Freak, Spike, Yin and Yang, carried carefully by Clipboard Girl, brought up the rear.

"Well that was a marvellous, stimulating night and soon there shall be nights even greater. It is close, the start of the end of the human race. Green Slime is to become part of everyday life and with the delivery of our dispensers following on; man may not be responsible for his *own actions anymore. Well, some of them anyway, in fact* many of *them. Yes, I's can't wait to let off a nuclear device, nor I, what fun that shall be!"*

"Oh boys, stop it. All this talk of Oppenheimer Day, it really is rather cheap. Did Hitler brag, Amin, Pol Pot, Stalin, well? Well, come to think of it, yes they did. Oh, it's late or early. I think I'm tired. I'll be in the palms having a lie-down if anyone needs me to kill anything of any bother. If anything else needs to be dispatched just ask Spike, I was pretty impressed with his stalking and assassination skills. Anyway, goodnight, good day, good morning or whatever!" said Freak.

Leap, and she was gone.

"She is a beast to be *admired, however one thing* does confuse I and I, not about her but about White and that Clipboard Girl flunky. Time to ponder!"

DOUBLE TROUBLE

"Hello everyone. Well, this is it."

Seth was addressing the team in the basement.

"Bandi and Steve, you sit in the rear of the Egg, Hannibal you in front of them in the little arm chair. It's for you to command the cockpit controls, stereo, air con, ride comfort, and anything else necessary."

"Fabulous!" said Hannibal as they all climbed in under the watchful supervision of Chief.

"Vincent, are you fully read up on all of the functions that the Commando has in its arsenal?"

"Yes sir, I mean Seth."

"Well, the onboard computer within the Egg will help you if you come across any difficulty. I recommend that you set a limit to your speed, we don't want you arrested by a constabulary on the way to blowing up a factory do we! If you would like Peuja to drive…"

"No, you're ok, Seth; if I need her I will give her a shout."

Vincent climbed on the Commando's black, softened leather seat, put on his helmet and gloves, turned to Chief and gave him a nod. The glass roof of the Egg slid closed and the motorcycle turned with the revolving floor to face the exit. Vincent lifted his visor, looked into his rear-view mirror and recognising Vincent's retinal signature, the Commando fired up. He reached for the accelerator and took a firm grip; the trapdoor hydraulics eased into action and then swiftly, the moonlight and chilling October air swept through the basement. As Vincent up the ramp to join the road, Seth turned to Maurice.

"I, for the first time, am a little nervous. It is you and I now Maurice, and Chief, of course."

And me!

"Yes, sorry, Peuja. You know, I recall a time, before this all began, when we were a meagre menagerie of nature's creatures, all friends, all relatively harmless." Seth paused for a moment in negative contemplation. "Something vile has happened to us, each one of us Maurice. We have gained human characteristics. It is true that our group seem to control our yearnings better than Yin and

Yang, but perhaps Freak, Escobar and Spike are really not telepathically controlled at all. Perhaps they have selected their actions using their own free will. So many conundrums, Maurice, there are so many. I think I have never felt so alone, even though friends and rabbits always surround me. I have butterflies in my stomach."

"I do too, but mine were in the soup!" He gave Seth a smile. "We cannot change what has happened, zo pull yourself together, Seth. You are the Rabbit King of England for heavens zake!"

"Yes, you're right." Seth shook his arms and legs.

"May the godz of the world take care of them," said Maurice

"Especially if they need Lecter," replied Seth. "Let's get to Peuja and follow their progress shall we?"

Shall I put the kettle on?

"She really does think she'z human!" said Maurice.

I heard that!

Sitting in the Egg and being driven through the hedgerows and country lanes of Cheshire towards the motorway, seemed quite exciting at first. The twisting roads and leaning Egg were all good fun for the first twenty minutes or so, but then Steve and Hannibal started to feel a little queasy. They hadn't taken to road travel quite as well as Garston had previously.

"Bandi, I don't feel too good," said Steve.

"Me neither," said Hannibal.

"Don't worry; that will pass after a while. It happens to humans, too," said Vincent talking through his helmet to Egg link, "it's called motion sickness. Humans have, over many years, learnt to adapt to the nausea, or take a tablet to ease the symptoms. It happens when we don't use our legs and rely on mechanised forms of transport. Just put on some music and have a snooze. That should make you feel better. I'll wake you all up when we get closer to Northampton."

"But I don't want to sleep," said Hannibal, "I'm too excited."

"Seth calling Egg, this is Seth calling Egg, can you read me, over?" Seth's voice was coming from a small speaker on the Egg's dashboard.

"Hi Seth, it's Bandi, how can we help?"

"Hello Bandi, it's actually I that can help you guys. Hannibal, there is a small bag to be sick in just under your seat, there is one for you too, Steve, and you Bandi, in a little pocket to your side. I added them to the interior specifications because I thought this might come about; I discovered its popularity during research. It seems to occur with canines more frequently, though. There is also some bottled spring water under the Commando's seat in the small holding area. I recommend you all re-hydrate yourselves before commencing the core part of your mission. However, the best thing you can do is, turn up the heat a little, get comfortable and watch the world go by. It will make you feel drowsy and eventually you will sleep through the journey."

Hannibal fiddled with the settings in front of him and soon enough, with the seducing intermittent bursts of dazzling yellow Motorway light and the hypnotic purring sounds of the Commando's beautiful engine, the Egg's mammalian occupants, one by one, dozed off. Vincent, however, rode comfortably and dreamily along the seamlessly endless tarmac laden veins of humanity. After an hours or so travelling, he found himself fighting his instincts to try and break the land speed record for a motorcycle, but he kept his discipline, resisted temptation, and rode pretty sensibly, well most of the way. At the appropriate junction he pulled off the motorway and began roving the lanes of England as he ventured deeper into the Northamptonshire Countryside. The Northampton factory wasn't located in the city; it was, in fact, located in the centre of a field surrounded by woods, which in turn were encircled by pastureland. The factory itself was an abomination of architecture, building regulations and sweaty palmed corrupt local government. Fenced off, with one way in and out, an uneven tarmac track through the trees, the structure was an ugly corrugated block, that seemingly broke all established laws of, planning with environmental due care and attention. Like a grotesque monolith, it stood glowing luminescent beneath the stark green night security lights.

"OK everyone time to wake up, we're close. Hannibal, could you please put us in tree frog mode?" asked Vincent.

Bleary eyed and with a stretch Hannibal set the required mode, Pufferfish mode which overinflated the tyres on the Commando to double their natural width. This enabled Vincent to guide the bike smoothly across the muddy grasslands to a desired spot near the fence where he slowed and came to a halt. Hannibal turned to Bandi and Steve to see if they were fully awake

"Ready?" asked Steve.

"Well, I'm ready," replied Bandi as the Eggs door slid opened.

Vincent climbed off the Commando, lifted the seat, and took out a bottle of water and a bowl from the storage compartment. He filled the bowl and placed it down for everyone to take drink.

"Through this fence and then the trees, is the field with the factory. It's about a hundred metres to the building. Good luck, follow the plan and there should be no trouble at all. I'll see you all back here when you're done. This is as far as I can go. Any questions?" asked Vincent.

Steve strode up to the fence and started digging, within seconds he had tunnelled to the other side and was shaking off the dirt. Bandi took a different route and hopped up onto the Commando to use it as a launch pad for an almighty leap to the grass on the other side of the eight-foot fence. Hannibal took the human option and climbed onto Vincent's shoulder. He the jumped to a nearby branch and ran from branch to branch until he had made it over to the other side and was standing beside Bandi and Steve. The three of them looked at Vincent through the fence.

"We love you Vincent," said Bandi.

"Be careful, I love you, too," he replied.

Like a slow motion scene from a Hollywood movie, where the heroes stride purposefully onward to save the world, Bandi, Steve and Hannibal walked into the woods and disappeared from sight. Vincent nervously looked at his watch. There was nothing he could do now, but wait.

***

The occupants of Arcadia slept peacefully, completely unaware of the fact that during their well deserved rest, two visitors had utilised the time to skulk around their home!

"Albert," said Garston whispering. "Can you take out the power box at the bottom of those palm trees? It seems to me that they must be the transmitting aerials. They are both covered in Freak's power conductive webbing. Be very careful though, Freak may be nearby somewhere."

"Yes, not a problem, darling and nicely deduced, but my eyes tell me that there is an armoured cable beneath the ground connecting them to a generator behind that pool house, so that will need disabling, too."

"That pool house isn't all it seems Albert, I snuck in through an air vent, and there is some kind of lab in there and some other unconventional bits and bobs."

"Did you find the prototype dispenser?"

"Well, yes, I did, but that's a little bit of a problem."

"Why is that, love?" Albert replied still whispering.

"Have you managed to have a look inside the main house?" asked Garston.

"Oh, Arcadia, Yes, absolutely gorgeous isn't she, such a wonderful example of neo-classical architecture and so tastefully decorated."

"Yes, well forget about all of that. Did you spot where everyone is?"

"Yes," Albert replied, "Spike is upstairs asleep in one of the bedrooms; Escobar is sleeping, head under wing in another bedroom and Yin and Yang are in the lounge. I can't find Freak."

"Well, the dispenser is in the aquarium with Yin and Yang, dispensing food"

"I thought that was just a reflection in the glass, how stupid of me! OK, so what's the plan, double 'o' Gerbil?"

"Destroy the box, destroy the generator, flambé the pool house and mug Yin and Yang for a dispenser. It's a delicate plan but I think we can pull it off!"

"How are we going to mug Yin and Yang, darling?"

"Leave that to me, if everything goes well, everyone will be occupied, if not just panic! Quick hide, someone's coming."

The pair took cover behind an ornate plant pot.

Mr White walked down Arcadia's glorious staircase, dressed in his bathrobe, holding a glass of water.

"That must be Mr White. Here, can you see what's on that computer monitor?" asked Albert. "It's the factory in Northampton look; can you see?"

"This is it. When I say take out the box and the genny…" Garston was interrupted.

"The genny?"

"Generator Albert, it means generator. You hit them and..." Albert interrupted Garston once more.

"Hit them?"

"It's a figure of speech, for Gnome's sake, just get with the vibe dude!" Garston was becoming infuriated.

"Gnomes?"

Ignoring the comments Garston ploughed on.

"And when I shout 'come and get me', fly down pick me up and fly off as soon as you can."

"Alright my love, just give me a second, I need to fly down to the bottom of the cliffs and pick up some ammunition!"

***

Bandi, Hannibal and Steve walked quietly through the trees to the grassy area surrounding the factory.

"Wow, it's a bigun," said Hannibal.

"It certainly is," Steve replied, "even though it's got no chestnuts!"

"Hey?" replied Hannibal a little puzzled.

"Err, shall we get on with it boys?" said Bandi, sighing deeply and trotting on. Hannibal and Steve stepped to it and followed snappily.

"Don't look now boys but we are being approached by a few thugs," said Bandi.

"Dobermans!" said Steve sniffing the air.

"I hate bullies!" replied Hannibal.

"Well, this Jackahuahua is gonna kick some dingleberry, see you inside!"

Steve put his head down and ran straight for the pack, whilst Bandi and Hannibal split left and right and headed for the delivery dock and side entrance respectively. Upon reaching the side door, Hannibal entered a code, which had been given to him by Maurice, into a numbered keypad. He poked his head around the door as it clicked open; saw the way forward was clear, and zipped inside. At the dock, Bandi hid behind one of the three delivery trucks and had a look around to make sure that no one was about. She didn't really want anyone to get hurt. Luckily she found it was all fine, the coast was clear, but she could hear yelping coming from the distant field. Worried that Steve may be in some kind of trouble, she began to run to his aid. She had only taken a few steps when she realised there was no need to fret, Steve was okay, indeed he was blissfully scattering Dobermans like bowling pins and having the time of his life! Bandi got back to the job in paw and efficiently set about slicing through all of the diesel tanks belonging to the parked trucks, as well as an oil drum that was tucked away in the corner. Her razor sharp claws made light work of it all and as a result, a pool of destruction seeped out and flooded the area.

Hannibal marched through the winding corridors purposefully, as if he'd walked them all his life and came to a door marked 'kitchen.' To his surprise, it swung open. He leapt behind it and took cover as three security guards ran out.

"Quickly, there's something definitely going on," one of them shouted.

Hannibal waited until they were out of sight and snuck inside. A blast of warm air suddenly hit the back of his neck. A shiver ran up his spine. Snarling and dripping with drool a big muscular Doberman was behind him. Hannibal turned slowly to face his bully but found himself backed up against the closed door with the Dobermans foul breath suffocating the air. He quivered with dread. The toned and towering mass of annihilation growled.

Hannibal mustered a whisper, "Oolaballuh!" And a few seconds later the haunting sound of a blood-curdling cry rang through the building!

***

"What did he zay?" asked Maurice.

"Oh no," said Seth. " He's about to live the oolaballuh!"

"Sorry? He said what?" Maurice asked again.

"It's a phrase Hannibal and I came up with for when Lecter is released. We and nearly everybody else in the world, including Hannibal, live this great 'hullabaloo' of a life, you know, just trying to get along best we can, struggling most of the time not living the life we dream and yearn for. Therefore, when Lecter is released, he lives the opposite, the oolaballuh! A life of freedom and joy, a life longed for and deserved. It's something that we all should be able to do, but life and circumstance often don't allow. Can you imagine living the life of your dreams all the time? Wouldn't it be bliss? It all started as just a bit of fun and a cryptic password, but it also seemed poignant and appropriate."

"I like it," Maurice replied, raising a single eyebrow!

Awakening of Lecter imminent.

"Oh dear, oh dear, dear," said Maurice.

Seth's ears covered his eyes.

"Here we go," he said.

Lecter awake!

***

Mr White sat up on the sofa and leant forward, his attention drawn by the live streaming action from Northampton on his monitor. His sudden movements woke Yin and Yang from their nap.

"*I do like this* continental sleeping in the middle of the day thing, it's *so refreshing. Ah, look* at White taking a *curiosity in our business*."

Mr White sat staring silently.

"S*omething's really* got his *interest."*

Escobar fluttered down the stairs, perched himself next to Mr White and turned towards Yin and Yang.

"What? Something's wrong with the dogs, what all ten *of them, there can't* be. What on this dull *decaying excuse of* a planet could positively misguide… sorry how many? Six, six I say. What possesses *maddened dogs to run* around *outside on the grass? Steve, I say! What! Steve, what's happening? I's are under attack I say, not us the dogs, by a mongrel. Well, he* won't get far. What, the cat's there too? Well, our dogs will eat that uppity old prissy feline; hold on, Freak said she was dead; *and a Monkey in* a *crash helmet. Have I's been* on *that Costa Rican paint thinner, Escobar*? *FREAK!"* they called.

Spike joined everyone in the front room.

"*Will someone get I's* out of this glass box, so I's *can have a closer look*? *NOW PLEASE!"*

Mr White stood up and lifted Yin and Yang out of the tank and sat them on his lap, they were a little irate to say the least. Freak slid down the balustrade and landed on the coffee table, skidding to a halt.

***

Maurice and Seth, as well as those at Arcadia, watched the black and white footage of Lecter's release. They winced and shuddered as the plot unfolded like a grainy, home made horror film, shot on a hand held digital camera. Eerily silent, the movie was hard going for any dog lover; it eventually came to an end with a frying pan to the nose, a testicular yank and the biting removal of an ear, all accomplished with the speed and fluidity of a rabid group of Piranha. The one-eared dog finally fled for its life by taking a lily-livered leap through the closed kitchen window!

"No more sleep, you can take my lunch but you can't take my FREEDOM!"

Lecter's tears filled his face as his helmet returned to its normal position.

"No. No, please!" he called to no avail.

Lecter disabled.

Threat eliminated.

A few limb twisting second later, Hannibal let out a satisfying yawn! With absolutely no idea of what had just happened, he gazed at the chaos surrounding him, shrugged his shoulders and quickly pulled himself together. Leaping up onto the gas hob, he turned all of the dials to full, whilst being careful not to press the ignition switch. Taking a moment, he popped over to the smashed window and watched the security guards tend to their whimpering dog team.

"Good old Steve," he said.

He then ran out of the kitchen and down the corridors to meet up with the others. They were in the main hall where Green Slime production was in full swing.

"Wow, Yin and Yang have been busy!" he said.

Huge vats of green liquid were gurgling and bubbling away like giant, brimming witches cauldrons. They systematically tipped and poured seeping, glutinous slime onto travelling conveyor belts beneath, which, in turn, transported the mixture towards enormous drying and packing machines. Hannibal found the stop button and the belts ground to a halt. The vats however, continued to pour out Green Slime and without the working belts to move it, it oozed sinisterly all over the floor.

"Blimey, it really does honk in here. Let's go guys, it's time to end this," said Steve.

"That's the smell of rotting seaweed," said Bandi.

"It's like ten year old cheese! Well, that's enough for me," he said, and ran towards the opposite wall. With a smash, he crashed straight through it, creating a Steve sized exit to the grassy outside world.

"You have to go now, too, Hannibal; it's alright, get back to Vincent. I will be with you in a minute," said Bandi.

Hannibal gave Bandi a cuddle and followed Steve out into the night. Bandi patiently watched him leave and then turned around, only to come across some company!

"Oh, boys, you really should be outside, it's going to get a little warm in here," she said.

Three Dobermans were stealthily prowling towards her.

"Have it your way."

The Dobermans kept coming. Bandi licked a paw and calmly sat down directly in front of them, closed her eyes and then, suddenly, in a blinding burst of light and heat, transformed herself into her beautiful fiery lioness form.

The Dobermans stopped in their tracks. The lioness looked at them for a second and then let out a roar so immense that the dogs scurried for their lives as if they had just spotted a box of fried chicken hanging from the back of a sports car. Now alone, the lionesss casually began a stroll through the factory. All around her, everything set ablaze. She slinked her way through walls, the hall, and then the vehicle dock.

'Boom', an explosion, 'Boom', another! The parked delivery trucks were tossed high into the air like kicked tin cans.

***

"Did she just walk through a wall, Maurice?"

"I think zhe did Seth and as the lionezz. Now, that'z a handy talent!"

***

"Wow!" said Steve, "Wow indeed," said Hannibal.

As they watched anxiously from the sheltered edge of the woods for a sign of their colleague, a final cacophony of explosions filled the night. In a choking mushroom cloud, twisted shards of splintered aluminium and steel flew high into the air whilst both security guards and dogs ran for cover.

From the chaos, the lioness cantered towards them.

"So how did she know she could do that again?" asked Steve.

"She just did, I suppose. She's so stunning," Hannibal replied.

Pulling up in front of her friends she closed her eyes, and transformed back to pussycat beauty.

"That was fun, we should really do something like that again sometime. It's nice to get out isn't it? Shall we get back to Vincent? I fancy a pilchard. I wonder if we've got any?"

Hannibal and Steve giggled and walked back with Bandi through the trees to the Commando, chatting all the way. On arrival they just hopped back into the Egg as if they were returning from a picnic.

"All good, was there any trouble?" Vincent asked.

"Not a sausage," replied Bandi.

"Ooh, I could murder a Cumberland," said Steve in reply.

The Commando growled and the group settled down and made themselves comfortable for the long journey home.

***

"Stage one complete Maurice, now we have to hope Garston and Albert are successful!" said Seth.

"I have all my slimy toez crossed," Maurice replied.

***

"Bastet, Fantastic!" yelled Mr White ecstatically leaping for joy.

"*What on earth are you so happy about*, Bastet! How, who, why? What was all *that about?* Did anyone else see that cat do that, what is happening? This is very *disturbing and undeniably unacceptable. I's understanding of what the* occurrence is, is limited to... hold on, White, what are you doing? Have I asked or even commanded you *to put I and I back in the tank?"*

"No you haven't boys," Mr White replied.

"*Why isn't he stopping,* he should be walking nonchalantly *to the drinks cabinet* and doing the Foxtrot by now and he's not..."

"No, I am not funnily enough."

Mr White placed Yin and Yang back into their tank of water.

"*Something's different about this tank... THE PROTOTYPE it's gone. Freak, kill him.* Kill him, *now!"*

Mr White turned to Freak!

"Now, you don't have to do that," he said, "all you have to do is follow your own beliefs and instincts, actually instincts is the wrong word. Use your own intelligence and..."

Freak leapt from the coffee table and extended her fangs to a strike position. Mr White calmly raised his hand, Freak's leap ended there! She found herself still, motionless and suspended in mid air, five feet above the marble floor. Mr White slowly circled her.

"*That's an amazing trick; you have* to give it to *him."*

"Oh, that's nothing gents, just you wait," said Mr White.

He casually poured himself some iced water from a jug sat on a sideboard and coolly drank it down.

"This is special," he said turning to the duo.

He tapped his drinking glass on the coffee table until it cracked and left a sharp edge whilst Escobar and Spike watched inquisitively. He then walked back over to the tank and looked down at Yin and Yang.

"Don't be concerned Freak, you will be alright, as will both of you, but things are going to be a little bit different around here from now on."

"I can't move," said Freak.

Mr White took the glass and cut his own thumb. He watched as his blood slowly trickled and dripped into the Yin and Yang's tank like drops of red rain in a clear pool.

"You see, the thing is that all species evolve at different rates and in different ways, and the fact that SPAFF, as you call it, accelerates that process, is something we all should never take for granted."

"You evil dog. You have SPAFF in your veins, I and I can taste it."

"Yes, well surmised. It, of course, means your terrepathic days are at an end for a while or at least for the period of time that the water-SPAFF-blood mixture that you swim in surrounds you. You see gentlemen, when humans are exposed to SPAFF they also gain a power. I, being a male of the species, can control through the gift of telekinesis, any living creature that has been infected with the fluid. I learnt I had this ability, when once attacked by a young small hungry monkey!"

"And what about mind control?"

"Not a single hope in the multiverse. The liquid protects me by forming a barrier beneath my skull."

"*You* scurrilous *fiend, so all of this time you* have not been under our control, but everyone else has? Cunning, very deceitful but how have you *communicated with the rest of us by…*?"

Mr White stopped them there.

"I can understand everything that is being said due to the speech programme created by Vincent Russell and a tiny little gadget I have in my ear called Junior."

"Traitor, Where is our prototype?"

"Well, while you were ranting at the monitor, I noticed, from the corner of my eye, an odd looking gerbil, fish it out with an extending tail; he's on the other side of the glass doors, standing on the Patio, at this very moment."

Everyone turned towards the glass doors.

"Garston!"

Garston froze, caught red clawed holding the dispenser. He smiled nervously at everyone and gave a wave.

"Now, Albert, now!" he called.

Albert bolted down from the sky at great speed whilst tightly holding pebbles from the nearby shore in his talons. As he approached his target, the power box at the bottom of the palms, he took aim and released his missiles. They smashed through the external steel casing of the box with a deafening bang, causing it to short out immediately, spark and burn. Albert swept, like a pilot, high into the sky once again.

The noise panicked the ladies in the house into all converging at the top of the stairs.

"Don't worry, it's nothing," Mr White called up, "I'm sure it's over…."

Boom! There was an explosion.

"Well, it may be over now. That's the generator, I presume," he said.

"Fire, it's on fire. The generator, the pool house," Clipboard Girl ran in form outside, hysterical, dishevelled and for some reason dressed in a silver lycra catsuit!

"Oh, they really didn't need to do that, not the pool house! Don't be concerned, the automatic sprinkler system will look after it."

"It's not working sir." Clipboard Girl replied.

A sense of urgent terror urged him into action.

"Quick ladies, to the pool house and grab anything you can that can hold water." Mr White suddenly became aware of Clipboard Girl's attire.

"What on earth are you wearing?"

"It's for Yoga!" she replied snappily.

There was a mad rush down the stairs into the kitchen and then out into the garden where Garston was standing fixed to the spot in the middle of the lawn. The stampede of ladies, with pots, pans and anything else that could hold water, headed towards him. However, he didn't panic, he merely, calmly, extended his tail and 'zip,' he was picked up by Albert.

Escobar stretched out his wings and prepared to take flight.

"It's alright Escobar," said Mr White, running outside holding a fire extinguisher, in time to see them fly off.

"Let them go. We will meet them all again very soon." He looked to the skies. "Can you smell that Escobar? It smells like rain." He turned to see Spike at his side. "Bastet, how wonderful, don't you just love a good snafu?" he said with glee.

There was a burst of thunder and then the rain fell hard and heavy.

"Something very odd just happened in that lounge, Albert, and I don't know what to make of it!" said Garston as he and Albert rose high above the clouds.

Clipboard Girl ran up to Mr White, cowering in the rain, with a very small saucepan in her hand.

"It's all I could find," she said being drenched by the deluge.

Mr White turned to her and smiled beguilingly.

"Don't worry," he said, "someone up there is looking after the fire."

A familiar raven squawked on Arcadia's roof.

"You know Clipboard Girl, there are two types of people in is world, those that make love like they make music and those who make music like they make love!"

Clipboard Girl looked at Mr White blankly.

"'The composers of life,'" said Mr White, "make music like they make love, with their hearts. They use all that they feel to milk their emotive souls into creating their scores of perpetual existence.

Now, 'The performers of life,' make love like they make music, with instinct and raw passion. They follow the rules set out for them within the composition and then just play away to their hearts content. One group is lost without the other, like oxygen needs fire; they depend upon one another."

Clipboard Girl still looked at Mr White blankly.

"You'll understand one day," he said. "Now, though," he paused for a moment and raised his arms in jubilation to touch the rain, "It's time to let the orchestra play the overture!"

Mr White turned and casually walked back into the lounge.

"Who are you, you blithering, human pomposity? And what is your objective?"

"Boys, if you think that this is all part of a little brainwave to create some chatting bunny fuzzies and a bunch of helpful creature cuties, well, you are miserably mistaken." Mr White grinned. "Welcome gentlemen to my world, a new world!" he said, with enormous pleasure in his voice.

Yin and Yang took instant offence.

"It's I and I's world White and we will rule it, *I's way!"*

INTERVAL!

#0066 - 110416 - C0 - 210/148/10 - PB - DID1420660